KT-393-105

HARRISON . C

AF(CR)

SEASON OF DARKNESS

Cora Harrison

Severn House Large Print
London & New York

This first large print edition published 2020
in Great Britain and the USA by
SEVERN HOUSE PUBLISHERS LTD of
Eardley House, 4 Uxbridge Street, London W8 7SY.
First world regular print edition published 2019 by
Severn House Publishers Ltd.

British Library Cataloguing in Publication Data
A CIP catalogue record for this title is available from the British Library.

ISBN-13: 9780727892751

Severn House Publishers support the Forest Stewardship Council™
[FSC™], the leading international forest certification organisation. All
our titles that are printed on FSC certified paper carry the FSC logo.

Typeset by Palimpsest Book Production Ltd.,
Falkirk, Stirlingshire, Scotland.
Printed and bound in Great Britain by
T J International, Padstow, Cornwall.

For Peter Buckman, literary agent par excellence. Persuasive, encouraging, tactful, enthusiastic, rigorous. 'Nullus est liber tam mallus, ut non aliqua parte prosit.'

One

'I wouldn't if I was you, Isabella.' Sesina opened the door of the kitchen range and placed her shoes on its black, leaded edge, hitching up her skirt to get the warmth on her ankles. 'You're taking a norful risk, you are, Isabella. You know what men are like!' *But there you are, wearing your best dress and thinking everything is going to go your way.* The words went silently through her head as she watched the other girl's face, lit by the firelight that left the rest of the kitchen in almost darkness. Dead obstinate. That was Isabella.

'I'm a match for any of them. Move over, Sesina, stop hogging the fire.'

Isabella wasn't going to listen. Sesina knew that by the stubborn expression on her face. *Oh, well, do what you want to do. Don't say that I didn't warn you.* But she saw how Isabella gave one more look around the kitchen and seemed to breathe in its shadows, its scents of baked bread, devilled kidneys and fried haddock. Almost like she was saying goodbye to them all.

Sesina made one more effort.

'Easy to say, Isabella. Here you are sitting in a nice warm kitchen, toasting your toes by the range. Not so brave you'd be, down beside the river in the fog. That's what I say. That Hungerford Stairs is a creepy place at night; you

1

know that as well as I do myself, Isabella. Why does he have to meet you there? Funny idea, that. Why can't he meet you in the place where . . . well, you know . . .' She finished there, purposely letting her voice tail out. Perhaps Isabella would blurt out the name of the place where she'd met this person, where she had first told him that she knew the secret.

'You shut up, Sesina.'

But Isabella, Sesina noticed, looked quickly over her shoulder at the pale oblong of street light that came through the basement window. Full of the jitters this evening, she was; that was sure. Her gaze kept flickering along the dresser shelves, kept being attracted by the light on the copper pans, on the stone bottles of prunes and the glistening glass jars of mushroom catsup.

'Told you! You're scared, ain't you? You can't fool me, Isabella,' she said aloud.

'Mind your own business, Sesina!' Isabella, as usual, was working herself into one of her furies, her voice sharp and shrill. Angry. That was her. Always ready to fly off a handle. Spitting out the words again, her voice shaking this time, 'Just you mind your own business, Sesina.'

She had seen something nasty in that fellow. That would be it. Isabella was as sharp as a needle. Should be a bit more sensible, now, but money had come into it. Money and the idea of a nice, easy life. No good talking to her when she had that on her mind.

'Do what you like. Don't care,' said Sesina with a shrug. Luxuriously, she hitched her skirt up above her knees and placed her shoes on top

2

of the range. Nothing like the heat of the fire on the calves of the legs. Took all the tiredness out of them. She reached down a poker and rattled the coals. Isabella was always stubborn. There was no arguing with her. One of those who never knew which side her bread was buttered on.

'He knows I wasn't born yesterday. As soon as I told him that I knew all about it, he changed his tune pretty smart; I can tell you that. It'll be all right.' But there was definitely a slight shake in Isabella's voice. Sesina gave her a sharp look. Biting her nails, she was. It'd been a long time since Isabella had bitten her nails. Had done it that night when they had nowhere to go, no place to sleep.

'What did you tell him?'

'You'd like to know, wouldn't you, Sesina. Mind you, there's a lot of guesswork in it. But I wasn't born yesterday. I just hinted at a few things, told him one or two of the things that I've found out and . . .'

'And then?'

'Well then, tonight, I'll tell him the rest. Show him what I've got. Then it'll be his turn, won't it? Told him what I wanted, didn't I? Some nice little lodgings and money punctual, every week.'

Sesina thought about it for a moment. Isabella was always one to give a smart answer, mostly a cheeky one. But would that work with a man who was being blackmailed?

'You think that he'll have a fit, when you tell him, don't you? You think he'll be kneeling at your feet? Be beseeching you to keep quiet? Be offering you all sorts of money? Be talking about buying you a new dress, a house of your own, a carriage? That's what you're thinking, isn't it?'

She waited for a reply. There was none. Isabella's expression had not altered. She sat there, soaking up the warmth from the stove, calmer now, her face slightly pink, wholly self-satisfied, her eyes full of dreams.

Sesina looked at her with contempt. 'You poor cow,' she said just as one of the bells on the wall agitated convulsively. 'Oh, drat that bell. What's that fellow want now?' she said.

'I'll go,' said Isabella, jumping up from her chair.

'No, you don't; I've got some more to say to you.' Sesina seized a broom. 'There! That's fixed it.' One quick pull with the head of the broom and the noise had stopped. 'Dead old, that wire. Snaps ever so easy! You sit down again, Isabella.'

'I'll tell the missus that you was the one that broke it.'

Isabella wouldn't tell, really. And she knew that Sesina knew she wouldn't. In the morning, they would both swear blind that the wire must have snapped by itself.

That's if Isabella was still here in the morning. Sesina still couldn't believe that this man had agreed to fix Isabella up in brand-new lodgings. And new clothes, everything. Told her not to bring anything with her and he would dress her like a lady. And then arranged this night meeting. That was suspicious, if anything was. Dead dangerous this going out at night to meet this man. And the Hungerford Stairs was a stupid

4

place to fix for a meeting with a man that you were going to blackmail. Not a nice place even during the day. And so near to the river, too. It would be downright stupid to go there.

And then she looked at Isabella. Hair brushed. Wearing her best dress. The one that she kept for Sundays. A bit faded now, but still the red and green colours shone out and they suited Isabella, suited her dark hair and her dark eyes. No, Isabella was determined to go. She had a vision; Sesina could see that. A picture at the back of her mind of a different future. A vision of escape. And she was determined to try her luck, thought Sesina. She scuffed the stone flag beyond the stove with one down-at-heel shoe, her eyes looking down, full of dreams, most like. What more could she say, thought Sesina. Isabella would walk out of the kitchen in a few minutes. Off to meet this mystery man.

Unless she could stop her. But she didn't think that she could. There was something about Isabella tonight. Something taut as a wire, as if she, too, would snap in two any moment, just like that wire on the wall.

Nevertheless, Sesina went back to her argument.

'Chances are that he'll knock you over the head and drop you down into the water. Why are you meeting him there in the dark, just beside the river if he's going to take you to new lodgings?'

'He's a gentleman, ain't he? He don't want to be seen talking to me in broad daylight, with everyone looking on. Use your loaf, Sesina.'

'I still think that you're taking a norful risk.

5

Why don't you get someone, someone else, to talk to him?'

'Like who?'

Sesina knew that question would come, but she said nothing, half-hoping that the same name would come to Isabella. Better if it did. 'No one can tell you nothing,' she said aloud.

'Well, go on then. Go on. Say it. Who can I get to talk to him for me?'

'What about Mrs Morson . . . or him, you—'

'Mr Dickens? What made you think of him? You mad or wot? You know what would happen? He'd be down to this place like a ton of bricks. Talking to the missus. "Very bad character, these girls. She'd blacken a nunnery." That's what your precious Mr Dickens said about me and I wouldn't like to tell you what he said about you, Sesina.'

'But if Mr Dickens did help you, he'd advise you. After all, if you've really found out something, something worth money, something you know about *him*, something that he'd give anything to hide, you needn't say the name to Mr Dickens, just ask his advice . . .'

'I've got something on him all right, but I'm not having that Mr Dickens interfering. After all my work in tracking down this fellow. I can just imagine what Mr High-and-Mighty Dickens would say. I know what he's like. If he did help me . . . Mind, I say, *if,* well, you know what he's like, don't you? He'd take over. Might get money, but would he give it to me? Not him. Would use the money to put me to school or something, send me off to Australia. Would be like that

6

Urania Cottage place all over again and getting lessons like we was little kids or something. Nah, I just want money from this fellow. Don't want nothing to do with the law or anything like that.'

'Tell us his name. Go on, Isabella, you might as well, an' then if anything happens to you, I'd be able to get the peelers on to him if he strangles you or something. That 'ud be some satisfaction, wouldn't it?'

'No, I'm not telling you his name, or nothing about him. I know you, Sesina, you'd be in there like a flash, you'd be after him with your hand out, getting your cut, and chances are that you'd spoil everything. No, you keep your nose out of everything. I'll be a rich lady and have my own carriage, just you mark my words.'

'If he gives you enough money to buy a place of your own, can I come, too?' *Stupid*, said Sesina to herself, just one of those daydreams that they had sometimes, chatting together by the fire. *What would you do if you was a lady?* But there was something about Isabella that made you think that she knew what she was talking about.

'I might consider you for a scullery maid, consider, mind you. Of course, you would have to address me as Madam. That would have to be the way of it.'

'Ta, ever so. I'll stay where I am.' Be better off, too, thought Sesina. Easy place this! Easy enough to fool Mrs Dawson. Dead stupid, she was. Pretend that the cat got the cheese; that the fishmonger gave short weight; that the crack in the window was caused by the errand boys throwing stones into the basement area; the missus was dead

7

stupid and would swallow everything. Isabella would be a different matter. She'd know all the tricks. *Still, I'd have something to hold over her.*

Aloud, she said, 'Here's the missus. I suppose that Mr High-and-Mighty's been complaining that the bell doesn't work. Quick, start scrubbing that soup kettle. She was on about that earlier.' Sesina, herself, energetically seized the handle of the knife polisher and started it whirling as Mrs Dawson waddled in and looked around the kitchen with a beaming smile. Sesina relaxed. Been at the lawyer's gin, again. Always did put the missus in a good humour. Sesina had heard Mr Doyle complaining about the level in the bottle going down so fast. Mrs Dawson hadn't let him get away with it though. Called on Sesina to witness that the bottle had been three-quarters empty when she had cleaned his room the day before. And, of course, for good measure, Sesina had sworn blind that there was even less than a quarter in the bottle first thing that morning; that she had noticed it immediately.

'Off to bed with you, girls,' said Mrs Dawson, suppressing a hiccup. 'The gentlemen have all turned out their lights, now. Off to bed, you'll need to be up early. The sweep's coming. One of you will have to let them in at five o'clock. We don't want them getting in the way of the breakfasts, do we? Which one of you? Want to toss for it?'

'I'll do it, Mrs Dawson. I'll let the sweep in.' Just as though butter wouldn't melt in her mouth.

Sesina looked at Isabella suspiciously. Perhaps she was going to be out all night. Downright dangerous that would be. Up to something, anyway.

8

'So off you go to bed, now, girls. Good night.'

'Good night, Mrs Dawson.' Sesina waited until the footsteps went back up the stairs again before saying, once more. 'I wouldn't if I was you, Isabella.'

'Yes, but you're not me, are you? You have no ambition, that's what's wrong with you, Sesina. I don't want to be a slavey all my life, do I? Sitting here in this basement. Not even a proper window. Look at that cheeky bugger trying to get a look at us. Go away, get away, you little guttersnipe! The wheel of that cart will roll over him if he's not careful. Pull down the blind, Sesina.'

But she did it herself, rapping sharply on the window and then pulling a face at the boy. Wound up like a clock, she was, thought Sesina. She looked across as Isabella went back over to the door. No good saying any more. Pig-headed. Always was. That was Isabella. Always crying for the moon. She shrugged her shoulders as Isabella took down her shawl from behind the door.

'I'm off now, Sesina. How do I look in my best dress? Want to look good for the gentleman, don't I? Suits me that dress. Mr Dickens picked out the material. I remember him coming when I was sewing it. "Red and green are just right for you, Isabella," that's what he said, so he did.' She pulled a bundle from behind the dresser and stepped out into the passageway outside. Sesina waited with a half smile, waited to hear Isabella rattle that locked door, but all she heard were soft rapid footsteps climbing the stairs to the upper basement.

9

Two

Wilkie Collins, *Basil*:

The evening, I remember, was still and
cloudy; the London air was at its
heaviest; the distant hum of the
street-traffic was at its faintest; the
small pulse of the life within me, and
the great heart of the city around me,
seemed to be sinking in unison,
languidly and more languidly, with
the sinking sun.

Dickens and I had walked forth from my lodgings in Lincoln's Inn; through the quiet gardens
of Temple Inn; then along the side of the river.
It was the hour of dead tide; the slime and ooze
stained the foreshore and birds picked busily
among the filth. We did not speak; we watched
the lazy roll of the water, listened to the cries
of the seagulls; each of us immersed deeply
within our different worlds of fantastical creation; until, silently, we turned away from the
river and into a muddy alley. It was dark there,
almost too dark for walking, but we rounded a
corner and saw a blue lamp flaring with a cold,
clean light in the murky air and casting the black
shadow of a man in a top hat on to the white
building. I started. I remember that. Somehow

it gave me a shock; as though it were an ill omen, a devil coming with bad news.

'Inspector Field! You are a long way from your home patch. What brings you here?'

I knew him then. An acquaintance of Dickens. One of the many who courted the great man and who were flattered by any recognition from him.

The inspector wore an expression of one who is bringing goods. He jerked his thumb at the door behind him. 'Dragged something out of the river not half an hour ago. Care to have a look? Might interest you. Come in, Mr Dickens, and you, Mr Collins.'

He led us across a paved and cobblestoned yard and into a small, icily cold, stone house at the back of the police station, only big enough to hold a marble slab and an iron pump. There was a girl there, quite dead, lying on the marble slab, her eyes widely opened, river water oozing from a faded red and green print dress, descending drip by drip into the drain below the slab. I gazed at the body in horror. The last dead body that I had seen was that of my own dear father, but he had been a tired, ill, old man. This was a girl younger than myself. Pretty, too. Smooth skin, lovely dark hair rippling out from an oval face, large black eyes, widely opened and staring up at me.

'What happened to her?' I blinked, wiped my glasses with an unsteady hand.

'Strangled and then thrown in the river. The surgeon hasn't seen her yet, but look at her neck. Been broken. That's what killed her, I'd say. Not

11

the river. Legs broken, bruises on her arms. Been beaten and strangled, that's what I think, anyway. The old story. She's dead now and that's the end of her.'

'Who did it?' The girl's face was unmarked. A pretty girl with dark hair. Someone had spread it out across the slab. The men who brought her in, I supposed. 'Who could do a thing like that?' I said the words half to myself and half to Inspector Field. Dickens was wearing one of his forbidding looks, his dark eyes angry, his mouth compressed. I saw him reach over as though to close the dead girl's eyes and then withdraw his hand.

The inspector shrugged. 'Probably not worth going to much trouble to find out, Mr Collins. Could be any one of hundreds. The Hungerford Market stays open until late. Lots of ships tied up at the wharf. Lots of sailors and porters around. Lads up from the country. Looking to do a bit of buying and have a bit of fun before going back home tomorrow morning. These girls, lots of them, do end up in the river. Not worth the manpower to find out who they are or where they come from. We'll put up a few posters, of course. But no reward; no information; that's the usual thing, unless there's bad blood between a couple of men, or women either. But you might get a story out of it, Mr Dickens; that's what I was thinking.' He offered that remark ingratiatingly, his large protruding eyes fixed eagerly on my friend, rather like a dog proffering a stick. 'Gives you an idea, doesn't it?'

Dickens, I remembered, had recently written

12

about Inspector Field in *Household Words*. The man now probably thought of himself as a partner in the book-writing business. He looked ready to supply a plot, but Dickens said nothing, just looked at the girl sadly and thoughtfully. It took him several minutes to rouse himself, and then he just nodded to the disappointed policeman and strolled out. This time he turned back to the river, and began to walk so rapidly that I had trouble in keeping up with him.

'A man would be better.' He muttered the words below his breath and then once again, aloud. 'Yes, a man. But there should be a girl, too. A girl and her father.'

'What do you mean?' I found him an interesting study when he was like this. Dickens, the family man; Dickens the entertaining host; Dickens, the would-be actor; Dickens the businesslike manager of his periodical, offering me a job, none of these were as intriguing to me as the novelist dreaming over the book at the back of his mind. He turned to look back as though surprised by my presence. His brow was knitted and I got the impression that he had been trying to put some unpleasant matter from his mind, but that it had persisted, had conquered his effort to think about a new book.

'I know that girl, Wilkie,' he said unexpectedly.

'You know what she might be like, might have been like. You know how she could fit into a story.' I could hear the eager note in my own voice. I was on the lookout for any useful tips into the novelist's art. But I had lost my friend's attention again. Dickens was muttering to himself.

13

'A waterside character?' There was a question in his voice.

'Is she going to be in one of your books?' I dodged a boy carrying a broken and rusty sieve with some small pieces of coal lying on it.

'No, I didn't say that.' He laughed suddenly and unexpectedly. 'Poor thing. She'd have liked it, I dare say. No, I was thinking of something else.' Suddenly he looked sharply at me as though noticing me for the first time. 'I was talking about a man. A riverside character,' he repeated the words, but this time with a satisfied air as though they had taken shape within his mind. He strode on, waving his umbrella in the air as if taking swipes at invisible insects.

I grimaced as I tried to keep up. One of the problems with Dickens was that the more thoughts that crowded into his mind, the faster he walked. I wished that I had longer legs. 'But the girl, Dickens, the girl, that girl in there, you said that you knew her.'

Suddenly Dickens focused, swung around, his eyes alert. 'So I did. Yes, I do. She was one of my girls, the girls in Urania Cottage, the ones that I was training up to emigrate and start a new life out in Australia. You remember, Collins, I told you all about it. I wonder what happened to her. A clever girl. Smart one, too. Not biddable, though. She was all wrong for Urania Cottage. We had to let her go. She was corrupting the others, getting up a rebellion against the matron. Even tried to argue with me. There was no reasoning with her.' A look of sadness, almost of regret, passed across his face, to be replaced by a look of anger.

'But this girl . . . what is her name?'

'Isabella Gordon; that was her name. I remember her well,' said Dickens. 'No, she wasn't right for Urania Cottage. Didn't want to start a fresh life. Wanted to go out at night, to go shopping by herself, to have some fun, if you please. She was disturbing all of the rest. Interfering with their teaching. Trying to get them to rebel, also. Spoiling their chances, as well as her own. "Well, young lady," I said to her, "you seem to have misunderstood this place. You'll have to go if you don't radically change your attitude." And so she went. And her friend, Sesina, followed her the following day. Bless my soul, that must be about two years ago now.' He wriggled his shoulders as though trying to banish an unpleasant thought or regret.

It was interesting, I thought, how he referred to the dead girl. Despite everything, she still belonged to him. Something quite paternal in his voice. I knew that hours and hours, so very much of my friend's time and energies, were bound up in this Urania Cottage experiment where girls about to be released from prison were selected as suitable to be given a chance of a completely new life in a completely new environment. 'One of my girls,' he had said.

'I wonder what happened to her in the meantime. Where did she go? And where has she been living? What do you think, Dick?' I mused on the girl while my companion looked straight ahead with compressed lips and narrowed eyes. 'I'd like to find out where she went. What happened to her? Who strangled her? People

15

shouldn't get away with strangling girls and throwing their bodies into the river. And the police not bothering about it unless there is a reward offered.'

I eyed my friend. 'You must be able to find out something, Dick. What about the other girls out in Urania Cottage? Wouldn't one of them know something? I bet they would! I know women. They always tell each other secrets. Let's go out to your Urania Cottage. It's not too late. Let's see what we can find out about the poor girl. You know something, Dickens, I think that girl will haunt me if I don't find out who did this to her.'

'Haunt you! Why haunt you?' He didn't like that. If there was any haunting to be done, Dickens would have to be the focus of it. 'Well, as you like,' he said, with the air of one giving into pressure, although I guessed that he himself was eager to trace the dead girl's killer. 'Yes, we'll go out to Urania Cottage. You can meet my Mrs Morson. I've talked about her to you, haven't I? A woman of strong character. I recognized that the instant I met her. I can always trust myself to pick out the right person for a job.' A touch of the bombastic Dickens, there, but then that look of sadness came over his face again. With the tip of his umbrella he swiped viciously at the head of a nettle that poked out from the stones.

'She was sorry about Isabella, too,' he said after a minute. 'Thought that the poor little thing might have been reclaimed, but no, the pull of her past life was too strong. She was sucked back, Wilkie.

16

That's all I know about her. It happens often enough. Almost inevitable. Just like the river sucks back what it has released on to its banks at low tide. We lose so many of them, so many of these girls. I try not to think of it or wouldn't sleep so well at night. She had to go, had to rebel. And now, look what has become of her.' His face darkened. 'Come on, Wilkie. At least I might have the satisfaction of catching the man who did this.'

And now in the way that he did these things, my mercurial friend was filled with a driving energy. Grasping my arm, he hurried me along until we reached the Strand.

Three

Sesina guessed who it was when she saw the profile through the glass of the front door. Hair swept back, that high, broad forehead, jutting chin outlined with a small beard; she had opened the door often enough for him at Urania Cottage to recognize him instantly. He had always brought trouble there, she thought venomously, and it wouldn't be any different now. She switched her expression to one of sweet innocence, checked it in the mirror of the hallstand and then unfastened the door and stood there silently, dropping a pretty curtsy and waiting for the gentlemen to speak. Perhaps the bastard mightn't remember her.

There were two of them there. She liked the look of the second fellow better. Didn't have those piercing eyes. A nice amiable fellow with strong glasses, a goofy-looking smile, going a bit bald, but sweet-looking, sweet as a chocolate drop. Chubby-looking cheeks, like a little lad. Didn't say anything, just gave her that smile, more like a little grin, really, and she found it hard not to smile back at him. But of course it was Mr Dickens who spoke and of course he was on the ball, as usual.

'Well, well, well, so who have we got here? If it isn't the pint-sized Anna Maria Sisini herself. So you're working here then, are you?'

He knew it all the time. He had been expecting

to see her. She was sure of that. In spite of his words, there was no trace of surprise in his voice. He was just pretending, just play-acting as usual. She curtsied again. Isabella had been missing now for over forty-eight hours. There had been that story about getting new lodgings, but somehow Sesina had never believed that it would really happen. Not much chance that the poor cow was alive, she thought. That's the way that life goes. You takes a chance and you pays the price. She waited. Let him do the talking; let him tell what brought him there. She looked into the dark eyes defiantly for long enough to show him that she wasn't afraid of him. The other fellow, well, she could see him look from one to the other, but she wasn't going to waste any time on him. He'd be like them all. Like Mrs Morson, like the Baroness Coutts, herself, like the prisoner governor, all of them obedient towards 'the manager'. And, of course, 'the manager' would expect her to fall into line, just like everyone did for him. All except Isabella, of course, she told him straight. *'I'm not a black slave from Africa, Mr Dickens, so don't you treat me like one.'* Sesina giggled to herself when she remembered that.

Poor old Isabella. She'd been missing for two days now. Not likely that she'd ever see Isabella again. Sometimes, she had half-wondered if Isabella had got her money and taken herself off. St John's Wood. Isabella had a great fancy to live in St John's Wood. More likely, though, that she'd been picked out of the river, like many before her.

'Well, then, Sesina, perhaps you could ask your

19

mistress to see us.' It must be Isabella. He didn't ask about her. He surely would once he had seen her. Knew that they had been friends, knew that they had left Urania Cottage at the same time. Poor Isabella. Must be a goner. Someone must have told him that she had been fished out of the river.

Why was he involved?

Unless, unless, Isabella had spoken the truth . . . unless, there was money somewhere . . . he was keen on money, was Mr Dickens. Mrs Morson was always saying that they couldn't waste anything, that she had to do her accounts. He'd come along and check them, too. Pretending that the girls were family and then making them scrub and cook and dust and mend and work the mangle and spend hours with the iron. Not much of a family, that, and him as rich as the Lord Mayor of London.

'The mistress, sir?' She could act dumb. That's the way that he liked girls – act dumb and he patted you on the head. Act clever and he got rid of you. That was what Isabella had said and she was probably right. He'd got rid of them, the two of them, didn't he? They had been the smartest girls in Urania Cottage.

'Yes, your mistress.' Beginning to sound impatient, now. That was like him. Never did have much patience.

'Oh, the housekeeper!' She made her voice sound surprised. 'These are lodgings, sir. Mrs Dawson is the housekeeper, and the cook.' She put that in so that Mrs Dawson wouldn't sound too important. She was dying for him to tell what had brought him there. Isabella was dead; that was pretty sure. But how did Mr Dickens and this friend of his get involved? She stood back and he came in, giving that look of his around the hall and up the stairs.

'I know the man who owns this terrace, Collins.' Talking to his friend now, just like she was a hallstand or something. 'An American. He lets out most of the houses, but I suppose this one is just a lodging house. I had lodgings myself in one of these houses in Adelphi when I was a young man.' Without even looking at her, he took a calling card from his wallet, made as though to hand it to her and then took it back and scribbled a few words on the back of it with his pencil before he handed it to her.

'Give this to the housekeeper, Sesina,' he said and she took it from him. *Mr Charles Dickens, Tavistock House, Tavistock Square.* She would read the rest while she was waiting for Mrs Dawson to tell her to come in.

A friend of Mr Donald Diamond he had written on the back. Trust him to know the landlord! Knew everyone who was anyone in London. That would be him.

'What does *he* want?' Mrs Dawson was taken aback. Not used to having people calling to see her at this time of the evening. One of the lodgers might put his head around the door, but that would be that. As for the landlord, well, Sesina had only seen him a couple of times during all the time that she and Isabella had worked in number five, Adelphi Terrace. But Mrs Dawson would know the name of Charles Dickens.

21

Everyone in London knew him. She would have to see him, like it or not.

'Says he's a friend of the landlord, Mrs Dawson.' Could read that for herself on the back of the card, silly old cow, but she was busy, scurrying around, putting away the gin bottle and the glass, taking a peppermint out from a box in the drawer and chewing on it while she straightened her cap in the looking glass. Been like a cat on hot bricks ever since Isabella had disappeared.

'Well, show him in, girl, show him in.' Mrs Dawson wouldn't make the connection with Isabella, of course. She didn't know anything about them really. Just before she had been turned out of Urania Cottage, Isabella had stolen some of Mrs Morson's writing paper and Sesina had written out references for both, sitting up in their bedroom, giggling, the two of them, and planning a life away from Urania Cottage. One good thing about the place, after all, had been learning to write so very well. They could both do an exact copy of Mrs Morson's handwriting and so Sesina wrote a reference, in a beautiful copperplate script, from an imaginary lady who was just about to depart to India and so had to dismiss two hardworking housemaids – the India business had been Isabella's idea and it had been a good one. Not surprising if there had been no reply to the request for references. By the time that Mrs Dawson had given up hope of hearing from this Mrs Robert Doncaster, Isabella and Sesina had been well settled into the house on Adelphi Terrace. Not a bad place either with the lodgers out all day and nothing but breakfast to serve for them.

Mr Dickens and his friend were standing looking up the stairs when Sesina came back.

'How many lodgers here in this house?' He looked at her sharply. Was always expecting you to tell a lie. That was him.

'Four, sir. One on the first floor, one on the second floor and two together on the top floor.'

'All single men?' He gave one of those glances of his up the stairs, just like he used to do at Urania Cottage.

'That's right, sir. Could you step this way, sir. Into the parlour.'

'Parlour and dining room on the ground floor, then there are three more floors above this one, Collins.' He said it just like he was going to buy the place, looking sharply up the stairs and then down towards the basement. Sesina walked ahead of them and rapped on Mrs Dawson's door. 'The two gentlemen, to see you, ma'am,' she said, making sure to close the door very firmly with a very definite click and then cautiously edging it open again so that she could listen to their conversation.

'I came to ask whether you employed a girl named Isabella Gordon here.' Very curt, his voice. He'd be different if Mrs Dawson was a real lady. Not that she cared about Mrs Dawson! No better than she should be. Isabella said that she had found out a few juicy little pieces of information about Mrs High-and-Mighty Dawson!

'That's right, sir.' Mrs Dawson sounded very nervous. 'Yes, she works here as a housemaid.'

23

'Here long?' He'd be looking around the room, just like he used to do at Urania Cottage, straightening a mirror, standing a cushion upright against the back of the settee, making Mrs Dawson nervous. There was a real shake in her voice when she said, 'About two years, sir. She and Sesina, the girl who opened the door to you, they both came at the same time.'

'References?'

'Oh, very good, sir, very good, indeed. I'd never take a servant into the house without references.' Mrs Dawson was beginning to recover. Sesina could hear her rummaging in that bureau of hers. She edged the door a little further ajar. He had his back turned to her. She could see the side face of the other one, the goofy fellow, but he didn't matter. She'd just give him a wink if he caught her looking.

Mrs Dawson had found the reference, now. Sesina wrinkled her lip. Old cow. Imagine keeping them. Luckily, just one sheet of paper. Not hers, then. Just the reference for Isabella. Would it fool Mr Dickens? They had copied it out of a book on household management that was on the shelves in Urania Cottage.

He was reading the reference now, holding it very close to his eyes. Even before she heard him grunt, she had known that he would guess. He and Mrs Morson were always writing letters to each other. He'd know her style of writing, that fancy copperplate. Sesina edged a little closer and saw him show it to the other fellow and then give it back to the housekeeper without saying a word. She took in a cautious breath.

24

'I'm sorry to have to tell you, Mrs Dawson,' he said, 'but Isabella Gordon has been found dead, strangled, I'm afraid, body dragged from the river. Poor girl.'

Sesina swallowed hard. She had been taken aback by the last words. She had expected him not to care, she had been ready herself for the news, but he had sounded a bit upset and that made tears prick at the back of her eyes. So Isabella was dead. The bastard. He'd killed her. No more than she had expected, but it was a bit of a shock, all the same.

'Oh, my God! Oh, Mr Dickens! Who was it did that terrible thing?' Mrs Dawson sounded like she expected an answer. Silly cow. As if the bastard who strangled Isabella and threw her body in the river would leave a calling card! She thought that he'd say something cutting. He was a great one for that. But he didn't.

He left a silence, just like he was thinking about the answer and then he said, very quiet like, 'I don't know, Mrs Dawson, but I'll do my best to find an answer to that question.'

The other fellow looked at him, then. Looked as if he were a bit surprised like. I wonder does Mr Dickens mean it, thought Sesina. He was a great one to be poking his nose into things, of course. The questions he'd ask! Would never take silence for an answer, neither.

'A terrible thing. Terrible, terrible, terrible.' Mrs Dawson seemed to think that she had found the right word. She repeated 'terrible' once again. 'I'll have to tell Mr Diamond. He'll be most put out.'

25

'Perhaps I could take that task from you. I'll see Mr Diamond.' Same as usual. A manager from start to finish. Mrs Dawson not too pleased, though.

'Oh, it's kind of you, sir, but I wouldn't dream of troubling you. And I'll have to discuss the staffing requirements with Mr Diamond.'

'Yes, of course, you'll need someone to take her place. I'll mention that to Mr Diamond when I tell him about Isabella.' As usual he rode over any objections. 'I'll pop into number one on my way back and have a word with Mr Diamond. I'm sure that he'll be most sympathetic. Good evening, Mrs Dawson. Come, Collins. We mustn't take up any more of Mrs Dawson's time.'

Just like him. Always hustling everyone. Sesina had barely time to get back into the hall before they came out, all three of them. Mrs Dawson looking very flustered. Mr Dickens, cool and calm. Mr Collins, well he had his eye on her, just like he found her interesting.

And then there was a click at the door. The turning of a key. Mr High-and-Mighty Doyle. The lawyer from the first floor. What brought him home so early tonight? Always in and out at all times of the day. A nuisance, he was. Irritated if he found you doing his room when his lordship came in, even at ten o'clock in the day. A barrister. No regular hours. That was what Mrs Dawson said. Barristers had no regular hours. Not like a solicitor or a schoolmaster, or even those two young journalists at the top of the building. Not that she would mind them coming in while she was cleaning. Nor Isabella, neither.

26

Great larks, that pair. Would talk as if you were human, not like the other two.

'Good evening, sir,' she said politely.

Didn't answer, of course. Never did answer her. Don't know how Isabella got him to talk. Though she might have been lying. Very likely. Sesina took up the two hats, with their gloves curled up like nestlings in the silk linings. She knew which was which. One of them was perfect, perfectly brushed, brand new, and expensive-looking. And the other, well, it looked as though it had rolled along the street, suffered a few bashes, dusty, too. Dust deep in the pile, the dust of years. She felt a bit sorry for Mr Collins. If she had been a housemaid in his house, she would give his hat a brush every morning before he went out.

Perhaps she could get a job in his house. And get away from Adelphi Terrace.

It was a bit creepy here now. She wasn't too keen on remaining unless the fellow who did that to Isabella was found and strung up.

Mr Doyle was just standing there, looking like he expected something to be happening, looking at the two hats. Waiting. What was he waiting for? Just like he expected something. Some announcement. And then he looked at the two of them, Mr Dickens and Mr Collins, pretended he had only just seen them.

'Goodness, you must be Mr Dickens,' he said, sharp as anything. 'Jeremiah Doyle, sir, barrister-at-law. What brings a famous man like yourself here, Mr Dickens?'

'How do you do?' Didn't sound too polite, Mr Dickens. Didn't want to talk. Just stood aside

27

from the stairs, almost willing the man to go up to his rooms. Sesina suppressed a giggle. Mr Dickens was a great one to get people to go up the stairs. There was that day when there was a big row with Isabella. Could hear it all over the house. And then Mr Dickens opened the door, walked past Mrs Morson, went across the hall and stood by the stairs, with his hand on the knob of the banisters. After a minute, Isabella came out, as bold as brass, looking all around her. Tossing her head, she was, pretending not to see him. But somehow he just sort of mesmerized her into going up the stairs to her bedroom, without saying a word to her. She picked up her skirts and waltzed up like a lady, but he was the one that made her do it.

And now, with Mr Dickens standing there at the foot of the stairs, Mr Doyle just gave a sort of bow and went off up without even looking back once. Sesina bit back a giggle. She could hear his footsteps on the first-floor landing and then his key in the door. He had two rooms there, a sitting room and a bedroom, best rooms in the house.

Mr Dickens waited until he heard the closing of the door. 'And now, Mrs Dawson, I won't detain you any longer. But perhaps I could have a quick word with your housemaid. I won't keep her more than a few minutes and then I'll be off to see Mr Diamond and I certainly will not forget to mention your need for a replacement housemaid. Thank you, Mrs Dawson.' And sweet as pie, Mrs D. turned around and went back into her room.

Sesina waited. She could see how Mr Dickens' friend gave a bit of a grin at that. And when he saw her looking at him, he shared the grin with her. A nice fellow, that Mr Collins. Once Mr Dickens had taken his hat, she gave the other hat a little dust with her sleeve before handing it to him. Mr Collins, she thought, didn't have a good servant to look after him.

'Let's go into the kitchen, Sesina.' Mr Dickens, of course, was quite at home and giving orders as usual. 'I suppose your lodgers just come in and out as they please, do they? And they'd all have keys,' he said, going in front of her, down the stairs, cool as a breeze, as though he owned the place, just tossing the words back over his shoulder, past his friend and back up to her. He didn't stop at the landing where the servants' bedrooms were, either, but went straight down the second flight of stairs right into the basement, just like he knew every room in the place.

'Goodness, your little legs must be worn out, going up and down these steep steps all day long.' Mr Collins lowered his voice a bit when he said that. He had a nice little smile on his face when he looked over his shoulder. A nice friendly smile, she thought.

'Yes, sir.' Sesina said the words quite loudly and saw Mr Dickens look back. Didn't speak to her, though.

'Good for the waistline, Collins.' That's what he said. Thinks himself very funny. Always did.

'We must be nearly down to river level now, Dick.'

'That's right. Cleverly built, these houses. The

29

terrace is on top of the warehouses and the Adelphi Arches. The Adams brothers terraced the whole place, two roads in front of the houses, the top one passes the front doors, and then the arches come out on to the lower road, makes a way into the kitchens and store rooms.' Knew all about everything; that was him!

By now Mr Dickens was down, opening the doors, one by one, peering into the scullery and the coalhouse, and then the washhouse. When he had opened and shut each door, he went straight into the kitchen.

'And the basement leads out to the arches, Wilkie. Handy for deliveries from carts. Very well planned, the whole of it.'

Mr Collins laughed then. A nice laugh, sort of a giggle.

'How on earth do you know all of those things, Dick? You're an extraordinary fellow!'

'I told you. I've been over one of these houses with the landlord, my American friend, Mr Diamond. Good kitchen, isn't it? Well furnished with everything.'

Sesina didn't ask them to sit down. Not her place, she reasoned. In any case, she didn't want them to stay too long. He made her nervous. He'd stare at you and you'd swear that he knew every thought in her head. She went and stood with her back to the window. Never did get much light in that area outside it. Never saw the sun, for sure, in that window. Nothing but the wheels of carts and the feet of the porters and passers-by. Mr Dickens perched on the corner of the kitchen table, only scrubbed half an hour ago, and Mr Collins just stood beside the range, warming his hands. Very small little hands he had, like a lady's. Delicate and very white. Sweet little fellow, she thought. Much nicer than Mr Dickens.

'So who else is in this house besides you and Isabella and Mrs Dawson? There's that Mr Doyle whom we've just met, but who else? Let me see, there are three floors, aren't there, in these houses, that's right, isn't it?'

'There's Mr Doyle on the first floor, sir and then Mr Cartwright on the second floor and two gentlemen on the top floor, Mr Carstone and Mr Allen.'

'You and Isabella have much to do with them?' Always a one to be shooting questions at a girl, from start to finish, nothing but questions and then writing away in his book, his casebook, written on the cover, for everyone to see. One of the things that Sesina hated about Urania Cottage. All those questions and being took down like that, everything that a girl said. She wasn't surprised when he pulled out a notebook from his pocket and started writing in it.

'We clean the rooms, sir.' Poor old Isabella. She was talking like Isabella was still alive.

'And?' He had lifted his eyes now and was staring at her.

'And what, sir?' Sesina could sound innocent when she liked, she knew just how to do it. Knew what he was getting at, of course. Wanted her to spill the beans. He was looking around the kitchen, looking at everything, at the copper pots and pans, at the three kettles, at the locked tea

31

canister, the toasting fork and the sides of bacon hanging from the rafters.

'You make breakfast for them all. That would be it, wouldn't it? They'd provide breakfast in lodgings like this, wouldn't they, Wilkie?'

'Yes, sir,' said Sesina when he looked at her. His friend hadn't answered, too busy staring around him, a bit of a sad look on his face, like he was picturing Isabella here in the kitchen. Nice little fellow, thought Sesina.

'And they have their breakfast in the dining room, is that right, or do they have it in their rooms? I see, in their rooms.' His eyes had been darting all over the kitchen and now they were on the four bamboo trays piled up on top of the press. Ever so nice, those trays. A slot on one side for a newspaper and one on the other side for the coffee or teapot and the milk jug. Isabella used to imagine having breakfast in bed from one of these when she came into her money.

'They have it in their bedrooms during the week and in Mrs Dawson's dining room on Sunday, sir.' Though why it should be called Mrs Dawson's dining room, I'm sure that I don't know, she thought. Seems the old cow thinks she owns the bloody place. *My dining room, my parlour, my gentlemen.*

'I see.' Now he had stopped writing and was staring at her with that wolfish grin on his face. *Charitable, him!* Isabella used to say. *He's not charitable. He's just looking for ideas for his stories. That's why he keeps asking all those questions.* Poor old Isabella, she thought. I'm going to miss her. I'd like to string up the fella that did that to her. 'The bell's broken,' he said abruptly. 'When did that happen?'

'The night that Isabella left, just before she left, sir.'

'That's interesting.' Thought he'd like that. He was staring up at it. 'What happened?'

'Isabella stopped it ringing, sir. Took a broom to it.'

'Hmm!' He was up on a chair now, examining the wire. 'Hmm!' he said it again when he got down. 'It's been broken,' he said to his friend.

'Bit of a mark on the whitewash, there. Bit of a scrape, wouldn't you say?' The friend peered up at the mark, but then he gave me a wink. 'Snapped, of course that was what happened, wasn't it, Sesina?'

'Yes, sir,' Sesina said and looked down at the floor. She'd have liked to give him a wink back, but didn't. It would be the very moment that Mr Dickens had swung around to look at her.

'First floor, that would be Mr Doyle, wouldn't it?'

'That's right, sir.'

'And the two young men at the top of the house.' He looked back at his notes. 'Mr Carstone and Mr Allen. What do they do?'

'Where do they work?' put in his friend. He had a bit of a twinkle in his eye. If he'd been on his own, she'd have given him a bit of a wink, but she daren't in front of Mr Dickens.

'They're both newspaper men, sir. I think they work in the same office.' Funny stories they had. Would have us in fits sometimes, telling about the tricks that they used to play.

'And Mr Cartwright?' He looked back at his notebook again. Just a ploy so that he could look back fast and catch an expression on her face.

'He's a schoolmaster, sir.' She waited for the next question.

'From London?'

'No, sir. I believe that he's from Yorkshire.'

'From Yorkshire?' Now that did get him interested. Reminded him of his own book. He didn't look at her this time, but across at his friend. She was able to study his face. Yes, he did look very interested.

'So, did you divide the work between you? It would make sense, wouldn't it? One to cook and one to carry. That would be the efficient way to do it.' Must think that he was back in Urania Cottage, making out his timetables and sticking them up on walls.

'Mrs Dawson cooks the breakfasts, sir. We do the carrying, the two us, Isabella and me.'

'So who took the breakfast to . . .' Again this pretending to look at his notebook. 'To Mr Frederick Cartwright, the schoolmaster.'

'Isabella, sir.' So he had noticed the Yorkshire business. Mrs Morson had read them a bit from *Nicholas Nickleby*, the bit where Nicholas had beat up the cruel Yorkshire schoolmaster who had been abusing the boys. She had told all the girls that these Yorkshire schools were very cruel. That there had been boys killed there. Mr Dickens had investigated and then he had written a book.

Sesina allowed a little pause to give him time to think about that. 'Isabella took breakfast to

34

the first and second floors and I took breakfasts to the top floor.' Not true, of course, but she could always pretend that she had been muddled if he thought to check with Mrs Dawson afterwards. Imagine Isabella giving up the fun of chatting and swapping jokes with the two lively fellas on the top floor.

That got him interested. She'd known that it would. He shut his notebook with a snap.

'Now tell me the truth, Sesina. Why did Isabella go out that night, two nights ago? Come now, don't play the innocent with me. There were just the two of you down here in the kitchen. She'd have told you where she was going and who she was meeting.'

'I think that she planned to go to the Hungerford Stairs to meet someone, sir.' That was safe enough. Mrs Dawson wouldn't give her the sack, lazy cow. Wouldn't want to have two new housemaids to train. 'I told her not to,' she added.

'To meet someone, a man?' He was staring at her now, boring into her with those gimlet eyes of his.

'I think it might have been, sir.'

'Think! You know it! Come on, tell the truth. You want that fellow to be caught!'

'Yes, of course, I do, sir.' But not until she could get some money out of him, first. Could be quite a bit; she'd pretend to know all about Isabella's little secret, of course. She'd be good at that. But who was it? She had a few guesses in her mind, but she wasn't sure. She put on her sweetest expression.

'I don't know who she was meeting, sir. I asked and I asked her. I begged her not to go. It didn't do no good, sir. But . . .'

He stared at her and she looked back at him. And didn't say any more. He was used to people telling him lies.

Let's see if you're clever enough to pick up a bit of hint. Sesina tried to send her thought to him. She knew what he was like. Tell him something and he thought that you were lying. Let him find out for himself by following up a hint and he'd be patting himself on the back about how clever he was in finding out the truth.

'Yes, she'd probably keep it to herself.' He said that, not to Sesina, but to his friend. 'That would be her. Isabella was always the queen bee. This one was just a hanger-on.' He gave a nod towards Sesina. Just like I was a dog or something, she thought.

'And what time did she leave?'

'About this time, sir, a little later, perhaps.'

'By the back door?'

'I think so, sir.' Now was the time for a little hesitation.

'Good, good. Might be able to find someone who saw her, perhaps even saw her meet someone.' He was talking to his friend again. But then he suddenly swung back at her. 'You think so?'

She looked at him blandly. 'I thought that she might have gone upstairs, sir, but afterwards I thought that I must have been wrong. It was probably one of the gentlemen going out. Just after she left. She wouldn't have gone out with

36

one of the gentlemen, would she, sir?' Let him do a bit of asking questions, get the man a bit jittery. That would be the best way of going about things. Now to get rid of him. 'Will that be all, sir? Mrs Dawson likes us, likes me, to get to bed early. We, I mean I, have to be up before six in the morning.'

'That will be all, Sesina. Which is the door that leads out to the arches? Out through the scullery, is that it? Come on, Collins, let's go this way. We can have a look round and then we'll go to see my wealthy American friend and find out if he has any information about his tenants.'

He gave her a nod when she showed them out, but his friend gave her a nice smile.

'Goodbye, Sesina,' he said.

'Goodbye, sir,' she said. 'Goodbye, Mr Dickens.' And then, just as he was going through the door, something occurred to Sesina. She hung her head and made her voice sound hesitating. 'I'll be going through Isabella's things, tomorrow morning, sir, after I finish serving up the breakfasts and cleaning the kitchen.' The light from the river was coming in through the open door and she could see a flash of interest in his eyes. She lowered hers, again. 'Should I tell Mrs Dawson if I find anything, anything to . . .?' She stopped there. Let him do the talking now.

He pretended to think about it, great play actor he was. Sesina had seen him at it, out in Urania Cottage, pretending that some girl was going to be thrown out and then pretending to give in to Mrs Morson asking for mercy.

'Well, you know, Sesina,' he said in the end,

37

'it might be just as well not to trouble Mrs Dawson too much about this affair. I'll drop in tomorrow morning and you can have a quiet word with me. We want this villain caught and put out of the way of harming poor girls, don't we?'

'And Mr Dickens is in touch with Inspector Field from the police.' Mr Collins put that in. There was a bit of a twinkle in his eye again. 'Inspector Field would be very interested to get any information to solve this crime.' And then he said, 'Poor girl!' in a very different tone of voice and Sesina liked him for that.

Mr Dickens nodded. 'And I'm sure that my friend, Mr Diamond, would want me to give as much help to the police as possible. So you have a very careful look, Sesina. You're a clever girl; I know that.' He gave her a little pat on the arm.

And then they went out, the two of them, Mr Dickens leading and Mr Collins following, out into the Adelphi Arches. Plenty of poor girls out there, girls begging, girls feeding babies, girls picking up bits of food that had dropped from some of the carts, bits of coal for the fire, girls trying to sell the only thing that they had to sell.

Poor girl; poor Isabella; that was right. She's dead now. But what about me, thought Sesina. I'm not going to be poor all my life. Things happen to poor girls. If you have money you're safe. She shut the door behind them, sat at the kitchen table and began to think hard.

Four

Wilkie Collins, *Basil*:

> . . . the place gave room for the air to
> blow in it, and distanced the tumult of
> the busy streets. The moon was up,
> shined round tenderly by a little
> border-work of pale yellow light.
> Elsewhere, the awful void of night was
> starless; the dark lustre of space shone
> without a cloud.

It was like a picture, I thought as I looked around,
just like a picture that my father would have
painted when he was alive. The rounded arch
framing the scene, the moon above the river, set
in a cloudless dark sky, and the ships lying
passively on the water's shimmering surface. Not
raucous, not sordid, not reeking of bad odours,
not at this hour. Somehow the moon and the cool
air of the night lent the place a certain beauty.
Dickens was looking around, just as I was. Both
of us caught by the strange beauty of the hour
and the place.

'Geniuses, those Adam brothers.' He was
enchanted. Quite moved. Almost mesmerized
by it all. 'What an idea, Wilkie, old man!' he
said enthusiastically. 'Dig out the Thames, keep
the mud at bay with all those underground

39

warehouses, build roads above ground and underground, those lovely arches to rest the buildings and the road upon. Like heaven and hell this place. Beauty above; ugliness and evil tucked away out of sight. And the poor, of course.' Suddenly the note of exaltation had gone from his voice and he sounded sad, preoccupied. He heaved a sigh and looked around at the miserable creatures huddled under the arches. 'Poor Isabella,' he said. 'Well, I did warn her.'

'She came out here, two nights ago. Where did she go then, Dickens?'

'Along the shoreline, I suppose. As far as Hungerford Stairs.' Dickens was always decisive. The words came out with a certain explosive power. One tended to believe everything that he said because of this certainty.

'So her friend said.'

'That's right.' He wasn't listening to me, hadn't heard the note of doubt in my voice. And then he started to walk briskly, back up through the arch.

'We'll see the landlord of the house, my American friend, first,' he said. 'On my way home, I'll drop into the police station and tell them that we know who the girl was and where she came from. I might have another word with Inspector Field.'

'Why do you think she was murdered?'

'Obvious, isn't it?' He had turned away from the river and was walking briskly uphill, under the arch. We had to stand in a few times to allow a carriage, pulled by tired horses seeking their stables, to pass by, but otherwise there was not much traffic around. Not many people either, just the few sad wretches who would sleep there all night under the shelter of the arch. On an impulse, I pulled a coin from my pocket and went across to one of them. She had three children with her and the boy almost looked as old as she did herself. I bent down towards her.

'Did you see a girl come out from that house, two nights ago, about this time?'

Mechanically, she stretched a hand towards the coin. A hand! It was more like a claw. I moved the coin away a little. 'A girl, a servant, she would have come out of that door down there, the door that myself and my friend came from. Did you see her?'

Her look sharpened. She opened her mouth. She seemed as though she was dredging up words from the bottom of her mind.

'Yes,' she said eventually, but there was no conviction in her voice.

'Did she have anyone with her?'

She looked at me as though trying to guess the right answer. Dickens had come back and stood impassively beside me.

'Yes,' she said again.

'A man?'

She nodded.

'Give her the money, Collins!' Suddenly Dickens was impatient. I could tell by the quick jerk of his head. 'Those children are starving,' he said to me. He took out half a crown from his own pocket and handed it to her. 'There you are, my poor woman. Send the boy to get some buns from the coffee shop. Make sure he gets one for each of you.' He waited until the bare legs had disappeared to the other side of the archway. Did not look at me and I was conscious of a feeling of shame. And then, as though suddenly making up his mind, he bent down to look into the woman's face.

'Did you really see her?' he asked, and the gentleness in his voice surprised me.

And she looked up at him then. The dazed expression on her face was not so obvious and her eyes had brightened a little. Her eyes went towards the arch. No sign of the boy. He and the money had disappeared and by now he might be buying the buns from a coffee shop on the Strand. She shook her head.

'No, sir, I didn't see no one come out of there that night.'

Dickens nodded. 'Make sure that you have one of the buns for yourself,' was all that he said, but he touched her shoulder gently, and then, almost as though feeling slightly ashamed of the gesture, he jerked his head at me and I followed.

'Pay first and ask after. You're more likely to get the truth,' he said as we walked side by side up the hill and emerged from the arch to turn into a steep side road.

'You're right.' I felt a little shame at the way that I had held that coin in front of the unfortunate woman as though she were a dog that I was enticing to perform a trick.

'Best leave that sort of thing to Inspector Field; he knows these people and he knows how to get the truth; he knows when they're lying. You're a softy; you would believe everything and anything,' he said. But he said it affectionately and I didn't resent it. He looked more cheerful now, far less grim, almost as though the bestowing of half a crown had opened a spring of talkativeness in him.

'You know, Wilkie, I have a feeling that there might be more in this business than meets the eye. She was a sharp young lady, Isabella Gordon. Can't see her risking her comfortable place in that house just to go out and meet the coalman or a porter from the Hungerford Market. No, I think if she went out when she was supposed to be in her bed, well, then she was expecting some money, quite a bit, not half a crown or even a sovereign. And, what's more, little Miss Sesina suspects something of the sort. And there was some strange business about Isabella pretending to go out by the scullery door, but not really. Going upstairs, perhaps. Whatever happened, little Sesina knows more than she is saying. I'd lay a dollar on that as my American friend would say. Turn here, Wilkie, old chap, now you can see we're back on Adelphi Terrace, back at the front doors again. My friend has the end house for himself, runs a sort of club for visiting Americans. Place is always full of them.'

The door of number one was opened to us by a well-fed, well-starched, middle-aged parlourmaid. She knew Dickens immediately.

'Well, Mary,' he said as he gave up his hat, 'Mr Diamond at home this evening?'

'Yes, sir, certainly sir, he's at home and all on his own. Will be glad to see you, sir. Let me take

43

your coat, and yours, sir,' she said to me. And, indeed, I was glad to be rid of it. The house, despite the cold damp November fog outdoors sweltered in an almost summer-like heat. There was a huge stove in the hallway, the flames burning with a blaze as it threw out such heat that one could not stand very close to it.

And then there was a roar from above, the voice travelling down the stairway where the vaulted ceiling seemed to add a majestic sound to the words. I looked up at it and admired the frieze and the decorated cornice. It would, I thought, make a magnificent opening to a play. There was a man standing on the top stair, arms outstretched.

'Mr Dickens,' said the voice with a strong American accent, 'Mr Dickens, you are more welcome than the Niagara Falls in a desert. Come in, come in.'

'My poor friend, are you as thirsty as that.' Dickens bounded up the stairs energetically. 'Shall we send out for a bottle?'

'Oh, I've got a bottle, Dick, got hundreds of them, all lying peacefully in my cellar. It's the company, man, the company. That's what I'm crying out for.'

Dickens' American friend, Mr Donald Diamond, was a huge man with an enormous paunch and a reddened complexion. He wore the largest and brightest waistcoat that I had ever seen on a man. And it advanced before him, swirls of red and yellow twinkling a welcome as much as his cordial face.

'Well, the company has come, Don,' said Dickens, shaking the enormous hand held out to him, 'and look what I've done for you. Brought you one of the most talented men in London! You should read his book, *Basil*. Spine-chilling! Blood-curdling! I predict a great future for him,' he said and I blushed a little, modestly, but thrilled with excitement as Mr Diamond pumped my hand up and down, the enormous diamond on his ring carving a glittering trajectory beneath the overhead gas lamp.

'Well, isn't that the greatest thing,' said our host. 'Mary, this calls for a celebration. A bowl of the Smoking Bishop, Mary and a few cuts of your pie.'

'Yes, sir. In a minute, sir.' Mary disappeared down the steps to the kitchen.

'Great girl, that, best girl in the whole of London. She'd work all day and all night, too, if I didn't stop her. "Don't you turn yourself into a slave, my dear," I say that to her. "I used to work like you when I was a young man and I've never forgotten it. Never have forgotten what my legs felt like at the end of the day, making those beds, cooking, cleaning, did it all." Made my money out of hotels and boarding houses, Mr Collins, you know,' he said to me, propelling me up the stairs with a large hand spanning the entire space between my two shoulder blades. 'Now come into the drawing room, the two of you. Come and warm yourselves. That's what I call a fire, Dick, just feel the heat coming from it. What do you think? Your Mr Pickwick would relish a fire like that, wouldn't he?'

He was a bit like Mr Pickwick, himself, I thought, as he propelled me into a chair beside

45

one of the most enormous fires that I have ever seen. I could see how Dickens looked at him with almost the fond smile of a creator. They had met on board ship when my friend was coming back from America. I had heard the story many times, but this was our first meeting. Dickens had told me that I would like him and I did.

'And so, you've had a book published, Mr Collins, well, isn't that a great thing.'

'Two; two books published,' I said and hoped that it didn't sound like boasting.

'Two! A young man like you. Well! How about that!' And the American accent made the words even more striking.

I smiled modestly, glad when Mr Diamond turned his attention to his fire, carefully placing a few more large lumps of coal in strategic places.

'Mary won't be long, gentlemen,' he said, as anxious for our comfort as though we were both starving with hunger and faint with the cold.

'We have brought you some bad news, Don,' said Dickens and I was glad that he had broached it before the maid returned. It seemed wrong to talk about that poor girl, Isabella Gordon – and I had a sudden vision of her lying dripping on that marble slab – while the Smoking Bishop and the slices of pie were handed around.

'It's one of your rooming houses, number five, a girl, a housemaid, she was strangled and thrown into the river.'

'Poor girl!' He was prompt in his response, but a bit puzzled, too. I could see that.

'I have an interest in the matter because she

was a girl that I had for a year or so in Urania Cottage – you remember that I've told you about the charity that Miss Coutts and I have set up, a charity to educate and train girls and give them a new life in Australia? You were good enough to give—'

'One of these girls, what a terrible thing.' I had a feeling that he interrupted Dickens before his generosity could be spelled out and I liked the man all the more for that. 'What happened to her, Dick?'

Dickens shrugged. 'She went out to meet a man. The old, old story, you'd think, but somehow, from cross-questioning the other maid, another girl from Urania Cottage, I get the impression that it was money she was after, not just a love affair or anything like that.'

'Money?' He seemed a little puzzled.

'Very possibly blackmail. And, I may be wrong, but I have a feeling that it might involve one of the men who lodge in number five.' Dickens, I could see, had made up his mind about that. He came to the point with his usual efficiency. 'What do you know about those men in your house, Don?'

Mr Diamond, I thought, looked somewhat taken aback at that. I could see the words: 'they pay rent' tremble on his lips, but he, like everyone else, was probably used to Dickens' determined character. Obediently he got to his feet, crossed over to his desk and pulled out a fat notebook. It had a label glued on to its front with the words: *Adelphi Terrace* written on it in a large round hand, an uneducated hand, I thought, looking

47

with interest at our host and thinking of him cleaning and making beds in boarding houses when he was a young man.

'I rent out all the houses on Adelphi Terrace except this one, but number five is the only one where I let rooms, not the whole house,' he said to me when he saw me looking at him.

I felt a little uncomfortable. It seemed a bit impolite to be cross-questioning a man about his tenants, just because Dickens had suddenly got some bee in his bonnet. I knew what it was, though. It had been that mention of the schoolmaster coming from Yorkshire that had started this train of thought.

Oddly enough, it was of the schoolmaster that the American spoke, first of all.

'Well, there's Mr Frederick Cartwright. He's the latest tenant. Took the rooms after a man who used to have them gave in his notice. Went off to be married to his boss's daughter. Mr Cartwright is a friend of his and he offered to take over the rest of the lease and then when that was up, well, he stayed on.'

'And how long ago was that, Don?'

'Just about six months ago, Dick, no longer, yes, that's right. I see the date here now. Just a week over the six months.'

'Gave references, I suppose, did he?'

'That's right. He's a schoolmaster at St Bartholomew's, got the reference from a clergyman there, at St Bartholomew's Church, all very respectable. Bank reference, too. No, I never worried about him.'

'But there was someone else, someone that you

did worry a bit about.' Dickens reminded me sometimes of a little terrier, named Ben, I had once when I was a boy, a splendid ratter with very upright ears and bright black eyes. He'd pounce on a rat in the way that my friend would pounce on a piece of information.

'You were going to tell us about another lodger, lodgers, perhaps: the two young journalists on the top floor, was it them?' Dickens, as well as I, had heard a hesitation in the American's voice.

'Naw! Not those two. Nice young lads, bit late with the rent once or twice, but you know what it's like, Dick, we were all young once.' The American beamed happily in a paternal sort of way.

'I was never late with the rent when I was young,' said Dickens grimly.

'Well, well, I can't say the same of myself, I'm afraid. Until I made my pile, that is. Has your friend told you about me, Mr Collins? Started off dirt poor, not a penny to my name, managed to get myself down to Georgia, over twenty years ago, it was; time of the gold rush. A young man, like you, would hardly have heard of the place, but I tell you, Mr Collins, there were some hearts broken down there. Gold, you see! Everyone after it. Digging all day long. Must have been about ten thousand of us down there then, all chasing gold. But you were interested in my lodgers, Dick. Well, that barrister fella, well he's a bit odd.'

'Late with the rent.' Dickens pounced again.

'Naw, naw, not that. Fact is that his rent is paid quarterly, paid by some law firm, not paid in his name, but by someone of the same surname, money in the family, that's what I reckon. Anyway, the rent comes in as regular as anything, Mr Jeremiah Doyle, Barrister-at-Law. Can't complain about that. But, you know, Dick, there's something funny about the fella. Doesn't seem to do much business. Upsets Mrs Dawson, complaining about the housemaids doing his room when he wanted to rest. Middle of the morning, too, according to her. You'd think he'd be busy with his law work, in an office, but no, he's in and out of the lodgings all day. Very irregular in his habits, that's what she said to me about him. Something a bit odd about him. Met him once down by the river. Stared at me as if he had never seen me before in his life. Had a dazed look in his eyes.'

'Drunk,' I put in.

'Naw, naw, not drunk, Mr Collins. No one minds a young man getting drunk.'

'Opium,' said Dickens decisively. 'I thought that there was something about him. Something about the eyes. Didn't care for his looks much, myself.'

'And he didn't look too young to me.' I put that in.

'Well, he wouldn't, not to you, Mr Collins. When you get to my age, lots of people look young.' The American beamed on me benevolently.

'I'd like to know a little more about this fellow, Mr Jeremiah Doyle. He is a bit old for a law firm to be managing his affairs. And paying his rent from a relative's account. What would you say, Wilkie? About thirty I'd put him, would you?'

As usual, of course, he didn't wait for my answer, just went on making one of his neat notes, and then drawing a mathematically accurate box around it.

'Strange thing is that it's paid by a man who lives out in America,' said Mr Diamond. 'I remember that now. A bank clerk had left a slip in when the rent was posted to me. It was marked as coming from the account of William Doyle, some place in America, can't remember where. I know, Georgetown, I think.'

'Perhaps the father of Jeremiah Doyle, what do you think, Dick?' I asked. 'Or even the brother, an elder brother. He might be the black sheep of the family, sent over to London to get him out of the way of a respectable family firm. Tea, perhaps. A lot of money in tea plantations. I used to work for a firm of tea importers, Antrobus & Company. Was never so bored in my life, Mr Diamond. That's when I took up the law.'

'And that bored you, too,' said Dickens with a grin.

'I might enquire about the name Doyle from Antrobus & Company,' I said, ignoring this. 'They're not far from here. Down at the end of the Strand, next to Trafalgar Square.'

'Best not,' said the landlord, looking a little uncomfortable. 'I wouldn't like to be seen to be betraying any secrets about my lodgers. In any case, I can't see that if a man likes to smoke a pipe of opium, not that I'd do it myself, but I can't see that it can have anything to do with the death of the housemaid in the house where he happens to lodge. It doesn't make any sense to me.'

51

'Once moral degeneracy sets in, then all is possible,' Dickens said in his firm way. 'Isabella Gordon would not be a girl to stand back from a little blackmail if she knew something to this man's discredit. And there's something else, too. Did you notice, Wilkie? When little Sesina was telling us about that night in the kitchen before Isabella disappeared. She said something about a bell ringing and then she looked up at the broken wire. I noticed it particularly when she said that, I wondered if it was anything to do with Isabella leaving so soon. Don't you remember? And when I looked up I saw that the label on that bell was first floor. First-floor lodgings, Mr Doyle's lodgings, that's right, Don, isn't it? The lawyer is on the first floor, isn't he?'

'That's right,' said the landlord. He looked a little uneasy, a little troubled, pulling at the lobe of his ear in a meditative manner. He hadn't liked my suggestion and I thought I wouldn't mention it again, though nothing would stop me finding out whether Doyle was a tea planter. Antrobus & Company had many on their list. I said no more, though, and listened to him quietly 'So you think that Doyle could be an opium addict,' he continued. 'And the girl Isabella finds out and she tries to blackmail him and then he kills her, strangles her and drops her into the river. Waal, waal, Dick, you're a great man to make up a story. I can see you writing a book about this. He's a genius, isn't he, Mr Collins?'

All very far-fetched, I thought. The man might take opium, but what was so wrong about that? Lots of people did. After all laudanum was just

52

opium mixed with a little brandy. My father, himself a most upright citizen, took that when he was suffering with his chest. I'd taken it myself, and so had my mother. Why should Mr Doyle pay Isabella to keep the secret, when it was probably known to his family and to his lawyer? I opened my mouth to say that, but then shut it again. Dickens was the kindest of men, but he did like to be the one in the forefront. And this was his friend, and his enquiries. He would not welcome me putting a spoke in. In any case, there was a sound of a door closing downstairs and then the sound of heavy footsteps. The maid was struggling up the stairs and the American crossed the room to open the door for her. Not something that an Englishman would do, especially not with company present.

'Just you smell that, gentlemen!' he was exclaiming as she came in. 'No one in London can make Smoking Bishop like Mary here. And wait until you taste her pies. Ambrosial, that's the word, isn't it, Dick? Here Mr Collins, just you taste that and give me your opinion on it?'

'Delectable,' I said, sipping it. 'The Romans would have appreciated it as much as the Greeks, Mr Diamond.' I wasn't sure whether he had appreciated my little joke, though he laughed heartily.

'There you are, Mary. You'll be finding yourself in these gentlemen's good books.' He laughed even more heartily at that pun and I joined with him. Dickens wasn't really listening, just frowning a little to himself. I thought that he sipped the Smoking Bishop and nibbled the edge of pie in a rather abstracted fashion. His mind was busy, I knew. He waited until the servant was out of the room before sketching his thoughts to us.

'Only two reasons why a man in his thirties would have a law firm looking after his affairs,' he said decisively. 'The first would be mental weakness and the second would be moral degeneracy. Now the man is obviously not of feeble wits – he's a barrister, apparently. You said that his lawyers wrote "barrister-at-law" after his name and no lawyer would do that without being sure of the facts. I met him, briefly, but that's usually enough for me. I'd put him as sharp, very sharp. What do you think, Don?'

'I'm sure that you're right, Dick. What did you think, Mr Collins?'

'He recognized Dickens,' I said.

'Ah, but did he recognize me as a genius? That's the true test of sharp intelligence.' Dickens mood lightened and then his face grew solemn again. He put down his glass and I knew that he was thinking of the dead girl. I had never met her in life, but even in death, there had been something about her, the mouth, the eyes, that luxuriant hair. And then I remembered how she had argued with Dickens, disputed his judgement. She would not easily have been forgotten.

I was not surprised when he said abruptly and impatiently, 'Nothing can condone murder. Nobody should be allowed to get away with murder, no matter who or what they are. I'll certainly look into this man Doyle. A suspicious character if ever I saw one. Don't worry, Don. Your name will never be mentioned. Now what

54

about these two young men on the top floor?' Dickens leaned back in his chair and now that he had taken a firm decision he seemed to be more relaxed and he took another sip from the Smoking Bishop. I accepted a refill from our host and took another one of Mary's pies while I waited for an answer to my friend's question. I had some questions of my own in my mind to ask of the landlord, but they could wait until the matter of poor Isabella was finished. *Gold Rush*, I thought. What a great book that would make. I imagined my hero, the hero of my next book, the trials, the tribulations, the disasters, the world-shaking moment when the wet earth fell away and when the sunlight suddenly struck, struck gold.

'They are journalists,' the American was saying. 'Came to me at the same time, both work in the same office. I have a feeling that they were in school together.'

'I'd like to meet them all.' Dickens was brooding on those four men and I knew that ideas were going through his head. I could see his eyes, very intent, almost blank, but at the same time full of energy, an energy that was in the background, that was kept cloaked behind an assumed air of indifference. 'Yes, that would be very interesting,' he said and his voice bore a flavour of indifference. Nevertheless, those eyes were now sharply focused on his host, almost as though he were waiting for him to produce a rabbit from the hat, a solution to the problem.

His American friend did not disappoint him. In fact, he looked interested, intrigued and eager to know more.

'I'll tell you what we'll do, Mr Dickens,' he said. 'I've been in the habit of throwing a dinner for my lodgers every Christmas, what say we do one now; what can we do in November? Some sort of anniversary, some commemoration, Trafalgar Day, something like that, what do you think? And I'll tell the tenants that it will be to meet the famous Mr Dickens. What do you say to that?'

'What about next Sunday?' Dickens was rising to the occasion with his usual quick-wittedness. 'Anniversary of the building of Adelphi Terrace; that's right, isn't it, Wilkie? Yes, that will be ideal,' he said without waiting for an answer from me. 'Sunday is a good day. Saturday, now, well they might have engagements, but Sunday is a dull day. You do that Don. We'll make it fun.'

'I'll get Mrs Dawson to do a slap-up dinner, and a few bottles of good wine, of course.'

'And a short speech from me, perhaps.'

'Or just a chat,' I said hastily.

Five

Sesina was up very early the day after Mr Dickens had visited the house. He would be back; she knew that. He wouldn't give up until he found out as much as he possibly could about the murder of Isabella. He'd be like a dog after a scent, she thought. And she would do her best to help him. Isabella might haunt her if her murderer wasn't caught. And she had a good idea of who it might be.

There must be some clues, she thought. Isabella was that kind of girl. She had brains, Isabella. She had been working things out. Sesina knew that. Sometimes, of an evening recently, she would be only half listening as Sesina talked, and any fool could see that her mind was working away, like doing those sums that Mrs Morson used to teach them. Adding up and taking away. That was Isabella.

But had it all been in her head?

Isabella liked writing things. That would be the way of it. Wasn't it likely that she kept things written down, pieces of information, fit them together like bits of a jigsaw. Mr Dickens used to bring jigsaws to Urania Cottage. He liked to see them all busy in the evening, singing, reading, listening to stories, playing parlour games and doing jigsaws. Isabella had been the best of them all at doing jigsaws. She'd have a picture assembled in the time that it would take some of the slow mugs to sort the pieces. Mr Dickens would know about that.

So where would be a likely place for her to have hidden the clues?

Sesina and Isabella had shared a bedroom since their arrival at number five Adelphi Terrace, two years previously. Mrs Dawson had offered them separate bedrooms, one in the upper basement and one in the lower basement, beside the cellar. She had explained that the house had no need for a kitchen maid or a parlourmaid since only breakfast was served and so less servants were needed. One of them could have the kitchen maid's room in the lower basement and the other the housemaid's room.

Well, of course, neither was willing to take the kitchen maid's room, small and damp, and in the end they decided to share the housemaid's room, just as they had always shared a bedroom in Urania Cottage, cosier, warmer and more fun as they liked to chat and share jokes before going to sleep. The kitchen maid's room was used as a dumping place by them, a place where they put stuff that they didn't want.

And a good place to hide anything that had been stolen or 'lifted' as Isabella would say. Some of the stuff had just been taken from the waste-paper baskets in the rooms, or other things lying around a room that could be quietly hidden behind a wardrobe until it was obvious that the owner had not missed the item, and then moved down to the basement. Others had been grabbed from stalls in Leather Lane on a day out. A pair of leather gloves, belonging to Mrs Dawson and reposing in a drawer until she had forgotten all about them. And the keys. They each kept one, neither quite trusting the other.

As soon as she was dressed, Sesina took her key from beneath a loose floorboard and then took her candle. She went softly and quietly down to the lower basement. Made up the fire in the kitchen first of all. If Mrs Dawson had heard her and came to investigate then she would make that her excuse for getting up early. For a while she warmed herself by the stove while she thought matters over and listened for footsteps. But there was no sound from upstairs and so she stole into the little room.

A slightly chipped inkpot and a couple of sharpened pens. The first discovery. Tucked into a drawer on the old clothes press. And then the calling cards. She remembered them. Rubbish she had thought them, but Isabella had taken a fancy to them. Twenty of them there had been, engraved, fancy writing, with gold decoration around the edges. Stored in one of the drawers.

Some missing.

There was a creak from upstairs. A warning that Mrs Dawson had deposited her bulk on the floor. No point in involving her. Sesina went back to the kitchen, put on her sacking apron and loaded her bucket with rags, brushes, black lead. She filled four coal scuttles.

Dragged your arm off, carrying these up the stairs, soon be gone, too and then four more to be filled.

And then she waited, toasting her feet in front

59

of the fire. Let the old cow make her own tea this morning, she thought. She began to prepare her speech and just allowed Mrs Dawson to get through the door before she launched an attack.

'Am I expected to do all the bedrooms, myself, again today, missus? When are we getting a new maid?'

'Don't know how you have the heart to talk like that, Sesina, with poor Isabella lying cold in a mortuary.'

'It's too much for one person,' said Sesina stubbornly. *And put that in your pipe and smoke it,* she muttered under her breath as she banged and clanked her way through the kitchen door. She didn't mind, though, too much. She had a plan in her mind and she was going to have money for herself before she was many months older. In any case, she had plenty to think about at the moment and didn't want to waste time instructing some ignorant girl in her duties. She'd make Mrs Dawson carry up Mr High-and-Mighty Doyle's breakfast, though. No point in letting her get away with murder. She'd bring breakfast to the two lads on the fourth floor, that was a pleasure and she didn't mind dodging the odd kiss, or even not dodging. They were so larky the pair of them that they made serving them fun.

And she would bring breakfast to Mr Cartwright. Now that wouldn't be fun. Him glaring at her from the pillow with a bit of feather stuck in his mutton chop whiskers, like as not. Daren't laugh, though. No, no fun with Mr Cartwright. That would be business. But she would have to be careful. No point in ending up like poor Isabella. She'd need a bit of help and she knew just the man to give it.

'No point in fetching a stick from the river if a dog will do it for you,' she muttered and then giggled a little to herself, managing to straighten her face before she went into Mr Doyle's rooms. Two of them. Two fires to clean out and two fires to light. Liked a fire in his sitting room as well as his bedroom, first thing in the morning, lazy fella. Would spend half a morning in there, lounging around, reading the newspaper. She'd do his sitting room first and try to be extra quiet when she did the bedroom. Ever so irritated he'd be if she woke him up before his breakfast arrived. Let Mrs Dawson take it up to him and see what a crosspatch he was in the morning. She almost held her breath while she cleaned out the bedroom grate, black-leaded it quickly and then kindled the coals. There wasn't a stir from him and yet she had a funny feeling that he was awake, something about the way he was breathing. Creepy fellow. You can't trust lawyers, that's what Isabella used to say. She was glad when she got out of the room and went up the next flight of stairs to Mr Cartwright's rooms. At least he didn't need his sitting-room fire to be lit until the afternoon.

'What's become of the other girl?' Mr Cartwright was already up when she slipped in through the door. In his nightgown, bare hairy legs, looking out of the window, looking over at the river. He was an early riser. Very particular about getting out of the house early, just in case there were

61

crowds on the street. Made a big fuss if his breakfast wasn't in time as he liked to get into the school half an hour before the boys arrived, or so he kept telling Mrs Dawson. He looked back at her and repeated his question impatiently. That great big ugly scar seemed to be cutting his face in two, and the patch of red-orange hair, Isabella used to say, made him look like that orangutan in Ashleys Menagerie on the Strand.

'Isabella, sir? Didn't you know?' She faced him. 'She's been found, sir, found dead. Dragged out of the river. Strangled.' She kept her eye on his face when she said that. He knew. He must know. Everyone else in the house knew. Mrs Dawson was telling everyone about it last night. The two lads, Mr Allen and Mr Carstone, they both knew. Had been talking about it. Popped into the kitchen last night. Were sorry about Isabella. Not at all as larky as usual.

'Strangled.' She could have sworn that his face went a little pale. 'Who found her? Who identified her? How did they know that she came from this place?'

'I don't know, sir.' That was the easiest answer. Funny questions, though. The lads on the top storey didn't ask any questions like that. Just said that they were sorry, and how much they liked her, and how Sesina would miss her friend.

Suspicious, him pretending that he didn't know, she said to herself as she went up to the top storey. She and Isabella used to leave these two to the last, used to argue over who would do them. She'd take up their breakfast. They were always dying for their coffee. Drinking the night

62

before makes you thirsty in the morning, they told her that nearly every day.

'Do the hall first thing this morning, Sesina; we'll be having the landlord, I'd say,' said Mrs Dawson as soon as Sesina had swallowed her own breakfast – and the remains of Mr Cartwright's rasher and egg.

'Not hungry this morning, sir?' she had said when she fetched his tray and he had given a grunt in reply. Bad conscience, she said to herself. As soon as she got back to the kitchen she gave it a quick heat-up and gobbled it down before taking her polishes out to the hall. Why shouldn't she have a cooked breakfast? Mrs Dawson always did.

Mrs Dawson was right. The landlord arrived. Bright and early, he was, too. Nice fellow. Came in. Opened the front door when she was polishing the hallstand, and slipped her sixpence. Wasn't alone, though. Mr Dickens and that friend of his, Mr Collins, came with him. Up early. She didn't think that Mr Dickens lived anywhere local. And Mr Collins looked half asleep. Giving a big yawn and then rubbing his glasses with his pocket handkerchief.

'I'll get Mrs Dawson, sir.' Wouldn't be too pleased to have her breakfast interrupted. Liked a good old sitdown by the kitchen stove at this time of the morning while herself and Isabella tore around like wasps in a preserving jar.

'Drat the man. What's he come so early for? Go on, girl, use your loaf. Put him in my parlour. I'll be up in a second.' Mrs Dawson sloshed some more tea into her breakfast cup and tried to wash down the rest of the food with it. Sesina went back up the stairs to find them standing in the hall looking all around them. Mr Dickens hadn't said a word yet. Not like him. What would she do if he said nothing and just went away without talking to her? She needed to get his attention, to make him interested in hunting down the murderer. When she reached the top of the stairs, she just addressed herself to the landlord.

'Would you like to wait in the parlour for a minute, sir? Mrs Dawson won't be a minute. She's just sorting the linen.' No harm in saying that in case the old cow was listening. He shook his head, though, and stayed where he was. Mr Dickens was looking around him, just like he did yesterday evening, but he stopped and listened to the landlord's question.

'All your lodgers gone out, are they, my dear – it's Sesina, isn't it?'

Yes, sir. I'm Sesina. The other housemaid was Isabella.'

Very silent, Mr Dickens, this morning. No harm in bringing in Isabella's name; she looked across at him when she said it, but he did not look back at her, just gazing up the stairs like he was wondering how they were built. She might get some information.

She allowed a few seconds to go by, to allow them to remember about Isabella before she added, 'No, sir, none of the lodgers have gone out yet.' She should probably ask them if they wanted to take off their hats and coats, but it would be bound to be wrong in Mrs Dawson's eyes. She was in a fine old mood this morning. Didn't like Sesina standing up for her rights.

And just at that moment, the sound of footsteps, heavy, firm footsteps, coming down the stairs. She knew who that would be.

'It's Mr Cartwright, sir, the schoolmaster.' Looking up at him now, she could see what a big, burly, heavily-made fellow he was. A bit like some of those prize fighters that you'd see at fairs, especially with that scar. Except that he was dressed all in black, with a black top hat. He took off the hat when he saw the landlord. Looked better with it on. Hid that orangutan hair of his.

'Good morning, Mr Diamond.' Just that. Never anything human about him. Didn't ask what brought the man here, didn't say anything about Isabella.

'Ah, Mr Cartwright. Off to the grindstone. How's everything going at St Bartholomew's School? Got your cane with you?'

That took the schoolmaster aback. He seemed to give a bit of a jump. Sesina moved to the back of the hallstand and began rubbing a bit of polish on to it. She usually didn't bother with that more than once a month or so, but she wanted to see his face. Looked furious, scar gaping, like an angry mouth. Didn't like that remark. No doubt about that. And Mr Dickens looked ever so keen when the landlord had said that. Watching the man's face. Listening. Listening to his answer when it came to his lips after that strange pause. A bit of a stammer when he replied. Sesina could see the faces as she

65

polished the dusty wood vigorously. Time for the schoolmaster to speak, now, but he seemed a bit uncertain, stammered a bit.

'N-not much need of that, Mr Diamond. The boys in St Bartholomew's School are all very well behaved. Nice boys from good families.' And then he was gone, out of the door, as fast as he could go. Sesina looked at Mr Dickens. Yes, he'd certainly taken an interest. Saw her looking too. He saw everything. And then he looked back at the landlord, waiting for him to do his errand, whatever it was. There was a sound of the kitchen door closing downstairs. Would take Mrs Dawson a while to get up those two flights of stairs, especially with the size of the breakfast that she had just put away.

'Ah, here comes Mrs Dawson, yes, I think I'll pop into the parlour now, my dear,' the landlord said to her in his American accent.

'I'll stay here, and have a chat with Sesina.' Cool as a breeze. Giving orders in another man's house. A quick look at his friend Mr Collins. When she came back from showing the landlord into Mrs Dawson's parlour, the two of them were still just standing there with their hats in their hands. Mrs Dawson hung around for a minute after saying good morning to them, but Mr Dickens just nodded at her and then ignored her. The housekeeper glared at Sesina who was standing holding the door open, but in she went, her head in the air. She'd make a stuffed bird laugh with her airs and graces.

And still Mr Dickens didn't speak. He just stood there, looking up and down the stairs and all around him. And his friend just twirled his hat on his ladylike little hand. Sesina didn't take too much notice of them. Let him wait, she thought, as she took up her polish again. She could hear Mrs Dawson. Making a big fuss about some dinner party that the landlord wanted her to give. Any excuse for Mrs D. if it was a question of her getting off her backside and doing some work. Could she do fish? Not her! *Just you come and look at the fish kettle, Mr Diamond. Can't say fairer than that.* She had the cheek to tell him to order oysters; that they were in season and wouldn't need no cooking. And followed that up with advising him to get some roast fowls – *from the pastry cook on the Strand; a dish of stewed beef, with vegetables – from the pastry cook; a raised pie – from the pastry cook.*

'Let's go down to the kitchen,' said Mr Dickens abruptly. Suddenly looking back at her as if he'd just noticed her.

Sesina nodded. She felt like keeping him waiting, just as he had kept her waiting, but she had something to tell him and couldn't wait to see his face. *I'll put you under an obligation to me, Mr Dickens,* Sesina thought to herself and so she packed up her polishes and followed him. Mr Collins came behind the two of them. He hadn't said a word, but he gave her a friendly smile.

'Not there, sir,' Sesina said when they got to the bottom of the stairs. 'Not into the kitchen. In here, Mr Dickens, into Isabella's room. I want to show you something.' It would be safe for the moment, she felt. The landlord would be talking or trying to get a word in edgewise, that would be the way of it. Mrs Dawson would have a lot of suggestions of ways for her to avoid any actual cooking for this dinner party that the landlord wanted to have. She knew her. It would be something else that could be bought in: *a raised pie and a dish of kidneys – from the pastry cook, of course; a tart, and (if he liked) a shape of jelly – from the pastry cook.* And various other suggestions. And, of course, the wine to be bought in, never mind that there was a stash of it in the cellar, left there by the previous owner of number five.

'So this was Isabella's bedroom, was it?' Mr Dickens had a look around. A bed and a clothes press. Looked all right, thought Sesina, but she didn't answer his question.

'Isabella was a great one for hiding things, sir, but I discovered this. It was under a floorboard.' Sesina took the flat piece of card from her pocket and handed it to him. 'I wonder could it be anything to do with who murdered her.'

The empty bedroom had made a great place to conceal a secret. And this was an explosive one.

'A calling card!' He read the words aloud: 'Mr Jeremiah Doyle, 54 Robert Adam Street.' He frowned suspiciously at it and did not turn it over. 'How did she get hold of this? Don't tell me, I suppose she stole them . . .'

'She didn't really steal the cards, sir,' said Sesina, making her voice sound virtuous and shocked. 'Mr Doyle threw them away. They were in the wastepaper basket. They were no good to

68

him, you see. They have the wrong address on them.'

He nodded. He would see the sense in that, of course, but Sesina kept her eyes fixed on him. A bit anxious, a bit worried, loyal to her friend, not wanting him to think badly of Isabella. She needed him to stir up things, to hunt down the murderer.

'What on earth did the girl want with them?' he asked and now his voice was a bit gentler, almost indulgent; almost a bit amused.

'She wanted to make a book, a book, that's what she told me. She was going to write something on one of them any day that something interesting happened and then she was going to turn it into a book. But it would be too expensive for someone like her to buy paper, of course, so she saved the cards.' *Mr Dickens would like that. Always very keen on self-help and being ambitious to improve.* 'Isabella wanted to be a lady, sir. She wanted to better herself.' Sesina kept her eyes fixed on him and her expression demure and respectful. 'That's what she told me, sir. She wanted to go on with her education. Do the things that you told her to do. See, she's written something on the back.'

And then he turned it over. Read it aloud. "'I've talked with him today. He's the one. I know that he is. I'll make that man pay for what he did." Who was this person, this man that she mentions, Sesina?'

Sesina knew that he would ask her that. 'I don't know, sir. I really don't know.'

'Nonsense, you girls would have been very

69

close, lived close to each other for years now, didn't you, shared a bedroom in Urania Cottage, if I remember rightly. Don't give me that nonsense. Of course you know who she's talking about.'

'I don't. I swear!' Sesina was enjoying this. He was always a one to think that he knew better than anyone else, always knew the truth. Let him find out the truth now. Let him find out that villain who murdered poor Isabella.

'Perhaps Sesina doesn't like to betray her friend. Perhaps she has sworn to keep a secret.' Mr Collins said that in such a kind way that Sesina wished she had something to tell him, just to him in private, a little secret between the two of them. And then she knew. Yes, she would tell him, but not Mr Dickens.

'It might be on another card, Mr Collins, the name of the man that she's talking about.' Sesina said the words softly, and just to him. She saw Mr Dickens swing around and look at her. Astonished that she would dare to speak without being spoken to. That she would dare address anyone else when he, the famous Mr Dickens, was present. Mr Collins, though, he was nice. He gave her a wink.

'You counted those calling cards, didn't you, Sesina; you know that there are some missing; you can see by them that some have been removed,' he said, quick as a flash.

'Yes, sir, well, it was Isabella who counted them really. There were twenty of them. Don't look like twenty, there, do they, sir?'

Mr Collins went over to the drawer that she

had left slightly sticking out and took out the pack of visiting cards, running them through his fingers. Nice nails, thought Sesina, pink and sort of polished-looking. She watched him count them; he did it twice.

'Only twelve here, Dickens,' he said. 'So she has written eight of these cards. You said that she was going to put them together to make a little book, when she was finished, is that right, Sesina?'

'That's right, sir, she wanted to make a book or a diary. Mr Dickens used to tell us that we should keep a diary.'

'Wonder what she's done with the rest of the cards.' He was talking to himself, but Sesina answered him, straight away.

'Hidden them, sir. She was set on hiding things. She would be afraid that Mrs Dawson would read them.'

'Or you, perhaps?' But he said it with such a nice smile that Sesina smiled back at him. She nodded.

'Or me, neither. She liked to keep a secret, did Isabella. That's why she didn't like Urania Cottage. You couldn't have no secrets there, sir, not anyways.' She said it confidentially, lowering her voice and standing on tiptoe to whisper in his ear. He looked amused. Mr Dickens, she noticed, was pretending not to hear, looking all around the miserable little bedroom with a frown on his face. She looked hastily at the window, then away, and then back again, leaning a little forward and narrowing her eyes.

And, of course, he saw the card that she was

looking straight at. She had left it there for him to find. Had taken it out from its hiding place in the window frame and then had put it back in again, but making it slightly more conspicuous. And it just stuck out, just a little edging of gold, but enough to catch the attention of someone holding a candle close to it. He reached out and twitched it from its place.

'Another one, Collins, look at this.' He had pounced on it and he pulled it out like one of them tricksters in Covent Garden taking a rabbit from a top hat.

'What does it say?' His friend was as excited as himself. Love a mystery, all of them!

'"Going to see the coachman tomorrow. I've found the place. The Saracen's Head".'

'I say, Dickens, this is jolly interesting. There's some sort of mystery here.'

Sesina looked from one to the other. A mystery, indeed. What could Isabella have meant? She began to ponder the matter in her mind.

'Come on, Wilkie. It's Hunt the Thimble time. Bustle about, my boy. You take that side of the room and I'll take this one. Six more cards to find. A bottle of wine to the one who finds the next one.'

He didn't mean her, of course. That was obvious. Not that she liked wine much. She had tasted some once when the landlord had given one of his dinner parties. A bit sour, Sesina thought, though Isabella had pretended to like it.

'Excuse me, sir, Mrs Dawson is coming down the stairs.'

That stopped them. Looked like a pair of lads

who had been caught larking around. Mr Dickens had taken the two cards. She'd memorized them, though. Bet I work out the story behind them quicker than you do, thought Sesina.

Mrs Dawson was bringing the landlord down to see her range. Just to show that she couldn't cook anything special on it. Sesina left the two of them to play about, Mr Dickens pulling out drawers, Mr Collins looking under the bed and she went into the kitchen to support Mrs Dawson.

'If only I could have one of them new stoves, the Leamington Kitchener, Mr Diamond,' Mrs Dawson was saying, 'Well, then . . .'

The sky would be the limit, that's what she means. On the day that I'm leaving this place I'll tell her a few home truths, Sesina promised herself. And the first one will be: you can't cook for toffee, Mrs Dawson. Leamington Kitchener or no Leamington Kitchener, you'll never make a cook.

But it mightn't work out. She mightn't be leaving this place. They mightn't be able to find out the name of the man who killed Isabella. And then her dreams of getting tons of money and living the life of a lady might come to nothing. She had better keep Mrs Dawson happy until the mystery of Isabella's death was unravelled.

'Missus is right, sir,' she said to the landlord. 'The range is ever so unreliable. Best get the fowls and oysters sent in and a few stews and the tarts. Then she can put her mind to the rest of the dinner.'

He was a funny fellow, the landlord, shrugging

his shoulders, looking from the stove to Mrs Dawson, and then he shouted out in his American accent, 'Dick, Dick, you're a man for gadgets. I bet you know all about something called the Leamington Kitchener!'

And, of course, Mr Dickens came in straight away, couldn't resist that. Always had to be the 'know-all', had to tell everyone the right thing to do. Sesina slipped out of the kitchen and left them to it. Mr Collins was still wandering around the kitchen maid's bedroom, tapping on walls and peeping into the chimney.

Sesina went right up, very close to him and whispered in his ear, 'I can tell you one thing, sir. I know that Isabella never went out by the back door that night.'

He gave her a kind smile, his big round glasses catching the light from the candle.

'How do you know that, Sesina?' he said. And he spoke in a whisper, just like they were having a little secret together.

'Because I took the key from the back door, sir and I hid it. I hid it in a place where she wouldn't find it. It was still there in the morning, sir, but Isabella had vanished. And that's not all. She didn't come back into the kitchen. I went to the door and listened and heard her go up to the hall and then I think I heard a creak on the stairs.'

Six

Wilkie Collins, *Basil*:

London was rousing everywhere into
morning activity, as I passed through
the streets. The shutters were being
removed from the windows of
public-houses: the drink-vampyres
that suck the life of London, were
opening their eyes betimes to look
abroad for the new day's prey!
Small tobacco and provision-shops
in poor neighbourhoods; dirty little
eating-houses, exhaling greasy-smelling
steam and displaying a leaf of
yesterday's paper, stained and
fly-blown, hanging in the windows—
were already plying, or making ready
to their daily trade.

I stood. I hesitated. I looked around at the London
traffic. I couldn't get Isabella out of my head.
My thoughts, my feelings were engaged with that
poor girl, with the dead girl that we had been
shown as I sauntered along the Strand, making
my way towards the Hungerford Market. I could
write a story about it. What was the beginning
of the story? Death. An awful finality about death.
Death was the end of everyone's story. And then

I had a sudden inspiration. I would do something quite, quite different. Something new. A book written backwards. Something quite different in the realms of literature. A book that started on the last page.

The last page, yes, that was the end of the story, not the beginning, the last page was when the dead Isabella fished from the river, dead and dripping, was displayed in the police station, lying there under the gas lamp. An object of curiosity, of perfunctory enquiry by the police and then consigned to one of those filthy, running sores that passed for the burial grounds of the poor in London.

And then my unseen reader lifts the page; turns the page over, just like opening a box of chocolate drops, reveals the next page. Two days earlier. The girl, alive, palpitating with a mixture of fear and excitement. Going to meet a man. What man? Was it a man? Sesina said that it was a man, but what if Isabella was going to meet a woman? A woman with hands strong enough to strangle. Arms strong enough to throw a body into the river.

And where did they meet?

Where to set the scene?

Hungerford Stairs?

I knew it well. Rotten to the core. Rotting wood, rotting houses, rotting men and women, diseased, drugged, corrupted, dying, dying from disease, dying from opium, dying suddenly and violently.

But was Hungerford Stairs the place where Isabella met her death? Her friend, Sesina, had said that. *I think that she planned to go to the*

Hungerford Stairs to meet someone, sir. I wandered down. Stood looking at the scene of desolation. I started to go on to the shore. A raucous flock of seagulls squabbled angrily over some prize towards the centre of the river. For a sickening moment, I thought I saw something rise, something that could have been a human hand. Several of the wretched scavengers had stopped their work, were standing rather still. Looking at me and then from me to one of their companions in misery. I began to feel uneasy, unsafe.

I stopped. Turned back. Went down Lower Robert Street, back to Adelphi Terrace. Came and stood on its lofty heights, on its terraced shelf above the restless river. Stood in safety and thought about my book; thought about Isabella and her wish to become a lady. There was daylight now. Or such daylight as one could have in the murk and fog of smoky London. But at night, away from the gas lamps? That was how I would paint the scene. At night there would be deep shadows. Shadows to hide a murder, to hide a murderer. I stood at the iron railing, placed a hand on their black painted surface, leaned over.

Perhaps the murder took place up here. My imagination sketched in the scene.

In my arms a dead girl.

Gathering all my strength.

A seagull soared above my head, dived. A perfect flight, straight as an arrow, it plunged down and hit the water.

But my imagination could not soar and dive with the bird. Even for a man with three times

77

my strength, a man strong enough to break a girl's legs and strangle the life from her body, even for a man like that, this was an impossibility. The body could have been dropped over the railing, but then it would have landed on the lower street, in front of the arches, not projected forward into the river. It would account for the bruises and the broken legs, but it was an impossibility for anyone, no matter how strong. I stayed there, wondering. There was a slam of a door from behind where I stood. Number five? I swung around. Yes. The schoolmaster. Late to his place of work. Saturday morning, of course.

And then I saw something that took my mind from Mr Cartwright. Down river. York Watergate. Oddly I had not really looked at it before, I knew it better from the work of one of my brother's artist friends than I knew it from life. Henry Pether's magnificent painting: *York Gate & the Adelphi from the River by Moonlight* was very much admired by me and most of the London world. But there it was, the real York Gate. Hundreds of years old. Beautifully carved from white marble, Italianate, a romantic place for a gentleman to meet a girl in strict privacy. I had seen for myself how my presence at Hungerford Stairs had drawn all eyes to me. But York Watergate, almost a stone's throw away from Adelphi Terrace, marooned in low tide, would be empty and deserted for most of the time.

That was it. That was the place. The place where a man could meet a girl in strict secrecy, could do what needed to be done without being observed by the tattered crows that haunted the

Hungerford Stairs. I had the setting for the second last page of my book. I turned words over in my mind, words that would serve to describe the midnight scene. The girl comes there, comes to meet a man. Not her first meeting, of course, though sadly her last. She comes to meet him, tells him what she knows of him; tells his deadly secret, asks for money, for a new life. I felt tears come to my eyes as I imagined how I would write that passionate plea. I could see her face. Big dark eyes, flowing hair, the pathos of that old dress, red and green to suit her colouring, chosen for her by a man who had wanted to give her a new start in life but who had been defeated by her stubbornness, by her zest for life, for fun, by her love of adventure, by her determined preference for the taking of chances above all dull security.

And then she had taken one chance too many, trusted to her wit, to her courage, trusted a step too far when she placed herself at the mercy of a killer.

I left the majestic heights of Adelphi Terrace, went back down to river level, thinking hard as I walked along beside the river. It was midday and the tide was low. The dry, soft sand rose in small puffs from the rapid movement of my feet as I walked, lost in my thoughts until a ripple of water touched the toe of my boot. The incoming tide from Gravesend was spreading up the river. Soon the water would reach the York Watergate Stairs. I would have to return by the Strand or by one of those subterranean roads built by the Adams Brothers. I moved a little faster, watching the moored boats rock and pull against the restraint of their anchor. In an hour's time there would be enough depth for waterside ferries to land on the slipway to York Watergate, but now the whole place was empty and deserted.

York Watergate. A perfect place for a meeting. About five minutes or less from number five Adelphi Terrace. No curious stares, no witnesses. I looked at the four tall white pillars of the gate and at the roofed area within them. It had been built more than two hundred years ago from the finest Portland stone. York House, itself, had disappeared, but its water gate still stood, now nothing but a place to shelter while waiting for the ferry. I stood on the slipway, my hand on the mooring post and gazed up at the Villiers' family coat of arms and looked at the arches that held up the roof. A little house. A perfect place for a secret meeting. I tried to imagine it; tried to visualize the two figures on that fatal night, seeing Isabella plainly, but failing with the man. A tall man, he must have been, bigger than Isabella, far bigger than me also, doubtless. He stood slightly in the shadows, and the girl was there, by that pillar, just where the watery moonlight would shine on her eager face as she tried to get money from him, blackmailed him. Isabella wanted to be a lady; that's what her friend Sesina had said. I dug deep into the murdered girl's mind, tried to imagine her words and then I saw something.

There, just beside the four-sided post, half hidden in some grass, was a large pocket watch, the silver dial gleaming. I bent down, picked it up. Unusually large, the black figures standing out against the white dial. A plain silver watch, definitely a man's watch. A silver chain, snapped in half. Could the victim have desperately grabbed at it, tried to avoid her fate? It seemed likely. I dangled it by its broken chain, turning it over. No name engraved upon it.

A movement, that was all. A movement from beside the white limestone of the nearest pillar. But I could have sworn that it was a man's arm, a glossy black sleeve, a glint of cufflinks. And then it was as if the air beside my right ear was split open. A small thud upon the wooden post beside me. Could someone have shot at me? For a moment I stared at the post stupidly, peered at it. I had even begun to lift my hand to feel for the bullet, still hardly able to believe that someone had tried to kill me, here in the middle of London. And then another bullet. This one skimmed my head, struck the gleaming silver of the watch and knocked it from my grasp. I looked all around, looking for help but there was no one near to me. I felt a heavy sweat break through my forehead, drenching the rim of my hat. I clenched my hands. The instinct to run away was very strong, but now all was quiet. And that watch might be the clue to poor Isabella's murderer.

I bent down. It was just there. The silver gleamed up at me. My hand almost touched it, and then a third bullet. This time I did not hesitate.

A moment of regret that I had got involved in the matter of the murdered housemaid crossed my mind. I was, I thought, only human, no hero, and I had a lot to live for. Self-preservation took over, and just as another bullet whizzed past my ear, I dug the tip of my umbrella into the soft ridges of the slipway and vaulted neatly over on the other side, landing on the soft river sand. I crouched there for a minute, my heart thudding. I had landed with a thud and a splash, the water was coming in rapidly and my feet were chilled with cold water. I had jarred my knee, and pulled a muscle in my arm. All thought of the watch left me and I yelled out as loudly as I could, repeating the one word, 'help!' as loudly as I could.

Useless, I thought. No one around. No one near. No one, except a murderer.

But then from out in the centre of the river, there came a shout. It was the ferry boat. A boatman was shouting. He had heard my voice, not the words, but he was waving his hand, pointing upriver, towards Hungerford. I understood him instantly. He was explaining that the tide was still too low to make a stop at York Watergate. I pretended to misunderstand him, though, wading into the river, shouting meaningless appeals and then walking along, still in the river, back towards Hungerford, keeping myself in full view of the boat and still endeavouring to keep shouting meaningless questions. I would, I thought, find a cab at Charing Cross and have myself driven straight back to my lodgings.

I dared not walk, but took a cab to Tavistock House that evening. Even so, I glanced nervously around and told the man to wait as I went up the steps.

'A cab! We can walk!' Dickens was appalled. He walked everywhere.

'No time.' I had thought about the matter for the last hour or so. No matter how often I reproached myself for cowardice, I could not get up the courage to go back to York Watergate. I was not the right man for these heroics.

'Get in, Dick,' I said, for once feeling in charge. And once I had given the address of the police station to the cabman I climbed in without a backward glance and he followed after a few seconds.

'Someone tried to kill me this afternoon.' I had waited until the cabman, above our heads, had whipped up his horses, before I whispered these dramatic words into his ear. The light was too dim to see the expression on his face, but his head whipped around.

'Why?' That was all that he said, but there was a note of intense excitement in his voice. I began to feel rather important. I jerked my thumb upwards, indicating the cabbie above us and then sat back. If I told my story now, Dickens would just take over when we got to the police station.

Inspector Field was disappointed in me. He and Dickens had listened to the early part of my story with a flattering display of interest, but my dramatic escape disappointed them. There was a silence and then the inspector said sadly, 'Didn't think to pick up the watch, sir.' His voice made a statement not a question out of the words. I winced and tried to make a joke out of it.

'Not too used to having shots fired at me,' I said feebly.

Dickens patted me on the arm. 'At least you are safe, old chap. But who could the man have been? Do you have any ideas about that?'

'I'm pretty sure of that,' I said. At least my brain had worked well. I kept them waiting for a long minute. After all, I was the one who worked out where the murder had taken place and I made them listen while I explained the logic behind my deductions about the site of the murder. 'And,' I said, 'when I stood on Adelphi Terrace and looked across to York Watergate, I saw the schoolmaster, Mr Cartwright, come out of number five. He saw me, I'm sure, saw me looking down river. He could have followed me there.'

'And then was scared that the watch might hang him,' said Dickens enthusiastically, but the inspector was shaking his head sadly.

'Pity you didn't come to me, first of all, Mr Collins. I'd have sent a man there. A couple of men. Search the place.' He didn't finish, but the expression on his face said that I had made a mess of everything.

'But you will send them now, won't you, Inspector? Mr Collins said that the tide was coming towards him. It would be good to keep an eye on the place and have someone there in hiding to see if the man comes back at high tide. And who knows, but they might find the watch.'

I could see from the inspector's face that he was not hopeful of results. I felt fairly sure that the schoolmaster, or whoever had shot at me, would have retrieved his watch very quickly and easily. I said nothing however. All was not lost even if the policemen failed to find the man or even the watch. They probably wouldn't! I knew, of course, that Inspector Field was one of only a very small number of detectives in the city of London. And that there were hardly enough constables on the streets to stop daylight robbery, let alone to solve a case where no one had been hurt.

However, I had a plan.

Seven

Wilkie Collins, *Basil*:

The Abbe was dwarfish and deformed,
lean, sallow, sharp-featured, with bright
bird-like eyes, and a low, liquid voice.
He was a political refugee, dependent
for the bread he ate, on the money
he received for teaching languages. He
might have been a beggar from the
streets; and still my father would
have treated him as the principal guest
in the house, for this all-sufficient
reason—he was a direct descendant of
one of the oldest of those famous
Roman families whose names are part
of the history of the Civil Wars in Italy.

Our guests were all assembled, clustered around
their landlord, Dickens' American friend, Don
Diamond, when we arrived on Sunday evening
and I felt cheered by the sight of them and by
the excellence of our host's Madeira. He pressed
one glass on me and then another while I
studied the faces of the four men who had been
asked to meet us. Which would be the face on
that second to last page of my book? Which was
the man who had lost a watch at York Watergate?
Which of these men murdered Isabella Gordon?

I looked at them with interest, but was glad of the numbers around the table. Safety in numbers, was my thought.

When there was a pause in the conversation, I took out my own watch, shook it, and held it to my ear.

'This watch of mine is always wrong. Who has got the exact time?' I asked, looking all around at them. I was pleased to hear what a very natural ring there had been to my voice. Even Dickens took out his watch, a prized possession presented to him by the people of Coventry.

The schoolmaster to my disappointment produced a battered old silver watch; Mr Doyle an expensive and smooth gold one.

But only one man there did not have a watch and that was one of the young journalists, Jim Carstone.

'Pawned it, did you?' said his friend Benjamin. 'Never did know such a fellow as you, Jim. Went the way of that medal you won in the King's Road shooting gallery, I suppose.'

Probably had pawned it, I thought. Young men did that sort of thing. I felt disappointed as I studied the other guests and tried each face for the mask of a murderer.

The lawyer first. He had a gold watch, suspiciously shiny. New possibly, but then everything about Mr Jeremiah Doyle seemed new and expensive. Not a name that I liked, Jeremiah. It had a stiff, self-righteous sound to it. I thought of the story that the landlord had told, of how this man's rent was paid for by his family's lawyers. During my studies at the Temple Bar I had met many barristers who by dint of paying for twelve dinners were qualified barristers, but who had done no studies and who had never had a single case. But what did he do with his time? Not a young man. Older than Dickens, I would have thought. He was an impressive figure, tall, well-made and the height of his forehead lent dignity to the bald head. He had a way of turning his whole head and shoulders as he asked a question, something that lent weight to his slightest utterance. He was talking to Dickens and I joined them. He shook my hand with the minimum of contact and turned back to Dickens as if he were more worthy of his notice. This irritated me and I addressed him abruptly, forcing him to return his attention to me.

'I understand that you are a barrister-at-law, Mr Doyle,' I said. 'Which inn do you frequent?'

He looked over his glasses keenly at me. 'Why do you ask?' he said.

I gave him a friendly smile. 'I've just been called to the bar myself,' I said proudly.

'I felicitate you,' he said pompously. He did not look at me, but still kept his attention on Dickens. He had very pale blue eyes, pouched and the candlelight on the table illuminated a tight, thin lip and one slightly drooping eyelid. I began to wonder how old he was in reality. Certainly middle-aged, but perhaps nearer fifty than forty. Yes, it was very strange that his rent was paid from a family estate, rather than from the man himself. He had turned back to me, his hands were now clasped behind his back as though he feared to give anything away and he stood with a slight stoop, peering at me through his spectacles. He hadn't replied to my question, though. Just as if there was some great secret about which inn he belonged to. Or was he a barrister, after all?

'What my friend means is that he's eaten the right numbers of dinners, got a new set of calling cards so that he can inform the world that he is a barrister-at-law. Didn't do any work, or any examinations, isn't that right, Wilkie? Just perused some law books in order to extract some plots for the novels that he plans on writing!' Dickens clapped me on the back in his exuberantly friendly manner.

That gave me the opening that I wanted. 'This will interest you, Mr Doyle,' I said innocently. 'I've been reading about a case, about a girl, just a servant girl, but with a brain as sharp as a razor, who learned very early on the secret of listening at doors, her ear to every keyhole. Soon she picked up secrets, blackmailed a guest, never a present employer, she was too clever for that, though sometimes, frequently, in fact, she black-mailed a past employer. I say a past employer,' I continued, noticing that others were listening and raising my voice slightly, 'past employer, because this girl, whether by forged references or whether by very good service while she stayed in a house, always seemed to have the best of references and easily got a new job. And in that way,' I said, looking around the room, where every ear seemed to be turned to my story, 'by hook or by crook, one might say, this pretty little

89

Anne Marie, moved from house to house through the district of Marylebone, until . . .'

'Until she was caught . . .' put in one of the journalists, young Jim Carstone. They had all gathered around to listen to the story.

'Wrong,' I said.

'Got a job with a lawyer and he blackmailed her,' said the other journalist, Benjamin Allen. Mr Doyle, I noticed, raised his chin above his high collar and looked down at him with the air of one who would say, *Do I know you, young man?*

'Wrong again,' I said.

'Some more Madeira, Mr Doyle,' said the landlord hastily. A bit wary of this man, I thought, as I plunged on with my story.

'You're right, though in one respect,' I said to Benjamin Allen. 'The last person that this girl worked for was a lawyer, but when she tried her tricks with him, he didn't hand her over to the police as a law-abiding lawyer should do, no, that was not the course that he took. And he didn't blackmail her, either. Not him. Blackmail is difficult and a dangerous measure,' I went on as little Sesina slipped into the room and began laying out hot soup plates. Her head had swung around as I said that word. I noticed that, but I carried on with my story. 'No, this lawyer took a more straightforward and surer path from his point of view. He withdrew from the bank every penny that he possessed, and I do believe that it was a tidy sum. And then he went down to the docks . . .'

'And drowned himself,' said Jim Carstone.

I shook my head. 'I doubt it; from what I read of him, from witnesses' statements, he didn't seem to be that sort of man.' Sesina, I noticed, was lingering over her task, conscientiously straightening every spoon and adjusting every linen napkin. She would be in trouble with Mrs Dawson if she stayed too much longer, but then, I supposed, Sesina was probably a match for Mrs Dawson. 'What do you think, Mr Doyle,' I said aloud. 'What do you imagine that our black-mailed lawyer did after he had been seen down at the docks?'

'I have no idea, Mr . . .' The pause he left after the omission of my name had an offensive sound and I noticed that the two young journalists exchanged glances and that one of them rushed into speech.

'Bought a ticket on a steamer, went back and murdered the girl, and then returned to the docks and disappeared for ever more,' said Jim Carstone.

'That's right,' I said cordially. 'The lawyer had probably been careful enough to buy a ticket under an assumed name, in any case, no one of his name had been among the purchasers of the ticket.'

'And so no one knows where he went.'

'Steamers going out by the dozen from Wapping,' said Benjamin with a nod of his head.

'The strangled body of the girl was found days later by the police, alerted by a milk delivery man, who saw a cat mewing at a window each day, but was unable to make anyone hear his knocks. The lawyer was never heard of again.

91

There was a certain amount of publicity. Picture of the girl in the newspaper and on posters. No one could find much about the lawyer, a man from Scotland, apparently, but the girl was recognized and the police received various anonymous contributions about her black-mailing activities.'

'Dinner is ready to be served, sir.' Mrs Dawson stuck her head in the door and I could have hugged the old lady as she came at precisely the right moment for me. Let Mr Doyle digest my story. I saw Dickens look thoughtfully at him before taking his place beside our host. I was on the other side, and Mr Doyle at the end of the table. Jim and Benjamin seated themselves beside me and Mr Frederick Cartwright, the schoolmaster, was between Dickens and the lawyer.

'So what brought you to London, Mr Diamond?' Mr Doyle wanted no more talk about lawyers strangling servant girls, I guessed, as Sesina adroitly poured soup into my plate. Mr Diamond seemed a modest man, said very little of what Dickens had told me about him, very little about the hotels that he had owned in America and about the vast wealth which had allowed him to buy the eleven houses of Adelphi Terrace, but concentrated on telling the story of how he and Dickens had met on board the ship *George Washington* on the way back from New York and how they had stayed friends when they came to London.

'And he showed me this terrace, well, I have to say to you gentlemen that I had never seen anything so pretty back in New York. First morning our friend walked me over here, there was a river mist and sun behind the clouds and they made such a picture, these beautiful houses, standing up there above the water. Told me all about the place. How it was built by the Adam brothers, and how Adelphi in Greek means brothers. Never knew things like that. Never had an education, not like you gentlemen,' he said modestly. 'I was out working at twelve years old, when I should have been in school. Let me give you a toast, gentlemen. To the Adelphi brothers who built this magnificent hillside by the river: John, Robert, William and James Adam.'

'To the Adelphi brothers,' we all echoed as we raised our glasses filled with excellent claret. I wondered was it really an anniversary for one of them, or for the building of the terrace, but none of the lodgers had queried this reason for the invitation to dinner. And I didn't think that with wine this good, anyone would have felt the evening to be a waste of time, even if Mrs Dawson's bought-in roast fowls and raised pies did not come up to scratch. Dickens, I noticed, was exerting himself to make an atmosphere of conviviality, telling a funny story about a near disaster in a play that he had put on in his own house in Tavistock Square. There had been a problem with one of the props: a big, heavy, carpenter-made pillar which fell over and the two men, Mark Lennon, a huge fellow and Walter Landor, another heavy-weight, struggled with it for minutes and then Anne Brown, his parlour-maid, who was watching from the wings, strode on to the stage, still wearing her apron and righted it in a minute.

'And, you know, gentlemen, when I thought about it afterwards, I thought that Anne has been in our service for about twelve years, and during that time she has lugged up and down stairs a few hundred carpets, twice a year at least, she has carried heavy, small children – I have nine of them, gentlemen, and Anne has been a friend to them all – I'd say that she has carried these children about a million times, has lifted wardrobes, cupboards and beds a few thousand times. We men can underrate the strength of women,' he said as Mrs Dawson placed the two roast fowls in front of the landlord. His eyes, I noticed, lingered on the woman.

'To Anne, the parlourmaid; stronger than any man,' said the American, raising his glass and we all pledged Anne Brown, the parlourmaid, while I looked at the stout figure of Mrs Dawson and wondered whether Dickens thought that she could have murdered the girl and thrown her into the river. Sesina, I saw with interest, seemed to be looking at Mrs Dawson also and on her face was a sharp look of curiosity. Don't be stupid, I told myself, why on earth should Mrs Dawson murder Isabella? Anyway, Sesina was sure that her friend was going to meet a man.

And then there was a toast to America, the country of free enterprise where a barefoot boy could rise to the heights of a millionaire, or make his pile, as Don amended Dickens' toast. And then there had to be a toast to Dickens, and his wonderful books. To the law, to Lincoln's Inn

94

and to the courts of Chancery as a source of great stories was my contribution and Benjamin toasted the maker of the raised pie, drunkenly waving a glass at Sesina as she came in to lay the pudding plates.

I leaned across the table towards the schoolmaster. 'You are very silent, Mr Cartwright,' I said as Sesina put a plate in front of him. I saw her glance keenly at me. Had he seen me this morning, looking across at York Watergate? Had he followed me? 'What did you think about my story of the blackmailing servant girl?' I asked boldly. I was rewarded by the sudden stiffening of the man's burly frame. Sesina paused a fraction of a minute behind him, her hand almost frozen on the edge of the pudding plate. He did not look at me, nor did he look at her. He looked down at the plate and then deliberately removed it from her grasp, almost as though he could not bear the tension of waiting for it to be released.

'You take an interest in crime, I'm sure,' I added, swallowing some more of the excellent port while I watched Mrs Dawson's sharp knife dissect some more of the fiddgy pudding on the side table. Sesina had now rapidly moved around to my side of the table and was standing behind me, her hand depositing a plate in front of me. I dug a spoon into my pudding and looked across at him.

'None, whatsoever. My interests are completely pedagogical,' he said pompously.

'Crimes happen in schools, too,' I remarked, trying to look wise and as if I had numerous examples up my sleeve. He was, I thought, a very big and very heavily made man. Though he had produced a watch readily, had it, perhaps, looked a bit too battered, the silver a bit too worn for a man with a good salary? Could it, perhaps, have been an old watch that he had hastily purchased from a pawnbroker when he had lost his own?

'Reported one of these a few months' ago, didn't we, Jim?' Benjamin's leg under the table, reached across mine to nudge the toe of his friend's boot.

'That's right.' Jim paused for a second, either to chew on his pudding or to think up a few details. 'That's right, Ben. Schoolmaster. No wife. Hires a girl from a reformatory. Girl seen shopping every morning. On Monday: no girl. Tuesday: no girl. Wednesday: no girl. Local baker; sweet on girl. Report to police. Body found cut up into pieces. Each piece precisely . . .' And here Jim looked all around the table. Every eye was on him, every spoon or glass was held poised in the air. He paused for another few seconds and then continued, 'Every single piece of that poor girl was exactly and mathematically the length of one foot, as though . . .' Jim drank a little port. 'As though,' he finished, 'it had been measured by a schoolmaster's ferule.'

'Bless my soul,' said Dickens, taking a little notebook and a small sharp pencil from his pocket, 'God bless my soul, what an extraordinary tale.'

The atmosphere was becoming a little uncomfortable. I could sense that. Mr Doyle put his glass slightly to one side, leaned across the table, his keen eyes surveying my friend.

'Do tell us some more about that reform school for prostitutes that you have out in Shepherd's Bush, Mr Dickens.'

I sat back and waited for fireworks.

Dickens took a sip of the wine and sat back, looking very directly across at the lawyer. 'Yes, Urania Cottage is in Shepherd's Bush. That part of your information is correct, Mr Doyle. But only that part. Urania Cottage is funded by Miss Coutts of Coutts Bank, and managed by her. And it is not a reform school. It is a home for unfortunate girls who have no homes of their own.'

Doyle took a swallow of his wine. A large one this time. It occurred to me that the man was slightly drunk. The slack skin beneath his faded blue eyes seemed even more pouched than earlier in the evening and his thin lips were twisted in an offensive sneer.

'Tell me, Mr Dickens, is it true that the girls in Urania Cottage have pianos? I've heard a rumour to that effect.'

Dickens' good friend, the landlord, looked anxiously from his tenant to the famous novelist. Mr Cartwright, who was lost in his own thoughts, brooded angrily over the remains of his port. The two young lads exchanged surreptitious grins, but Doyle smiled openly, a mocking smile as he awaited a reply. It was not long in coming.

'Oh, certainly,' said Dickens with a nonchalant shrug. 'A grand piano for every girl in the parlour, a cottage piano for each in the bedrooms, and,' he paused, deliberately flicking a crumb from the table, and finished with, 'and, of course, several small guitars in the washroom.'

'Bravo,' said Mr Diamond, with a burst of genuine laughter. 'There you are, Mr Doyle, you've got your answer!' He was, I thought, glad to lighten the atmosphere. Nevertheless, I saw him look across at the brutal face of the schoolmaster, now flushed with wine, and I saw his lips tighten. Not a man to shield the murderer of a poor housemaid in a house that he owned. That was my feeling about Mr Diamond and I warmed to him.

Eight

Sesina waited impatiently in the hall. Time they were all gone, she thought as she fiddled with the cloth used for dusting the hallstand mirror. The two journalists had left; she knew what they'd be up to, down to Covent Garden, she'd lay a bet on that. Jim had pinched her cheek. Benny had snatched a kiss and asked her to save what was left of the fiddgy pudding for their breakfasts, but she didn't mind them. Wouldn't hurt a fly, either of them, she would bet on that. They were a good laugh, that pair. Wanted to know what it was all about, this dinner for the lodgers; no surprises in that, pair of bright boys. Guessed that it might be something to do with Isabella's death. She told them. Not everything. Of course not, but a bit about herself and Isabella. About how they came to Urania Cottage. About Mr Dickens. About how he came around to the prisons and to the reform schools. She made a good story about Urania Cottage. The mark books where girls got marks for good behaviour and marks subtracted for bad behaviour, about the piano, the singing lessons, the sewing lessons, the handwriting lessons and reading lessons, all that education for the girls so that they could become good servants. Benny and Jim had fun with hearing all about Mr Dickens' pet charity for homeless girls. She gave them a good imitation of one of his favourite little talks before the pair of them went off. Down the Strand. On to Covent Garden. Sesina wished that she could go with them. Anna Maria Sesini! That was her proper name. Was it the name of her mother or her father? Benny Allen thought that it sounded Italian when she told him about it. Said that Italy was a lovely place. Very warm, very friendly. She should go back there and find her family; that was what Benny said. Told her that if he and Jim made a fortune in some way, that they would take her there on a holiday.

As if!

The schoolmaster had gone up to his own room. Eaten as much as a hog, she reckoned. His stomach looked larger than ever.

But the other four were sipping brandy and swallowing coffee in Mrs Dawson's parlour. Her ladyship was in a fine old bad mood; she liked a nice sit-down there of an evening, *her parlour, if you please*. It was a good job that the landlord had allowed her to hire a girl who was to do the washing-up. Otherwise she would have Sesina at the kitchen sink the minute the dining room had been cleared. Her ladyship was down there, in the kitchen. Bullying the poor girl now, she was. She'd be there finding fault for the next half hour, hopefully. Sesina felt in her pocket. She had been really busy all day long, but she had found time to go into the little damp cold bedroom on the lower basement floor and look all around it carefully, searching for possible hiding places. And then she had discovered the water tank. Good job that I don't sleep here; that would keep me awake all night, was her first thought, but her second was: *good hiding place*! Thick in dust, the top of it was, but it had been a good hiding place, a good place to find a card.

'Let me see that soup kettle as clean as a whistle next time I come down! You just mind your manners, too, missie, or you'll feel the back of my hand. No making faces when I speak to you!'

Still bullying that unfortunate mite, thirteen, if she's a day; pity someone doesn't give Mrs Dawson the back of their hand, thought Sesina. Drat! She's coming back upstairs, will be hanging around; currying favour with the landlord, bobbing to them all. In desperation, she stole back into the parlour, making believe to be checking the coffee pot. The landlord was telling them all about his time in the gold rush, as he called it. Out in a place called Georgia in America. Everyone going there trying to make a fortune. Most of them ending up poorer than they were when they arrived. Sesina wasn't surprised. The landlord had the right idea. Might find gold, or might not find gold, but as sure as eggs is eggs, all those people who were flooding out to Georgia, trying to make a fortune, each one of them would need a place to lay their head at night, a place to eat a cooked dinner, a place to have a drink in the evening. Setting up hotels and boarding houses was a surety, though very hard work compared to finding a bit of gold, and a lot slower results too. Most of these quick ways to make money turned out badly in her experience.

Pity that poor old Isabella didn't think a bit harder before she went off that night to make her fortune.

Sesina waited patiently, half listening to the landlord's story about his hotels, until Mr Collins' eye was on her and then she edged the calling card slightly out of her apron pocket, making sure that the gold edging caught the light from the candelabra overhead. That Mr Collins was a sharp little fellow. His eyes were on her instantly; she saw his glasses flash in her direction. Sesina replaced the coffee pot and left the room quietly without a backward glance. Once she had pulled the door closed behind her, she waited and listened. There, that was his voice.

'I think, if you gentlemen will excuse me for a minute, I'll just smoke my cigar out-of-doors. A bit too much of your very excellent wine, Mr Diamond! A smell of the river and a few gulps of fog will have me right as rain in five minutes.'

Mr Dickens said something about young men, nowadays, laughing with the landlord and in a moment Mr Collins was beside her in the dark recess of the parlour door. He held out his hand and Sesina put the card into it.

'Found it on top of the water tank,' she whispered to him.

'You're a great girl,' he whispered back. She thought that he might snatch a kiss, but he was too much of a gentleman for that. He put the card away in the breast pocket of his coat and then slipped his hand into his trouser pocket. 'That's for you, Sesina.' His lips were almost at her ear, bending down over her, and patting her on the back with his other hand. A shilling, no less; Sesina could feel the shape and size of the coin as it nestled in the palm of her hand. He kept his hand on her back, keeping her with him as he walked towards the front door.

'Where's the York Watergate, Sesina?' He asked the question quite loudly. Must be a bit drunk. Yelled the words out! All the other gentlemen must have heard him. But perhaps it was that he could hear what Sesina could hear, perhaps. Old Mother Dawson coming puffing up the stairs from the kitchen. Sesina waited until the housekeeper had opened the door into the hallway before answering.

'It's down river from here, sir. You can see it from across the road.'

'Come and show me, won't you?' Now he pretended to see the missus. 'You don't mind, Mrs Dawson, do you? I'll just borrow Sesina for a few minutes. I don't know this part of London very well. Oh, and Mrs Dawson, what a wonderful meal that was! Don't know when I enjoyed a meal so much. You must be exhausted. I hope you'll have a nice rest when we're all gone.'

Sesina could hardly keep a smile off her face. Struck all in a heap, she was, the silly woman. Her fat face smiling, showing every one of her yellow teeth. Eyes looking down, dropping curtsies, *Oh, sir!* No one could imagine her threatening to give the back of her hand to a poor little starveling ten minutes ago.

'Would you like to take your hat and coat, sir?' Sesina said, nice and soft. Not putting herself forward. The missus wouldn't like that. A great one for telling you to know your place; that was Mrs Dawson. Pretending to be a lady with *my parlour*.

103

'I'll risk it. Not far to go, is it?' He didn't wait for a reply but went through the front door as soon as Mrs Dawson had opened it. Sesina was after him before she could think of anything to say. Let *her* hang around the hallway and wait for the landlord and Mr Dickens to come out.

It wasn't too dark outside. There were four gas lamps at the edge of the pavement, one of them quite near to number five. As he stepped off the pavement a carriage came around the corner from Robert Street. Empty except for the coachman. Whipping his horses. Nearly went into Mr Collins. Sesina grabbed his sleeve and hauled him back. Had a bit too much to drink, she thought, once again. His breath, when he turned back to face her, smelled of wine.

'Thank you, sweetheart,' he said and took her hand and squeezed it for a second before dropping it. This time he looked up and down the roadway in front of the eleven houses before he crossed over to the railings. 'Brrr,' he said pretending to shiver and taking her hand again. 'Strange place. The fog, the river mist, the gas lamp. Feels like being on the moon, doesn't it?'

'I'm used to it, sir,' said Sesina. For a moment she thought that he had forgotten about the card and wondered how to remind him. She felt a moment's impatience. She looked down at the river. That river where poor Isabella found a last resting place. Not very nice that. Being dragged out, cold and dead. No more fun; no more great plans. A man who had done that deserved to be hanged. If only she had the money, the power, the right to nose around, just like those two men!

She'd have to give him a nudge. Chances were that he might forget all about Isabella, standing there, smoking his cigar and looking up at the moon.

'Can you see well enough to read the card, sir?' she asked.

'You read it, sweetheart, your eyes are better than mine.' A bit drunk, she thought knowledgeably. He had difficulty getting the card from his pocket. She snatched it from him before he allowed it to fall.

'This is what it says, sir: "Found something in his room today. He was the one who beat my poor brother to death. I'm going to make him pay for it!" That's filled the whole card, sir.'

Mr Collins took the cigar from his mouth. 'What!'

Sesina read the card to him again, memorizing the words before she handed it to him.

'This is terrible.' He seemed very moved. There was even a crack in his voice. Suddenly she felt rather fond of him. Nicer than most men. Perhaps he would be the one who would get vengeance for poor Isabella. She was a little doubtful of how forceful he would be, though. Mr Dickens, now. If he wanted something done, everyone else ran around doing his bidding. Still, perhaps the two together would be the best way. She was clever enough to deal with both.

'"Found something in his room today." That must mean . . . Well, Sesina; that does seem to indicate, you know, to show, that it must be someone whose room she visited.'

'Isabella was a good girl, sir.'

'Yes, yes, yes, of course.' He took the cigar from his mouth and waved it in the air. 'No, I didn't mean to hint anything else, Sesina. Don't think that. I know that she and you clean the bedrooms here. It's just that if it was in this man's room, well then . . .'

Didn't like to say it out straight. Gentlemen are like that, she thought. Not Mr Dickens, though. A great man for straight talking. *I'll tell you straight, Sesina,* that's what he would say. For a minute she half wished that it was Mr Dickens who was standing here with her now beside the river, listening to these words. He'd pounce, like a dog after a rat. He'd guess straight away.

'We both go into men's rooms, sir,' she said with a nod in the direction of the terraced houses behind them.

'Yes, yes, of course.' Seemed a bit upset. Thinking that he might have offended her. As if!

'And what's this about a brother?' He put the question in quickly, like he wanted to pass over this business of gentlemen and their bedroom. Thinking about the maid who cleaned his bedroom, perhaps. Wondering if she would find out anything about him.

'Isabella had a brother, sir. She found out about that. She went to the workhouse on her day out. The place where she was brought up. Her brother had been adopted, sir. She told me that.'

He took a few more puffs from his cigar and then he flung it into the river. Waste. Hadn't been properly finished. He didn't turn towards her, just stood there, watching it as it went flying down, a bit like one of them seagulls swooping on a bit

106

of rubbish. When the red spark was gone he turned back to her.

'Where was the workhouse?'

'Don't know, sir. But I think that one of the men on the top floor gave her an idea, one of them newspaper men. She was full of it one morning when she came down. Wouldn't tell me, though. Very close, she was. That was Isabella. Washed up the breakfast ware and then went off on her day out. Once a month, sir. That's when we get our day out.'

'Mr Allen and Mr Carstone? Is that right?'

'That's right, sir.' *Except that we call them Benny and Jim.* 'She told me a long time ago that she could remember the workhouse, but she didn't know the name of the place. I didn't take much notice.' No point in looking back. Never any use in it. Sesina hadn't wanted Isabella to start on that. Much more fun to look to the future. To plan a good life. But she had been a long time upstairs that day.

'And when she came back from her day out, her cheeks were all red. Like they had been blown by the wind.'

He didn't say anymore. Just stood there, staring at the river. She thought that she should remind him of Isabella, bring him back to the puzzle of her death.

'What do you think she means, sir? "I'm going to make him pay for it!"?'

He gave a big sigh. 'I'm very much afraid, Sesina, that she meant that she was going to blackmail him. And thus she met her end!' He lit another cigar and puffed at it for a moment.

There was the noise of a front door creaking open and Sesina knew that sound. She turned. Of course, Lady Curiosity, Mrs Dawson, was standing there. Immediately Sesina leaned over the railings pointing down to the east.

'Can you see it now, sir? That's York Watergate. Look the mist has lifted a little. It's a very fancy place. All fancy stonework. Boats sometimes land there, sir.' Her voice would carry across the road in that still, foggy air.

He was not so drunk that he didn't play along with that. 'Ah, you're right, Sesina. What wonderful eyes you have. I couldn't see it before.'

Then there was the sound of a door closing, just a careful click. Mrs Dawson wouldn't want Mr Collins to see her spying on him.

'Did your friend ever mention York Watergate to you, Sesina?' Now he sounded quite sober.

Sesina turned to face him. 'No, sir,' she said, but her mind was working fast. Could that have been the place? Was he on to something? Clever enough, she thought. 'I want that fella hanged!' There wasn't much light here by the railings, but there was enough to show the surprised look on Mr Collins' face. Didn't expect that tone of voice from her. Didn't understand. Families never meant much to people like herself or Isabella. Families deserted you, left you at workhouses, sent you out on to the streets when you were old enough or sold you off to anyone who would give some money for you. She wouldn't know her own sister if she walked in the door. But she and Isabella, though they quarrelled like two cats on the roof top, well, they looked out for each other. Whoever did that to Isabella Gordon wasn't going to get away with it, not if Anna Maria Sesini could help it.

'You can leave it to us to keep after the police,' he said.

'I'll do everything I can to help you, sir.' And she knew that her voice sounded sincere. He patted her on the shoulder.

'Good girl,' he said and took another puff of his cigar. It seemed to give him energy, because he turned around to her and when he spoke his voice sounded different. Enthusiastic, keen.

'I wish you could find some more of those cards, Sesina.'

'I'll do my best, sir.' Sesina glanced over her shoulder. Mrs Dawson was probably peering out of the dining-room window at her. It wasn't safe to stay any longer.

'I'll run down to the lower road, sir, and go in by the basement door and have another look. If Mrs Dawson sees me, I'll tell her that I've gone to give the hired girl a hand with the washing-up.' And if her ladyship demanded to know why she had done this, she could always act humble-pie and pretend that she didn't like to knock on the front door like a lady. Sesina smothered a giggle as she thought of how she would act out that scene.

'Do that.' He sounded a bit absent-minded, a bit sleepy like. Then he suddenly seemed to sober up, throwing away the second cigar. 'I've thought of somewhere that she might have hidden one of those cards. You know when I was about thirteen and living out in Italy, I was a very naughty boy and got up to things that thirteen-year-olds shouldn't get up to. Do you know what I'm talking about, Sesina?'

'No, sir.' Well, she had to say 'yes', or 'no' and it was a fifty-fifty chance, either way, of which was the answer that he was expecting. He didn't seem bothered, just patted her hand, smiling to himself.

'Well, I kept a book, a diary, I suppose, but I called it a book, silly boy that I was, but of course I didn't want my parents to see it so I unscrewed the knob on my iron bedstead and kept it in that hollow space. It was a bed just like the one in poor Isabella's room.'

'I'll try, sir, and the next time that you come, I'll slip it to you, quiet like.'

'That's a good little girl. Here comes my friend now. We'll find some excuse to visit again and then you can slip it to us. It will be our secret, won't it, Sesina?' He was patting her hand again. Getting all spooney, he was. Drunk, of course. Would have to get him safely across the road. No harm in him. Pity that Isabella didn't find someone like Mr Collins. Still, who knows how ugly anyone, even the quietest are like if they're in a blue funk.

'Yes, sir,' she said aloud and listened for the sound of horse hoofs as she escorted him back across the road. 'Good night, sir,' she said as she slipped past Mr Dickens. He already had his hat, so Mrs Dawson had lowered herself into giving it to him. Mr Collins' hat was still on the hatstand and she gave it a quick brush with a clothes brush that she had found since his last visit. Should save money on those cigars and buy himself a new hat. Not a dressy man. He was telling the landlord now how he thought pyjamas and dressing gowns were the most comfortable clothes to have dinner in.

'Your hat, sir,' she said, offering it to him. And then, to her surprise, Mr Dickens slipped her a sixpenny piece.

'You're doing well, Sesina,' he said. 'I've asked Mrs Dawson about you and she said that she was satisfied. Good girl.'

Trying to sweet-talk her, that was sure and certain. Still, they were on the same side, the great and famous Mr Dickens; Mr Collins, who, according to the landlord, would soon be famous and Anna Maria Sesini who had never seen her father and had only a very shadowy memory of her mother.

But when it came to brains, she thought, as she shut the door behind all of them, when it came to brains, she'd bet she could run rings around the two of them.

And what was all that story Mr Dickens had told about the servant being as strong as any man. Not a surprise to her, of course. But the people at the table had looked surprised. And, she thought, he had given a very strange look at Mrs Dawson. And so had Mr Collins.

Naw, she said to herself, naw. It were a man.

But could she be sure. After all, Isabella had said quite a few times, something about Mrs Dawson. *Needn't be so high and mighty. If the landlord only knew what I know about her. No better than she should be.*

Didn't take much notice at the time, thought Sesina. But what if Isabella was only up to her usual tricks when she said it was a man? What if it was Mrs Dawson all of the time that she expected to get money out of? She wouldn't be too surprised. As soon as Mrs Dawson came bustling out, she gave her a long, thoughtful look. Ever so put out, she was. Something had really rattled her. In a real bad mood. Or was it that she was a bit frightened? She'd try her out.

'Did you hear the story that Mr Dickens was telling about a woman who strangled her maid?' Sesina asked the question in her most innocent fashion, but she saw Mrs Dawson give her a sharp look. Needle her a bit more. That might bring something out. 'Mr Collins was telling me another story when we was outside looking down the river.' She pretended to hesitate, gave a little giggle. 'About a housekeeper who murdered one of her employers. I don't suppose that woman would like to have anything like that told about her. She'd pay a few pounds to have that kept a secret, that's what I say.'

'And what I say is that you should get in there and sweep the crumbs up and do the job that you are being paid for, and not stand around talking rubbish,' snapped Mrs Dawson.

'Yes, Mrs Dawson, certainly Mrs Dawson,' said Sesina. Be fun if I found a few pound coins lying on my bed tonight, she thought, as she collected the small hand broom from the press near the stairs.

'And you can tidy out that press when you finish the parlour,' said Mrs Dawson viciously.

112

She took the door from Sesina's hand, looked as though she might slam it. She was in that kind of humour. Sesina's ears were ready for the bang, but when she turned back, before opening the door to the parlour, she saw that Mrs Dawson was staring up at one of the high shelves. Spotted something that she could steal, perhaps.

When Sesina came down to the kitchen, she found that Mrs Dawson was in a good humour. 'Made you a cup of soup, Sesina, put a drop of brandy in it too, so if you taste anything funny, that's what it will be.' The words had rushed out just as if she had practised them.

'That's nice of you, missus.' The soup did look good and it did smell of brandy. She picked it up and moved it closer to her lips. 'Just joking about the story, missus,' she said. 'Mr Collins didn't say anything of the sort. He's a very nice man.' And then something came to her mind. Mrs Dawson peering up, looking at the top shelf in that press by the back stairs. Sesina suddenly remembered what was up there.

Rat poison!

She moved across the room, blowing the top of the soup. 'God! Can't wait to have it. I'll just cool it at the window.' She had the window open in a second, made loud slurping noises and hoped that Mrs Dawson would not hear the sound of soup dripping down the ivy and into the area below. When she turned back into the room, licking her lips and exclaiming with delight, she saw a strange look on Mrs Dawson's face. Was it fear? What was she afraid of? Perhaps, even, was she sorry that she had done such a thing?

Nine

Wilkie Collins, *Basil*:

In the ravelled skein, the slightest
threads are the hardest to follow.

'Not a sign of that watch, I'm afraid, sir. And no
lead to the man who fired at you, Mr Collins.
Though there was a bullet buried in that wooden
mooring post. So you didn't dream it, Mr Collins.
And not clue, sir, not a single, solitary clue, to
the man who killed that girl. Could be anyone,
couldn't it?' Inspector Field had shaken his head
sadly when we dropped into the police station
on our way home. The inspector did not show
much interest in finding Isabella's murderer. Only
his esteem for my friend Dickens had prompted
him to make a few enquiries – people that had
known the dead Isabella in the streets near where
she lived, butcher, baker, candlestick maker, all
of the men who had delivered goods to the basement door of number five Adelphi. 'Not really
any clues,' the inspector had said with a finality
which drove us both out-of-doors again, wandering
along by the riverside, and when we had parted,
Dickens had repeated the inspector's words, but
in a thoughtful way. And then, quite suddenly,
he exclaimed, 'But that's not true, is it, Wilkie?
We do have some sort of clue, thanks to Sesina's

find. Let's meet at two o'clock tomorrow and we'll walk up to The Saracen's Head, I know the place, Snow Hill, near Smithfield, you must know it, Wilkie, don't you? Let's see what we can find out. Energy and fixed purpose, will achieve wonders. We'll put a few clues on a plate for Inspector Field, what do you say, my boy? Remember, two o'clock sharp outside the Temple Inn.'

I spent the night in my mother's house and woke at eight on the following day, with a strong conviction that some time in my sleep I had seen the face of the man who had strangled Isabella. I watched sleepily as the servant put the finishing touches to the blazing fire, wondering what I should do to spend the morning before meeting my friend. I could work on my book, I supposed, but somehow I had lost interest in it for the moment. I needed to allow my thoughts to mature.

'What's the day like, Annie?' I asked.

'Raining, sir,' she said and drew the curtains to prove it to me, I suppose. Now that my eyes were properly open I could see that she herself looked wet from her trip to the coalhouse, her hair still slightly dripping.

'I think that I'll have another little doze,' I said, moving further down in the bed. 'Don't bother about breakfast until I ring.'

I slept instantly and dreamt of clues while I was sleeping, of one large calling card that had the word 'CLUE' in large capital letters upon it, but which I found impossible to turn over. And the torment of the dream was that I knew this held the secret to everything that was puzzling about Isabella's murder. When I woke again it was only ten minutes later by my bedroom clock. But now I was fully awake and the rain had stopped, leaving a miasma of fog behind it.

I rang the bell, ordered breakfast in the dining room and pondered over the word, clue, as I washed and dressed. I had come across a reference to it during my desultory readings at the Temple Inns. The original word was 'clew', meaning a ball of thread and like the ball of thread that led through the labyrinth, the 'clew' led one to the solution. Perhaps today little Sesina would have something for me, something that would lead us to the heart of the mystery, lead us to the secret that Isabella had thought, poor girl, would make her fortune.

I was not an early riser normally, but I was so eager to solve the mystery of poor Isabella Gordon's murder that I was within the Adelphi Arches soon after ten o'clock. The place was busy. Fish carts, meat carts, men wheeling barrels, housemaids flapping mats, it was a hive of activity and made me feel somewhat guilty about my lazy life when I seldom bothered to change from pyjamas and dressing gown until about noon in the day.

I lingered for a while. And then a cart came up, driven by a surly-looking butcher, taking his ill-humour out on his horse. I hate cruelty to animals and I stepped forward to remonstrate with the man. He pulled up. Not because of me. He hadn't seen me. He jumped down and hammered on the door of number five. I abstracted a handful of hay from an egg cart and fed it surreptitiously to the unfortunate horse, stroking the poor fellow's ears, while the butcher was waiting; his face to the door.

And there was little Sesina, looking trim and neat. She saw me. I was sure of that. I saw her eyes go to me instantly before she started to berate the man.

'Very tough, that last lot of beef, Bob. No good at all. The missus was ever so angry about it. Said to tell you that she won't put up with such poor stuff.'

An angry man. His voice came across to me. The voice of a man who had little control. 'Don't you give me that malarkey; you cheeky little *mot*. Look what happened to the other *mot* with the smart tongue.' There was a heavy and threatening note in his voice.

'I heard that, my man.' I stepped forward instantly, leaving the horse to munch in peace.

He stiffened. He didn't swing around. Didn't stare aggressively at me. He just stayed very still for a moment.

And then he nodded; no, more bowed his head. 'Sorry, sir,' he said and sidled past me.

'And don't let me see you mistreat that poor animal of yours again.' I felt rather brave saying that. I don't think that I would have dared if he had not shown himself to be such a coward in the face of a few words. He behaved almost as though he were afraid of me, averting his eyes from me and muttering a few excuses. I watched him go back, mount to his seat, shake the reins of the horse and turn it to go back, all in a strangely different manner to the way in which he had arrived. I had no illusions about myself. Soft voice, soft hands, a bare five and a half foot tall, a good five or six inches shorter than that brute. Why had he taken so much notice of my words?

Had Dickens and I been misled by Sesina's strong conviction that Isabella had left the house through the front door on her last night? And that, perhaps, she had left in the company of one of the gentlemen in the house; that there was something strange about the snapped wire of the bell. I had noted the wires running along the hall, above the hallstand and had thought the ringing of the bell might have been a signal. But what if we were wrong. What if Isabella had a spare key to the basement door and had gone out that way, locking the door behind her?

Surely, it was more natural, more understandable that she had been murdered by one of her own kind? This butcher, for instance. I looked towards Sesina. I would question her about this man, I thought. She turned away, looking back into the house, still holding the dish in her hands. I wondered what the poor, homeless people who sheltered under these arches thought of the riches of food that were daily brought to these back doors.

'Just bringing the meat in, missus. And then I'll do the mats.' Sesina called into the house. She gave me a quick wink, which amused me and then went back inside, shutting the door behind her. I made my way into the shadows of the archway and stood there. The unfortunate poor woman that Dickens and I had spoken to was still there. No baby in her arms now. I tried not to speculate about the baby. I fumbled in my pocket and silently gave her half a crown. She said nothing in return, just kept the coin in the palm of her hand, gazing at the money in a dazed fashion. The children looked at me in silence. The boy was coughing badly.

Sesina was back out again in a flash. She had a couple of mats with her and started to bang them vigorously against the railings by the river. I went to join her, not standing too near, but making an appearance of someone who is observing the boats. There was a police launch there, moving rapidly down the river. A rope behind it. Towing something. I turned away. I didn't want to know.

'Didn't find anything, I'm afraid, sir. That was a good idea about the bed, but there was nothing there.' Sesina had moved a little nearer to me. She did not look towards me as she said the words, but bent down to add the last mat to the ones which she had already shaken.

I slipped her sixpence, anyway, as she passed me. Not the girl's fault. We still had the other two cards to go on, poor Isabella's pathetic attempt at making a book, perhaps in imitation of the man who had rescued her from the streets and seeing that she had an education. It had been quite a feat. I took the two cards from my pocket and brooded over them. The handwriting was beautifully formed, the handwriting of a gentlewoman. This Mrs Morson who managed Urania Cottage must have had a great influence over the girls if they modelled their handwriting on hers.

I walked away towards the Temple Inn, called into the porter's office to see whether there were any letters for me, did a little reading in the library, looking up old law cases, looking for inspiration that would bring me a few steps further along the dreary path of the book that I was trying to write. I had not planned it properly. I could see that. I had been lazy, had thought that the idea would carry me on, but now I found myself, like a traveller in a moorland who has no map and no real destination in mind. I took a sheet of paper and neatly numbered it one to thirty, down the left-hand margin. I would do no more, I resolved, until material sufficient for a booklet, was sketched in beside each one of these numerals. Thirty booklets, each published fortnightly in Dickens' magazine, *Household Words* and then put together to make a book – a book that would make me famous.

But somehow inspiration eluded me.

I pulled another piece of paper towards me, folded it in four, took a soft pencil and began to draw. The eyes were the first thing that I drew, not dead eyes, but large, dark eyes, looking directly at me, their creator. I tried to put in the light that must have been there when she was still alive. And then the hair, not so difficult. Hair remains when the light is extinguished from the eyes. Black hair, easy to do with a pencil. I had an India rubber beside me but I made no use of it. My pencil twirled over those lustrous curls. I was no artist, not like my father or my younger

120

brother; competent, would be all that I would class myself, but today I was inspired. I sketched the outline of a pair of slim shoulders beneath those tumbling skeins of hair. And then the dress. I had no colours with me, but I remembered the patterned strip on the flounces at the end of each sleeve and along the hem of the dress.

And last of all I drew the mouth. The girl looked out from the page at me with a half-smile, half enchanting, half appealing, asking a question.

We were a silent pair, both Dickens and myself when we met at two o'clock. He would have been up at seven in the morning, splashed under his famous cold shower, the most vigorous in the whole of London, he used to boast. Then he would have eaten his breakfast, in silence, probably thinking about his morning's work. And at nine o'clock, as punctual as any clerk, he would go into his study, shut the baize-lined door, shut out the world, and get on with his creations until the hour of two struck. And then he walked for the afternoon, thinking his way through the next instalment.

And so today when we met, we walked along in silence. Me thinking hard about the complexities of my plot, building scene upon scene; how I could sculpt it by bringing in the surprises one by one. And Dickens, immersed in the final stage of his new novel, *Bleak House*, was thinking also. He was walking rapidly along, his lips moving in a silent pantomime of speech. From time to time, I was tempted to confide in him a sudden new and original twist that I contemplated in the story of the deaf circus girl, but a glance at his face stopped me. I knew better than to interrupt him. There would be only one girl in Dickens' mind at the moment and that would be his creation, Esther Summerson. And yet as soon as we climbed the steep heights of Snow Hill, I could see that he had banished his imaginary world from his mind and was now looking around him with great interest. By the time that we walked into the yard, he was alert and keen, observing the coaches which were lined up, the stables with the patient heads of horses looking out, the coffee room above where the travellers could be glimpsed. There was a bar at the back of the yard and he led me towards it with the air of a man who knew the place intimately.

There were a number of coachman in an outer room, not much better than a stable, protected by a roof, propped on rough beams, but open on to the yard. We could see them inside there, seated on long forms, around a heavy table, downing pints of beer and Dickens went straight towards them, producing a half crown from his pocket, throwing it into the air and catching it neatly. The silver caught the light from the gas lamp and sparkled. There was a sudden turning of heads. One man got up and came towards us. Dickens gave him a keen look, but raised his voice slightly so that all could hear him.

'Good afternoon to you all,' he said briskly. 'I'm looking for a man who spoke with a girl, dark hair, wearing a green and red dress. May have been a few weeks ago.'

'She would look a little like this,' I said,

producing my sketch from my pocket book and handing it to Dickens.

'A lot like that.' He nodded vigorously. 'A very good likeness, indeed.' He showed it to the man who now stood beside us.

I looked eagerly at the fellow. He had glanced at the sketch, but now his eyes were on the half-crown.

'Don't remember her myself, sir,' he said, still retaining the sketch in his hand. 'I could try to find out, sir, if I can take the drawing with me.'

Dickens instantly handed over the half-crown. A man of decision, always.

'Wouldn't do to have all the drivers coming out here around us in the yard,' he said in an undertone to me as the man went back towards the seated coachmen. 'Management wouldn't like it,' he added. 'This man will do the work for us.' He reached into his waistcoat pocket and produced another half-crown. This time he didn't toss it up and down, but held it concealed in his hand. This time he would require hard information.

We could see our friend inside the dimness of the bar. He was moving from one to another. As far as I could see, he hadn't produced the sketch. It still seemed to be in his pocket. I watched him, narrowing my eyes to distinguish his tall figure among the other shapes. 'I hope he is not going to cheat us,' I observed uneasily.

'Shouldn't think so. Had an honest look about him. Earn good money, coachmen. No need to cheat.' Dickens' eyes, also, were narrowed as he gazed fixedly at the bar where the coachmen were busy filling up their stomachs, while their horses munched hay in their stables. And then he stiffened. The tall figure of the first man had moved towards the yard and was followed by another, a much smaller figure with bright red hair.

In a moment they were outside. Didn't come towards us though. The tall man had stopped first. Took a half-smoked cigar from his jacket pocket and handed it to the other. And then, while the cigar was being lit, quite casually, he produced my sketch, holding it under the light of the gas lamp. The man stopped, match still kindled and looked intently.

'Is that her, Sam?' he asked. To my disappointment the man seemed to hesitate, screwing up his eyes and tilting his head to one side.

'That's her,' he said eventually and looked over towards Dickens. I saw his eyes go to the closed hand.

'Thank you, my friend.' Dickens moved forward and subtly dismissed the tall man. We were left with the smaller and red-headed man who was still staring at the sketch. Then he shrugged and handed it back to Dickens, who passed it over to me.

'So you remember her,' observed Dickens.

'Nice little girl, taking ways, she had. Trying to trace her little brother. He had been stolen from a school in Yorkshire. That's what she told me. Had been brought to London by a man, about three months ago. A man with red hair, mutton chop whiskers and a big scar, right down his left cheek. That's what she told me. Wanted to know whether I had remembered him, was asking lots of us that question. Some of the lads were joking her, but I took it serious when she asked me if I had ever taken a man like that from Yorkshire to London. In September, that's what she said.'

'And had you?' Not a muscle had moved on Dickens' face but I was excited. *A man with red hair, mutton chop whiskers and a big scar, right down his left cheek.* A perfect description of Mr Frederick Cartwright, the schoolmaster who lodged on the second floor of number five Adelphi Terrace.

'Yes, I had, sir.' The man had a nice straightforward manner about him and I felt that his evidence could be trusted. 'Yes, I remembered the scar. A very bad one, it was, like a mouth almost, right across his cheek. He was anxious to get to London. Wouldn't enjoy a drink with the other passengers. After me all the time, that's what he was. "How much longer, driver?" pestering me, like. That's when I saw that scar move, open and shut like a mouth, it did. It was him, grinding his teeth. *You've got a fair old temper and it's led you into a bad fight sometime, a fight with knives, my fine fellow*, I was saying that, in my mind, of course, sir.'

'And the boy?'

'Well, I had to disappoint her, there, sir. No, no boy, I told her. Take many of them up to Yorkshire, but I disremember any coming back and that's the truth, I'm afraid.'

'And this was a few weeks ago, was it?'

The man seemed uncertain. His eyes were still on the half-crown in Dickens' hand. 'Wouldn't have thought it was as long ago as that.' He

125

thought for a moment. 'Could be, I suppose.' He sounded a bit doubtful.

Dickens opened his hand and gave him the money. 'And would you remember the name on the waybill, by any chance?'

The man, honest fellow, shook his head. 'Sorry, sir, get so many of those people up and down the country, week in and week out.'

'If I gave you a letter, C; two letters: Car . . .'

'That's it, sir, Carson, no, that's not right, Carter; that would be it.'

'Near enough, Wilkie, don't you think,' said Dickens as we walked away. 'Carter, Cartwright, not too great a difference for a man who transports hundreds of people up and down the country week in, week out, as he says himself. But where does that leave us?'

'She was looking for her brother?'

'Do you know, Wilkie, I wonder if that was a little romance that she made up. A great girl for romancing. The lies that girl told me, well, Isabella, I said to her once, perhaps you should write a book, Isabella. You're the world's best at making up stories. Never met anyone to beat you.' Dickens chuckled a little, but then became serious. 'I looked up her history in the book that I keep at Urania Cottage. She said she was apprenticed to a shoemaker, well, that may or may not be the truth, but if it was, well, when you talk about apprentices, Wilkie, in the case of these parish children, it's a bit like slavery. Isabella ran away as soon as she could, got herself to London; you can imagine how she managed to keep body and soul together on the streets of

London. She was in prison when I met her. Educated, you know, that was one of the first things that I noted about her, could read well, write well, spell and everything. Nothing but trouble in the cottage though. Why bless my soul,' said Dickens warmly, 'I do think that girl could have started the French revolution single-handed, just to amuse herself in a period of wet weather. Herself and that little Sesina. Great friends they were, birds of a feather.'

'So you don't believe the business about the brother.' I mused a little on Isabella. Pretty, clever, educated. 'That handwriting,' I said aloud.

'She copied that from Mrs Morson, some of the girls did. But not many could do it as well as Isabella. Poor girl.'

'So why has she gone to the trouble of researching Mr Cartwright?' I asked.

Dickens laughed. 'I can guess,' he said. 'She picked up a hint, poking around in his bedroom; that would be Isabella. Picked up a hint that he was from Yorkshire. Mrs Morson had read to the girls some of my book *Nicholas Nickleby* – the girls all relished the part where the wicked schoolmaster got thrashed by Nicholas the hero; I remember Mrs Morson telling me that. And so our Isabella might have decided to do a little blackmail. Found something, threatened to go to the school, to St Bartholomew's, nice school that. Yes, that would be her. Doing a bit of blackmail, I wouldn't doubt. You remember, Wilkie, how taken aback he was at our American friend's little joke, about his cane. He may well have got the job by a recommendation from his friend and they may have suppressed the Yorkshire connection. St Bartholomew's wouldn't have wanted any schoolmaster with a record of violence and Yorkshire, helped by *yours truly's* book, did have a very bad reputation for ill-treating boys. Perhaps Isabella threatened to tell the school that he had been in some sort of scandal in a Yorkshire school.'

'But the cards, the book that she was going to write?'

Dickens shrugged his shoulders. 'She was going to write another *Nicholas Nickleby*. I suppose that I should take it as a compliment.' He had an amused smile on his lips.

'Poor girl,' I said. And his face hardened.

'I'll see that the fellow who did that gets hanged,' he said with a quick swish of his umbrella, which alarmed a couple of gentlemen passers-by until they saw who it was and then they just whispered excitedly to each other.

'What about Inspector Field?' I asked the question tentatively and then when he looked at me with some surprise, I said hastily, 'I wondered whether we should mention it to him.'

His face relaxed into amusement. 'My dear Wilkie,' he said, 'Inspector Field is a very busy man. I think that we'll sort out this little matter ourselves, don't you?' And then he began to walk very rapidly, swinging his umbrella and staring fixedly ahead. From time to time a passer-by would suddenly stop, swivel his head around, nudge a companion, but Dickens took no notice. *Fame*, he would say, if ever I pointed out the excitement that his presence on a street could cause, *fame, my dear Wilkie, is nothing. Money, now, that is important! The labourer is worthy of his hire, that's something that you must keep in your mind and I foresee a brilliant future for you. Give the people what they want, give, but don't forget to take, also.*

Tavistock House, where the schoolroom was large enough to hold seventy people, all invited to witness one of his plays, was a very notable reward for his industry. I brooded over this while we walked briskly down the hill. My father had been a rich man, had made more money from his paintings than ever did the recently deceased Turner, though many would whisper that the latter was the better artist. But the landscapes and seascapes that my father had turned out so capably were prettier sights on a drawing-room wall than ever was a Turner. And my father's industry had meant that his wife and his two sons lived their lives amid ease and plenty and after his will was read, I knew that there was no urgency upon me to earn my living. Fame, though. That was what I wanted. Fame and the satisfaction of producing a notable piece of writing. I thought about this as we went along and decided not to rush into writing my next book. I would give it time to mature in my mind. Perhaps write something different. *The Dead Secret*, I thought. That would be a good title. The secret would be about the parentage of a girl; she finds out that she is not whom she had thought; that her mother is not her mother and that her father is not her father, either.

129

'Dickens, I have such a good idea,' I said eagerly.

'Don't talk about it,' he said and his voice was kind, not dismissive. 'The trouble with you, Wilkie, is that you let out too much. You talk too much about your ideas. And then when you go to write them down your find that they have seeped away from you. Keep that idea of yours wrapped up safely in your mind until it matures. Expose it to the air, now, before you have written your book and it will tarnish.'

I nodded my head. What had worked so well for him should, *would*, I vowed, work for me. And so, in silence, we walked down the hill and on until we reached the crowded pavements of Fleet Street. I did my best to keep my mind away from my idea and on Isabella and her quest after her parentage.

We had planned to dine together, probably at his favourite restaurant, Rules, where the head waiter would always find a place for Dickens, no matter how crowded the room was. And I knew, as soon as we entered Maiden Lane from Covent Garden, that Dickens would suddenly shut down that section of his mind and turn his attention back to the dead girl and our quest after information about her.

But not before. Now he was brooding on his book, again. I knew that by the expression on his face, by the way that his lips moved as he walked rapidly along the pavement. At some minute soon, he might turn to me as though seeing me for the first time and make some facetious remark. Until then I knew enough to keep very quiet and to allow his mind to work. Probably though, he would wait until we reached Rules.

And so I was surprised when he suddenly stopped in the middle of the pavement, just beside a coffee shop.

'Isn't this the place that those two young newspaper journalists were talking to you about? The place where they get their supper, usually?'

'That's right.' I was surprised that he had been listening into our conversations. He had seemed, during the dinner party, to be much occupied with the lawyer and the schoolmaster, each sitting on either side of him. 'Yes,' I said looking upwards, 'this is the place.'

'Let's go in.' He was through the door before I could reply.

'*Two for his heels*,' yelled a voice as we pushed open the door of the upstairs room. It was still early in the evening, but Benjamin and Jim were at their supper, a tankard of steaming purl beside each and a plate of bread and beef in the middle of the table. But most of the table was occupied by a cribbage board and a pack of cards, spread out.

'*Go*,' groaned Ben as Jim inserted another peg on his side of the board.

'Good evening, gentlemen. Mind if we watch your game?' Dickens carried over a chair and placed himself at the table. 'Another bowl of purl, and two more tankards,' he said to the waiter who drifted up looking as though he hoped we weren't going to be too much of a nuisance to him, took another look at Dickens and then straightened himself with a look of recognition in his eyes. 'Yes, sir, certainly, sir, any food, sir?'

'No, no food.' Dickens cast a quick look at the dry beef and unappetizingly curled slices of bread. He had told me once that he had been poor when he was young and that I had been lucky to be the son of a rich man, a man whose pictures were purchased by royalty. Nevertheless, he was as fastidious as an earl in his tastes. He took some of the purl, though, when Jim ladled it out for us into the two extra tankards and we watched their game patiently, listening to the cries of 'hauling lumber!'; 'one for his nob!'; 'muggins!'; 'Raggedy Ann!' until the final call of 'Up Sticks!' meant that Jim had won the game.

Jim gravely shook hands with himself, with a muttered, 'Well done, Jim, boy!' Then he patted himself on the back, proposed a health to himself and emptied a tankard in his own honour while his friend mopped imaginary tears with an imaginary handkerchief. Dickens watched with an amused gaze. Surreptitiously, he slid his notebook and pencil from his pocket and made a note beneath the screen of the tablecloth.

The two of them might well know quite a bit about the servant girls, I thought. They were just the type. About seventeen or eighteen, I reckoned, and wondered whether they reminded Dickens of the time when he had been a newspaperman of about the same age as these two youngsters.

'Ever play cribbage with Isabella or Sesina at your lodgings?' enquired Dickens. It seemed an innocent question. He had told me once that the girls in Urania Cottage played cribbage which he thought was a harmless game when played with buttons and good for their arithmetic. He had personally selected some cribbage boards for the place.

Ben and Jim, however, were a little alarmed at that question. Neither replied. Over the rim of the tankard, Ben's large, pale-blue eyes slid across to his companion. Jim took another gulp from his tankard and raised the ladle invitingly at us. I took a little more, but Dickens shook his head.

'Excellent stuff,' he said, taking a sip, a very small sip, and then another with the air of a connoisseur. He didn't repeat his question, but just waited patiently for the two young journalists to finish their drink.

'Didn't see much of them,' said Jim after a minute.

'They'd clean the room while we were out at work,' said Ben.

'And we'd always eat out,' added Jim.

'So I understand,' said Dickens soothingly. 'Really good purl, this.' He held up his tankard and admired the steam oozing out from it, inhaling it with a smile of appreciation on his lips, then putting it down after taking another small sip.

'I suppose the only time then that Isabella would have to talk to you would have been when she brought you your breakfasts. Which of you was it that helped her to find the workhouse?'

It was a shot in the dark, uttered very quickly. Dickens had put down his tankard and was looking straight across the table, first at one and then at the other. Neither was a match for Dickens. Jim looked accusingly at Ben and Ben succumbed.

'She was talking to me about it, one morning. Just after she brought up my water for shaving. She said that she was very young when she was taken away but she remembered the look of the place.'

'Did you think that she was telling the truth?' Dickens asked the question quietly.

'Never thought about it at all,' said Ben. He looked across at his friend. 'What did you think, Jim?'

'No reason to lie to us,' said Jim with a shrug.

'True,' said Dickens. He gave a little nod to himself. I guessed that Isabella had told him a different story when he interviewed her before she came to Urania Cottage. He had told me once that he always checked the girls' stories, checked police records, gaol records, but early life was not easy to check and most girls made up some fantasy about poor, but honest and loving parents who died from a fever necessitating their children to scatter around the streets of London.

'And what were her memories?' he asked.

'Well, ships, that's the funny thing; she remembered ships. Ships going up and down.'

'By the sea? At the seaside?'

'We thought the river, didn't we, Benny?'

'That's right, Jim. We did. From the way that she described the place. She talked about the ships being enormous and very near. She said that she was frightened of how huge they were.

134

She was only little then, about three or four, she thought. Well that's what she told us, anyways.'

'And a very steep hill; she remembered that, didn't she, Ben, and rolling down the hill and being beaten for getting her pinafore dirty.'

'And so in the end, we came up with Greenwich. Jim had gone there to do a piece about the naval college and he described it to her and she thought that was the place that she had been in when she was small.'

'And her brother?'

'Didn't say nothing about a brother, did she, Benny. Don't remember nothing about that. She just talked about other girls, the girls that she knew in Urania Cottage and about the time she had before she went there. Made up a lot of it, I'd say,' said Jim, with a wry, man-of-the world air. He fingered a wisp of whisker lovingly. I grinned, passing a hand over my mouth to hide the involuntary twitch of my lips. Not that long since I was his age, I thought, more idle than he, but I remembered also worrying about whether my whiskers would ever grow.

'There is a workhouse there, at Greenwich; I know that. Did she ever go there?'

'Went on her day off. Very pleased with herself the next day, wasn't she, Benny?'

'Said that she was going again on her next day off. I remember that,' said Benny.

'And she found out something about her family, did she?'

'Some sort of stuff about her being just left temporary like. About her mother had promised to send for her.'

135

'The workhouse most like says the same thing to everyone. Makes it sound better,' said Jim wisely.

'But Isabella believed it,' I put in. I thought about it for a moment. It seemed very sad to think of Isabella being full of excitement about the discovery of a mother who had abandoned her. 'I wonder why she was going to go back again. Perhaps it was to see someone who would remember her mother, some member of the staff who had their day off when Isabella arrived. Did she say anything about why she was going back again?'

They looked at each. There was a slightly furtive, slightly guarded look about them both since Dickens had asked them about Isabella. Up to then they had been two typical young men, just having an evening meal in the coffee house, but once the subject of the dead girl had come up, they had been uneasy.

'No, I don't remember, do you, Jim.' Benny buried his nose in the comforting scent from his tankard. Jim fiddled with the pegs in the cribbage board, arranging them in a zigzag pattern. Dickens beckoned the waiter.

'Some more purl,' he said.

That did the trick. They both relaxed and began to boast about how streetwise they were, knew everything to be known about London. Could tell any out-of-town person where to go, no matter whether he wanted a hat or an eel pie.

'And if I wanted a ticket for a play?' asked Dickens with a little smile.

They fell over themselves telling him about the

cheapest place to go and to uncover their knowledge of ticket touts.

'What about a birth certificate?' Dickens' tone was casual and he buried his nose in the tankard of purl.

'Easy, Somerset House,' said Jim.

'And you directed Isabella there.' Dickens crumbled some bread in his fingers and then wiped them with his pocket handkerchief.

'That's right,' said Jim carelessly and he tossed back some more purl.

Dickens got to his feet. 'Well, gentlemen, we've disturbed you at your evening meal. Isabella was an inmate in a charitable home which Miss Coutts set up for girls and as her assistant in the work I have an interest in the girls that stayed there. I trust you'll forgive our questions, when you know the reasons behind them.'

'And that's very good purl,' I added seeing they looked even more uncomfortable after that little speech.

They were glad to get rid of us; that was apparent. And when we went through the glass door and I turned to shut it properly, I could see both heads, the dark and the fair one, close together, and both young faces were very serious.

'I wonder whether Isabella had sworn them to secrecy,' I said to Dickens as soon as we were on the busy pavement.

He didn't answer. I glanced at him, wondering whether he had heard and knew by the expression of his dark eyes that he was thinking very hard.

'Fancy a trip on the river steamboat tomorrow

137

afternoon, Wilkie?' He didn't wait for me to answer but went on, 'We could visit the place where Isabella might have spent her childhood. I think that I could get something out of them. I know something about that poorhouse and work-house, I know about the precious villain who set it up. We'll call into Adelphi Terrace first, though, and see if we can get anything more out of Sesina. Wouldn't be surprised if that young lady knows more than she is saying.'

'I got the impression that she is very keen for everything to be done to find the murderer of her friend,' I said a little stiffly. I thought that Dickens was a bit schoolmasterly with Sesina. 'She might confide in me more readily than in you,' I added.

'God bless my soul, Wilkie,' he said impatiently, 'you don't know those girls like I do. Up to all sorts of tricks, every single one of them. There were times when I was coming back from Urania Cottage that I had to laugh. Gave the cabby a fright a couple of times. Thought the world had exploded somewhere in the region of his knees. I was thinking of all the lies that I had heard and laughing to myself so hard!'

Ten

Sesina stared at the card. One or two of the words were blotted out by the smudge of smuts smeared across its surface. It had been many a long year since a fire was lit in that damp little bedroom, but the chimney was still encrusted with soot. Still, it was readable. She pondered over the words. Despite all the stains and the splodges, almost all of the black ink of the ornate curled copperplate letters stood out clearly.

My mother had to get me away from him. She couldn't keep me. He'd have killed me too. If he doesn't pay me to keep my mouth shut I'll go down to that school. One more . . .

The last word was missing. Sesina turned over various possibilities for it in her mind and then shrugged her shoulders. Let Mr Clever Dickens work it out. After all he spent most of his time writing books and writing articles for newspapers – sob stuff, the sort of stuff that would make well-off people keep reading and reading as they sat comfortably on soft chairs in front of roaring fires; sort of spice on the roast beef, she always thought, makes you appreciate what you've got when you read about people in misery. Of course, what rich people didn't know was that they had fun sometimes. That girl that Mr Dickens wrote about, lying there in front of the workhouse,

139

taking his five shillings and then going off silently without saying nothing, that girl, most like, just laughed her head off when she got around the corner. She had done it herself sometimes. Didn't mean that it wasn't real, being hungry and cold; but a bit of laughing made it seem better. And knowing what rich people were like; that's how to get money out of them. Bare feet better than dirty broken shoes, Isabella said to her once. And a clean face, too. Rich people don't like dirt, don't like torn clothes, think that you should wash and mend. But they like to tell their rich friends how they gave money to a barefooted girl. Or write about it in the newspapers, of course. Like Mr Dickens!

I miss Isabella; the place is a bit of a morgue without her, Sesina thought, as she went into her own bedroom and tucked the card behind the small mirror that stood on the chest of drawers. I'll get some money out of the fellow that did for her and then I'll move on. Her imagination ranged over how much she would need. Perhaps a place of her own wouldn't be such fun, after all. A shop, now, that would be nice. Or, better still, a coffee stall. Practise a bit of cooking. *Too much for you, Mrs Dawson, let me help, show me what to do.* She'd have a coffee stall in Covent Garden. Serve breakfast to stallholders and the delivery men in from the country and even some gentlemen coming home after a late night. Plenty of backchat; that would be fun!

But first she had to get evidence against him. No point in asking for money until she had enough on him to give him a fright. She'd give

140

his room a good old turnout, today. That char-woman who came in each day to help with the cleaning could busy herself with his lordship Mr Doyle's rooms and with the hall and parlour. A quick flick around the top floor – the lads wouldn't notice as long as the fire was burning when they came home – and then she would really turn out Mr Frederick Cartwright's place, search his sitting room, his bedroom and his dressing room. Didn't usually bother about that once she had emptied the bowls and the slop pails.

Sesina went into the kitchen. She'd make a good pot of tea, she decided. That would put the missus in a good humour. There was even a slice of sponge cake. She had found it in Mr Cartwright's room – well it had been half a cake when she had found it, but the remaining slice should do the trick if presented to Mrs Dawson. *Cake, sir? Well, I'm sure I don't know, sir. Hope there ain't mice around, Mr Cartwright. I'll tell Mrs Dawson. We need a new cat. I'll tell her that.*

'Keep your strength up, missus,' she said, as soon the housekeeper came yawning into the kitchen. 'You're looking a bit peaky. You don't want to collapse after all the trouble that you've been put to. Just you eat that bit of cake. Got it special for you when you sent me out on an errand yesterday.'

'You're a kind girl, Sesina,' said Mrs Dawson graciously. 'It's all been a shock to you, too, as much as to me. I must get another girl to replace Isabella when my nerves are better, but I've been thinking that for the moment we might just manage with that charwoman – she seems willing; what do you think?'

'Perhaps we could get that young girl in to scrub the kitchen and the front steps, what do you think?' asked Sesina. She had left a few moments' pause, long enough for the slice of sponge cake to do its work in sweetening Mrs Dawson. 'That would leave me a bit of time to do the shopping, go to the market and get some proper fresh stuff, something for our supper, that sort of thing. You don't want to have the burden of that, what with the shock that you got and all,' she ended in virtuous tones. If that didn't work with the old hag, well, nothing would.

Mrs Dawson meditatively mopped individual crumbs from her plate with a wet forefinger. 'I'll think about it,' she said. She took a large bit of the cake, chewed it and then another swallow of tea. It did the work. 'Yes, I was thinking the very same thing myself yesterday,' she said affably. 'Your young legs could do with stretching and if you take over the shopping, well then I could keep a close eye on that young one and on the charwoman today. I'll have a word with the landlord about keeping the two of them on for a few weeks until we are ourselves again. He won't mind, I daresay. That young one comes cheap and the charwoman is not expensive, neither. We'll see what he says. He promised to call in some time today or tomorrow.'

'And now I best do the bedrooms,' said Sesina, adding some scouring powder to her bucket. 'I'll leave the third floor for the charwoman. These two aren't fussy. I gave the first floor a good

142

going over yesterday so I'll start with Mr Cartwright's set this morning.'

If ever I have a house of my own, I'll have a cupboard for cleaning stuff on every floor. Not dragging my guts out every day carrying all this stuff up six flights of stairs. And then she thought that if she did have a big house like number five, she would have three or four servants. Let them haul up the loads, she thought. No one ever bothers their head about me, so why should I bother my head about them? And as she toiled up the stairs, she planned her servants. A parlourmaid called Jane, she decided. A nice old-fashioned name. Jane would be from the country, she decided. And then a cook called Mrs Burns, from Scotland. Could have some good laughs with a name like that. And two housemaids, Susan and Sarah, she decided. And she'd lie in bed in the morning, sip hot chocolate while Sarah lit the fire and Susan brought up hot water. She wouldn't be too familiar, but not nasty, neither.

Now for something to hold over him. She unlocked the door to Mr Cartwright's bedroom and went in. Had a good look around. Scattered tealeaves over the carpet and let them settle while she searched the dressing room. It had a high clothes press in there. Even standing on a chair she couldn't reach the top of it. In the end she tied the hearth brush to the sweeping brush, knotting the duster around it and swept from side to side and from back to front. Nothing there but a cloud of dust and a couple of dead moths.

Drat! She thought. Lucky that it was just varnished boards in here.

Then she searched every pocket in the two suits, the dressing gown and the summer raincoat that hung there.

Nothing.

Floorboards? No, not a single one of them was loose. He'd be the sort of man to complain if one of them was.

She tried behind the washstand, sent her brush along the top of the door and then went into the bedroom and stretched herself on the bed while she had a good think.

Mr Cartwright was a tidy man, and a suspicious one, too, she thought. Not one to hide things in rooms that were cleaned by servants. But Isabella must have discovered something? Perhaps there was nothing now left to be found. Still, she was determined not to give up. Even if she couldn't get money from him, at least she could see him swing for what he did to poor Isabella.

There must be something. She got off the bed and did a little dusting. The furniture came with the rooms, of course. Furnished lodgings; that was what they were. But that little desk on top of the table by the window, could that be his own, something that he brought with him? She gave it a good dust while thinking hard.

What was she looking for?

Letters, she supposed. And letters would be kept in a desk. Mrs Morson had had a desk like that. Whenever she'd got a letter, she would read it, and then lock it in her desk.

This desk was locked, too, but Hannah in

144

Urania Cottage had shown her the trick of that and Selina managed to click it open with a nail file from his washstand in just a few seconds. Very, very tidy, his desk. No letters there. And, come to think of it, no letters ever came for him to number five. Writing paper and envelopes, stamps, too. All very neat. And then she touched a spring and a drawer slid open. Just one thing in it. A big envelope with 'Receipts' written on it. Very good handwriting. Month and year, everything filled in. It wasn't sealed so she pulled out the sheets of paper. 'Paid in advance. Three months' rent.' 'Paid. For making and fitting one black suit of clothes.' 'Paid. For the repairing of pair of leather boots.' Nothing but receipts for clothes, rent and goods. She was going to shut the desk again when she spotted something. One of the pages. Same good thick paper. Sesina noticed it because it had a dirty smudge on the bottom corner, as though someone with dirty hands had picked up the page and waved it through the air to dry the ink. She examined it. In Mr Cartwright's handwriting. 'Received in full payment. £20:0:0.' Twenty pounds, she thought. That was a lot of money. And no mention of goods or services received. And the handwriting of the signature was quite different. A mixture of capitals and small letters. Very bad handwriting, she thought, not at all like the handwriting which Mrs Morson taught to the girls of Urania Cottage.

A dirty thumbprint on the bottom of the page. Perhaps a man that worked with his hands. This man had got twenty pounds sterling from Mr

Cartwright. Sesina felt a rush of excitement. Perhaps that was what Isabella had discovered. Something about this man. She peered at the handwriting. 'Tom', she thought. And then something beginning with the letter G and an R somewhere in the middle of the word. She took it to the window, slipped through the heavy net curtains, glancing down at the pavement before she examined the page. Mrs Dawson was outside the door, taking the air like a lady, looking up at the sky, wondering whether she would need an umbrella to pop down and see the landlord. Sesina retreated quickly. No point in the extra light from the window, anyway. Didn't make it any clearer. Still she had something. Perhaps that Mr Collins could help her. He was the type that she could run rings around. She replaced the envelope in the secret drawer, pushed it in until she heard the click and then closed up the lid of the desk. But the lock that had worked so perfectly with a quick turn of the nail file when she had opened the desk, now refused to close. Again and again she tried, but there was no sound of a click. She felt a dampness on her forehead and sweat soaked her dress, under her arms and between the shoulder blades.

And then she stopped, feeling the sweat turn to an ice-like chill. Surely it couldn't be. Eleven o'clock in the morning. Not him, surely. And yet she could have sworn it was his voice. A slam of the door. The heavy front door. Steps on the stairs. Her mind refused to believe what her ears were telling her. It couldn't be. The second set of stairs. She heard that creak on the third step.

In a sudden panic she dived beneath the bed. Stupid! She had a perfect right to be here. Why not be dusting? Cleaning a window? Too late. A rattle of a keys. A rush of cold air from the staircase. 'Stupid little bitch!' That would be meant for her. Hadn't liked finding the door left open. Would he go to the desk? She held her breath. And then stretched rigid. The springs creaked and dipped down, almost touching her shoulder. She flattened herself as much as possible, lying face down. Waiting.

Taking off his boots. A pair of trousers dropped on the floor beside her. Did he know she was there? Would he rape her? She tried to edge towards the other side, but his weight pinned her, immobilized her. Now all of her dress was soaked with icy sweat. She waited to see the face peering down at her; to feel his hand pulling her out. She could scream, she told herself. But the house was large, Mrs Dawson wouldn't hear. And if she did? Would she ignore it?

The springs lifted. He had stood up. Even in stocking feet she heard the thud of his steps. Crossing the room. A drawer wrenched open. A gag, perhaps. Back now. Cautiously she wriggled towards the opposite side of the bed as far away from him as she could go. A striking of a match. Smell of a candle. As Sesina watched, the candlelight illuminated the floorboards. He had lowered it down. Was looking to see what was under the bed. No, not yet. Shining the candlelight on the heap of clothes. Brown trousers, white flannel knee-length drawers. He had stripped both off.

147

And then she saw it. Almost a circle. Bright red. As red as a blood moon.

Blood. That was the stain on those flannel drawers.

Now he was sitting down again. She edged even nearer to the other side. He was pulling on a fresh pair of drawers. She could hear him grunt with effort. Now for the trousers. This was her moment. She couldn't stay there. Who knew how many girls that man had murdered? Not giving herself time to be afraid, she wriggled out from under the bed, her fingertips pulling her forward, slid across the floor and beneath the closed curtains. In a moment, she was on her feet and had thrown open the window. At least now she could scream. She climbed out on to the window-sill. Not a soul on the road. Just her luck. Nevertheless, she stayed there. She and Isabella always did the outside of the windows together. She found the handle grip on the side frame, but missed the reassurance of a friend on the inside, ready to grab a dress, ready to steady her.

He felt the chill after a minute; she knew he would.

'What's that? Who's there?'

He had his fresh pair of drawers on, his trousers pulled up and was sticking one arm inside his braces when he came to the window and jerked back the curtain. Sesina looked down desperately. A cab had rounded the corner. Went up to the top of the street, turned and came back. No passenger in it, pulled in across the road, beside the railings, waiting for a possible fare.

He would sit there with his window open and listen for someone to whistle him up.

Sesina did not hesitate. Didn't care if he managed to get her sacked. Anything was better than ending up in the river with her neck broken, just like poor old Isabella.

'Ahoy, there, handsome!' she screamed and waved her hand at the cabbie. He was out of the cab in an instant. Looking up at her, grinning.

'Don't you fall, sweetheart!'

'Not a chance. And don't you come any nearer, neither. No looking up under my dress! I know you cabbies!' She would pretend not to have heard Mr Cartwright, not to have seen him come into the room, she thought. Give him a chance to get his trousers pulled up and buttoned.

'Anyone want a cab?' Full of cheek, some of them drivers. Owned their own cab and horse. Never took much notice of no one. She blew him a kiss. Keep him watching.

'What are you doing there, girl?' The schoolmaster was just beside her. With one shove he could have her on the ground, swear that she fell.

'The windows, sir?' Sesina kept a firm grip on the metal handle, but waved her other hand to show the two-paned windows on the second floor of the building.

'Hm!' Didn't seem too interested. 'Look, there's a red ink stain on those flannel drawers. You can get that out, can't you? Don't know what I can do with the trousers.' Now he was back sitting on the bed. She was across the floor in a second and was at the door leading out to the landing. *Red ink!* A likely story. Still he was muttering to himself, 'Clumsy idiot of a boy. Still, I made him pay for it!'

She didn't wait. Shut the door on him and was down the stairs in a flash. She had reached the next landing when the door was flung open. He had come out, was standing at the top of the staircase.

'Get back up here!' Sesina's heart skipped a beat. She stopped, hesitated. Mrs Dawson came out from the parlour on the ground floor and looked up at her.

'Get back up here!' The command was repeated.

'Sesina,' hissed Mrs Dawson, flapping her hand upwards, 'are you deaf, girl?'

'Yes, Mrs Dawson, just going back up, missus.' She'd be safe while the housekeeper was there. 'Just finished doing Mr Cartwright's room, missus,' she said loudly and clearly as she went back up as fast as she could.

'You forgot this!' He thrust the stained pair of drawers at her. Red ink. Definitely red ink. Too bright a colour for blood. She felt weak with relief when she got away from him, waved the pair of drawers at Mrs Dawson and ran rapidly down towards the kitchen.

It was only as she turned the handle of the scullery door that she remembered the unlocked desk.

Eleven

'No problem at all. Very nice man. Takes an American.' Mrs Dawson pulled the warmed-up remains of the raised pie from the oven and divided it unevenly between the two plates on the kitchen table. 'Very generous people, the Americans,' she went on. 'He agreed with every word that I said. Quite happy for me to hire the charwoman and the young girl until we get ourselves settled. Said he'd been to the police, but there was no news. No one found to have killed poor Isabella. Asked me if I had a notion, but I told him that she was a good quiet girl and that she never had no man friends. Bit of backchat with the butcher sometimes, but I didn't say anything about that. Nothing but a bit of high spirits. Just put a drop of that gin in my glass, Sesina, and take some more potatoes for yourself. You're looking peaky. We can't have that.'

'I suppose that the police don't take no interest, seeing as she was nothing but a servant,' said Sesina. There was going to be a fuss about that gin. Might be a high-and-mighty gentleman, Mr Doyle, but not so high and mighty that he couldn't see the level of his bottle sink every few days.

'No, I don't suppose that they do,' agreed Mrs Dawson placidly. 'Anyways, London is full to the brim of men and which one of all those fellows done for her? Well, that's a hard question.'

'Perhaps it was a woman,' said Sesina, resentfully eyeing the amount of meat that Mrs Dawson had managed to put on her own plate. 'Women can be meaner than men, sometimes. Just as strong, too.'

'Never!' said Mrs Dawson. She sounded a bit irritated so Sesina thought that she should change the conversation.

'Ever heard of a man called Tom Goldman or sommut like that, Mrs D.?' she asked casually.

'Can't say that I have,' said Mrs Dawson, taking another sip of her gin. 'Why are you asking?'

'Remember Isabella talking about him,' said Sesina. She got up from the table and carried the dishes over to the sink. Time for her ladyship's little nap now; her voice was already quite sleepy. No point in encouraging her to talk. Sesina had lots of thinking to do and wanted to be left in peace. No point in her going to the police with anything, though. They'd not listen to her. I need a messenger boy, a famous one. She giggled a bit at her thoughts as she scoured the pie dish. The girls at Urania Cottage used to say that Mr Dickens could see into their minds when he stared at them with those gimlet eyes of his. He'd get a shock if he could see into her mind.

Mrs Dawson was still quietly bedded down on the sofa in her parlour when the front door knocker gave a sharp tat-tat. Sesina had the door open before a second knock could be sounded.

'Good afternoon, sir,' she said with a quick bob at Mr Dickens and then another at Mr Collins. Mr Dickens stepped in across the threshold immediately, but Mr Collins stayed for a moment, looking over his shoulder at the river. There were a few rays of sunshine this afternoon and they sparked a glint from the gold rim of his spectacles.

'And how is Sesina today?' Had a nice friendly way with him.

'Very well, thank you, sir.' She made another bob in his direction, but looked closely at Mr Dickens. *Got a job of work for you to do, my man.*

Good thing that he couldn't see into her mind. She had to choke back a giggle at the thought. He wouldn't, of course. That was the thing about these gentlemen, and ladies, too. They listened to the words that servants said to them. Never stopped and wondered what was behind them. She gave a quick glance over her shoulder. Not a sign of Mrs D. Fast asleep and snoring. Rapidly she pulled out the calling card from her pocket and held it out to Mr Dickens. He took it from her quickly, like an eel pounces on a worm.

My mother had to get me away from him. She couldn't keep me. He'd have killed me too. If he doesn't pay me to keep my mouth shut I'll go down to that school. One more . . .

He read it over, a couple of times, probably. Sesina studied his face. Getting on a bit, Mr Dickens, aren't you? Getting a bit pouchy under the eyes. Eyebrows a bit bushy too. His wife should trim them for him. Mr Collins, now, he had nice soft skin. Pity he had to wear glasses. Still they made his eyes nice and large.

'*School!*' So he cottoned on to that one. No

153

fool whatever you liked to say about him. That was the word that had stuck in her own mind, too. Not talking to her, of course. Oh no! Handing her his hat, but looking at Mr Collins.

'Where did you find it, Sesina?' That was Mr Collins. Nice face, nice mouth, ever so soft-looking. 'Down a well!' Just like his sarcasm. Even his jokes had a bit of an edge to them. She would love to have said smartly, *Bottom of the river, sir* but she needed him.

'I found a loose brick in the chimney, sir. It was tucked in behind that.' She said the words to both of them and Mr Collins gave her one of his sweet little smiles.

'Strange girl! Why didn't she hide them all in the same place?' Mr Dickens said the words half to himself, but half to Sesina and she responded immediately.

'I was thinking about that, sir. I reckon that she was afraid of them being found. One on its own wouldn't make much sense, would it, sir?' Very polite, very deferential.

'Well done. Very good reasoning.' Looked at her with approval. Should have been a school-master. Would have suited him. Wouldn't have made as much money, though. Not like what he got for writing the books. Wouldn't have so much influence, either. He'd serve her purpose better as he was. The great Mr Dickens. She dropped a quick bob. No harm in keeping him sweet.

'Well, Sesina,' he said. 'I'm still trying to look into the matter of Isabella's death. I want to find out who might have murdered her. To see if there was anyone who might have had a reason. I'd have thought Isabella would have enough sense to look out for herself, that she wouldn't have gone with any strange character. What do you think? You'd have known her better than any of us. Was she meeting a man for some purpose?'

'We were wondering if she knew something about someone,' said Mr Collins. 'Enough to make them give her a present to keep quiet. What do you think, Sesina?'

You might be right, sir. I was wondering about that, too.' No harm in giving them a bit of help. Had to hand it to them, though. The police would think that a girl like Isabella would only meet a man for one reason. Mr Dickens, though, he knew Isabella; knew that she was clever, and no innocent.

'We were talking with the lodgers on the top floor, Sesina.' He had decided to take her into his confidence and she couldn't help feeling a bit flattered. 'Apparently,' he went on, studying her with those sharp eyes of his, 'apparently, Isabella told them what she remembered of a workhouse. They thought that it might be Greenwich. Would you know if she ever did go there, Sesina?'

'Yes, she did, sir. On her day off. She went there and she discovered that she had been left there by her mother, left temporary like, that's what she told me. She was going to go again.' That was enough information for them, thought Sesina. No point in distracting them over some nonsense, in spinning a fairy story out of it, like one of those stupid books that lady visitors would read to little nippers in the workhouse.

And then the bell rang. Even up here in the

155

hall, they could hear the jangling very clearly. Sesina raised her eyes to the wires that ran above the picture rail in the hall. She could see the two men looking up, also. Six wires, parlour, dining room, first floor, second floor, third floor. This was the second floor. Making a great old racket, he was. Even woke up Mrs Dawson. She came staggering out, her cap askew, her lips ready to say something unladylike, but she spotted the two men just in time.

'Sesina, dear, why don't you answer the bell? Don't you hear Mr Cartwright ring? Good afternoon, Mr Dickens, Mr Collins.' A nice little bob to them. Old hypocrite.

'Just going, Mrs Dawson. He's just rung this very minute.'

What does he want? Not like him to ring at this hour in the afternoon. In a great hurry, too. Not waiting. Door thrown open. Banged against the wall. Heavy footsteps on the stairs. Thundering down. Going at quite a pace, too. Actually running. She'd never seen him run before. Past the lawyer's door. He'd skid on that rug if he didn't slow down a bit and now down the next flight of stairs, swinging from the newel and thundering down on the steps. He was in the hallway in a second with a face as black as night.

'Mrs Dawson, may I ask who cleaned my room today?' He had the voice of a brute and the face of a brute, hands clenched like he was just stopping himself from punching someone. Gave Mrs D. a fright. Looking at him with her mouth open.

'It was Sesina, Mr Cartwright. Sesina, you cleaned the second floor, didn't you?' As if she

156

had fifty servants, and couldn't remember what each one had to do.

'Yes, Mrs Dawson.' Sesina looked innocently at the housekeeper and hoped that no one could hear her heart pounding. This man could kill, had killed, perhaps.

'What seems to be the problem, Mr Cartwright?' Mr Dickens, cool as a breeze, very good at that kind of voice.

'I beg your pardon, Mr Dickens. Didn't observe you in the stress of the moment. Your servant, Mr Collins!' The brute made a sort of a bow to both of them. 'I'm very distressed and upset. My desk, a little portable desk, something left to me by my late mother, it has been damaged, the lock has been broken. Goodness knows what has been stolen. I demand to search that girl's room.'

'I didn't touch the writing desk, except for to dust.' Sesina spoke as loudly as she could.

'Did you steal anything from Mr Cartwright's room, Sesina?' Dickens asked her. None of his business, but somehow she had a feeling that he was on her side.

'No, sir, no, Mr Dickens. I never! Didn't take nothing from that room. Nothing but dust and ashes and what was in the slop pail.' And even nastier than usual. Must have been taking medicine. Anyway, she was pleased to hear how well her voice sounded in that tall hallway. Nice and loud and very sure of herself. A good conscience, that's what she had. A good conscience is the most valuable possession that anyone can have. The parson in the prison chapel used to preach that and he had right on his side, she thought.

She tried to make herself tall, and stand there, stately-like, and look everyone in the eye.

'I want to search that room of hers. I demand to search it.' He was sticking to it. And now he was probably wondering if she had seen that receipt for twenty pounds. If she was on to his dealings with this Tom Gorman or Tom Goulding or whatever that name was on the bottom of the receipt?

'Wouldn't it be more usual to send for the police?' Mr Dickens' voice was very cool. Sesina felt her mouth go dry. Whose side was he on, anyway? Goodness only knew what the police would fasten on you.

'No, no, I don't want anything to do with the police. Just want to search that girl's room and make sure that she hasn't stolen anything from my desk. There was a ten-pound note inside one of the drawers.'

'I don't mind,' said Sesina boldly. There were beads of sweat on the man's forehead. *Didn't want the police. Well, well, well, wasn't that interesting?* She looked virtuously at Mr Dickens. 'It would be very unpleasant for Mrs Dawson to have the police in the house after all that she's gone through, sir,' she explained in her softest voice. 'I wouldn't cause her any trouble for the world. If Mr Cartwright wants to search my room, he's welcome to do it. I'd like to have this matter cleared up.'

'Well, in that case, I think that Mrs Dawson should be present, should be the one to handle the girl's clothing and belongings. I'm sure that you agree with me about that, ma'am, don't you.'

He didn't give her time to answer, just held the door to the back stairs open, ushered her in, gave a curt nod to Mr Cartwright and then followed them. Of course he took it for granted that he would form one of the party. Imagine Mr Dickens not having his finger in every pie!

Mr Collins, however, didn't go. He sat down on the bottom step and patted the space beside him invitingly. He had a nice little smile on his face.

'What did you find, Sesina?' he whispered.

Twelve

Wilkie Collins, *Basil*:

The cry for mercy was on her lips, but
the instant our eyes met, it died away
in long, low, hysterical moanings. Her
cheeks were ghastly, her features were
rigid, her eyes glared like an idiot's;
guilt and terror had made her hideous
to look upon already.

'I didn't like the look that fellow gave that little girl, Dick. I hope that she's safe in the house with him. That housekeeper wouldn't be much help, I think. Always smells of gin, to me. I'm a bit worried about Sesina. Hope that she's got a key and can lock her door at night.'

Dickens shook some ash from his cigar over the side of the steamboat and watched the glowing embers fall down into the water for a moment before he replied. 'I might have a word with my American friend about his lodger. You're right, Wilkie. A sullen fellow, that schoolmaster, isn't he? With an uncontrollable temper, I'd say, wouldn't you?'

'Reminds me a bit of Bill Sykes in *Oliver Twist*. I looked at him sideways when I said that. We would both have very clearly in our minds what Bill Sykes did to a girl. At that very moment, the

160

steamboat was passing Jacob's Island and the well-dressed passengers on the boat looked silently across at the scene that Dickens had described so chillingly in his book: '*dirt-besmeared walls and decaying foundations, every repulsive lineament of poverty, every loathsome indication of filth, rot, and garbage: all these ornament the banks of Jacob's Island.*' Dickens looked too and there was a brooding aspect to his dark-featured face. It was a minute before he spoke, and by then the steamer had chugged past the sight of those crazy, tumbledown houses.

'Yes, he was a nasty, sullen, bad-tempered brute of a fellow, too, wasn't he?' he said thoughtfully.

I was usually amused when Dickens spoke of one of his characters as a real person, but now I was too worried about little Sesina to tease him about it.

'This business needs to be straightened out, Dick, and the truth about it needs to be known,' I said emphatically. Dickens was usually the vigorous one of the pair of us, but now I felt roused and troubled about the girl, responsible for her, somehow. Such a little thing. Would hardly come up to my chest. Never met a girl so small.

'And Cartwright does come from Yorkshire,' I added.

'My dear Wilkie, my much esteemed friend, might I just suggest – just suggest, mind you – that there may be some perfectly respectable men from Yorkshire.' Dickens said the words lightly, but his face wore a troubled look. He tossed the butt-end of his cigar into the Thames and we both watched the small glowing tip curve through the foggy air and then disappear from sight.

'He doesn't even have a Yorkshire accent. That shows, doesn't it, that he probably went there to work in one of those schools,' I argued. 'Isabella's words were "beat my poor little brother to death". He came back down to London because of a scandal.'

'If Isabella had a brother, and we can't be sure of that,' said Dickens. 'She never mentioned a brother to me, but that's not surprising, you know, Wilkie. I've noticed that. Families don't mean much to these girls. But if she did have a brother, then why in Heaven's name should he be up in Yorkshire? And at a boarding school? One of those disgraceful schools where there are no holidays, little food and little or no education? What took him there? Someone had to pay something to keep him there in the first place. Mostly, as far as I could find out, the boys in those schools were unfortunates whose parents were not married or where the mother was a widow who had married again and her second husband wanted to get rid of the boy. Doesn't make sense to me, Wilkie. I know that girl's background. Isabella was on the streets, in prison, on the streets, and in prison again. Was there when I met her first. How did she come to have a brother in a boarding school in Yorkshire?'

'Perhaps we'll find out when we get to Greenwich,' I said.

'Perhaps,' he said. 'Now tell me, did Sesina confess to opening and searching Mr Cartwright's desk? She did, didn't she?' He was watching me with a smile on his lips and I had to smile back.

'Well, yes. She didn't take anything, though.'

'No, I thought that she didn't.' He nodded with satisfaction. Dickens liked to be right. 'She looked quite placid about having her room searched,' he said. 'If she had stolen anything, she'd have made a great fuss about protesting her innocence. Since she hadn't, she didn't bother wasting time and energy. But I thought that you'd get it out of her, though. She's taken a fancy to you.' Dickens took out another cigar, examined it and then put it away. He was always very strict with himself about the number of cigars that he smoked and the amount of wine that he consumed.

'Well, she did see something,' I admitted. 'He kept an envelope full of receipts and there was one for £20 to someone. "Tom", she thought. And then something beginning with the letter G and an R perhaps somewhere in the middle of the word. Could be "Gordon", couldn't it? Well, that's what I thought. Sesina said that the paper was very dirty, just as though it had been handled by someone with dirty hands.'

'Seems unlikely.' Dickens crossed his legs, admired the shine on his boots and poked a piece of orange skin with the point of his umbrella until it was lost from sight beneath the seat.

'Unlikely?' I queried. I felt a bit annoyed that he had dismissed this interesting story with two words. Perhaps he was annoyed that Sesina confided in me rather than in him.

'Well, who was this Tom Gordon? Isabella's

163

father? Not likely. Her brother? Even more unlikely. Why should her brother pay Mr Cartwright? Sesina probably made up the whole thing.'

'Why should she?'

'To make herself seem important.'

'Can't see that it made her particularly important. I had to coax her to get it out of her.'

Dickens laughed. 'My dear Wilkie, if you knew these girls as well as I do, you'd know that they lie in the way that someone like you and I tell the truth – automatically. They lie for the sake of it. And they are up to every trick in the book.'

'Poor things,' I said. As a boy I had once had a dog who had lived, and starved, on the streets of Marylebone until I insisted on taking him in. Even in his old age, when he was fat as butter and spoilt by the entire household, he never quite trusted anyone near his plate. He would push it into a far corner and as he ate, a low growl would rumble from time to time. My father had painted a picture of him when he was lean and hungry, standing over his plate, growling and baring his teeth, but no one had wanted to buy it. Not something that people want on their walls, he had said and had given me the picture. I never had that courage to tell him that I had burnt it secretly, years later, at the bottom of our garden, when he and my mother had gone to visit friends. I could not bear to see how thin and frightened my poor Rover had looked then.

'Greenwich,' I said, pointing at the distant hill rising like a green cone with its observatory crowning the steep hill.

The workhouse was down at ground level near to the river. A huge building, three storeys high, its roofs dotted with immensely tall chimneys. I wondered why it had to look so gloomy and decided it was the immensity of it that made it look inhuman. One part for men, one for women, one for children, a hospital for the sick and a school where a busy murmur, too muted and too monotone to be likened to bees, seeped out through the windows.

'Isabella could read and write well when she came to us,' observed Dickens and I noted a sadness in his voice. He looked around him, surveying the whole building with a rapid glance and then led me unerringly towards the office where a large, immensely fat lady almost fainted at the sight of the great Mr Dickens.

'Oh, Mr Dickens, oh, Mr Dickens, I have every one of your books! Oh my goodness, if only I had known that you would be here today, in this blessed office, oh, my goodness, Mr Dickens, to think of you walking in that door, just like any human being. Excuse me, Mr Dickens, I must pinch myself!' She gave a little giggle and I flinched at the idea of those rolls of flesh being pinched and oozing forth an oily fat, but she was running on with her flow of words, punctuated by nothing but commas. 'And looking like your picture, that woodcut, very severe, I imagine your head, all full of those Pickwicks and little Oliver and Rose and little Dombey and just to think of hearing your voice here in this place, this gloomy old place, you'd be used to having tea with the Queen, you'd be at home in

165

Buckingham Palace, I'm sure and reading to her, I'm sure I've heard that you read aloud beautifully and all of your books standing on my shelf and if only I had them here!'

And then the large fat lady ran out of steam and collapsed, leaning on her desk for support. She not only owned all of Dickens' books, but would find herself a character in one of them, I thought with amusement, as I noticed the small, involuntary movements of my friend's hand, as though he were taking her speech down in his rapid shorthand. It would be lodged securely within his mind, on the shelves of his mind, as he put it, himself, and would rise to the foreground in the middle of some book, still unborn.

'What a thing to find a friend,' he said with his usual charm. 'And now I'm sure that you will be able to help me. I am trying to trace a young girl, an inmate once of your orphanage here. She would be in her early twenties now, but I wouldn't be too sure of when she left you. Perhaps quite early. Her name,' he paused there for a second, was going to put the past tense, and then got out of his difficulty by saying decisively, 'the name that I am looking for is Isabella Gordon. Here as a child, I understand, but, I imagine that she would have left you . . .'

At the earliest possible opportunity; that would be Dickens' thought. From what he had told me of this Isabella, she would not be one to hang around a workhouse for a minute longer than necessary.

'Isabella Gordon, well, that's familiar.' The lady clerk resumed her businesslike air. She opened an imposing dark brown leather ledger on the desk before her and turned back a few pages.

'There you are,' she said with satisfaction. 'My sister always says to me, "Never knew anyone like you, Pauline. Don't know how you do it." That's what she says. "Got the memory of an elephant, that's what you have."' The enormous woman giggled happily at her sister's description while she chatted happily and Dickens' forefinger wrote rapidly in the air below the high ledge of the desk. The woman had a different accent to London people upriver from her. Cockney, yes, but there was a different intonation, a different emphasis on the ends of words and perhaps quite a strong flavour of the Kentish accent as an overlay.

'Had a young lady in here, there we are. Three months to the day. Well I never! Asked me the very same question. Look at it there. And you won't believe this, Mr Dickens, it's just like God whispered in my ear, "Pauline, don't you put them records away. A dark stranger will come *aquesting* them." You just sit on that there chair, Mr Dickens, and your friend, too, and I'll get them for you in two shakes of a lamb's tail.'

And then she was off, calling lustily for someone named Mary Ann.

'Looks like she did come here,' said Dickens softly. 'Can't think who else might have been interested in Isabella Gordon.'

'The police,' I queried, but he smiled pitying my ignorance. By now, I guessed, the police had forgotten all about Isabella Gordon. She had been buried in a pauper's grave. I had found that out

167

from him. By now the quicklime would have dissolved her flesh, if she was lucky. If not her festering remains would corrupt the air and poison the inhabitants of the small narrow streets near to the cemetery.

'Here we are!' Cheerfully the elephantine Pauline came into the room carrying another series of ledgers. Lying on top of it was the first one of the serial editions of *Bleak House*, stitched into its blue cover, bearing the words '*Bleak House* by Charles Dickens' and festooned with Mr Browne's illustrations around the centrepiece.

'I've got another one, I think,' she said panting with excitement. 'Please, Mr Dickens, could you write your name in it while I go and have another look.'

'Looks as worn as though a thousand Paulines have read it on a daily basis,' said Dickens when she had disappeared again. He signed his name to that one and to the fourth booklet when that turned up and listened patiently to Pauline's raptures before steering her back to the subject of Isabella Gordon.

'Yes, a nice young girl, remember her well, wanted to know whether we might have any records of her, had them of course, my goodness me, everything here is documented, Mr Dickens, not a person comes and goes without a note in the ledger, and gracious, I just thought what I will have to write today, the proudest note that I have ever written will be the one that I will write today of your visit.'

Dickens didn't look too pleased about the idea

that his visit would be documented. I saw him open his mouth, but I jumped in quickly.

'And this Isabella Gordon, she came here twice, did she?'

'Yes, she did.' Pauline turned to me as a very much lessor luminary.

'This is Mr Wilkie Collins. You must read his magnificent book. It's called *Basil*. A great book.' Dickens was always very kind about broadcasting what little fame I had, but I didn't think that Pauline looked too excited. She was slightly embarrassed, though, about confessing that she had never heard of me and to hide her blushes opened the second ledger and scrutinized it carefully.

'I remember now,' she said. 'The first time that she came I told her that she was down as being temporary and that her mother had left her. Most of them pretend that it's someone else's baby, or they found the child, but it's written here, not my handwriting, Mr Dickens, this is the handwriting of a lady who is retired now. But it's all here. "Mother says that she wants to reclaim the child as soon as she comes back."'

'And where was she going?' I asked the question. Dickens, I could see, was still absorbing Pauline's slightly sing-song delivery, reducing it to a mental form of shorthand.

'Doesn't say. They have these ideas, all of them, going to make a fortune, going down country, going to marry a farmer, poor girls!' Pauline gave an enormous sigh that almost lifted the page of the register. 'I showed it to the girl, to Isabella. Poor thing, no one reclaimed her.

Still, I suppose that it was something to her that her mother had planned to come back for her. Thanked me anyway. I remember that. Nice manners. Better than some.'

'But you say that Isabella came back. Why was that?'

'Well, she came back a month later. She must have. Here it is in the same book, only a couple of weeks old this entry.' She peered at it. 'Not my handwriting. Yes, I remember now. She was so persistent. Some of them are like that, Mr Dickens, poor girls, like that girl in your *David Copperfield*, well, she was so full of questions, don't know how she could expect me to know everything, doesn't know how many of those children who come in and go out of that there gate you see behind you, but as I say, Mr Dickens, she was persistent, so I says to her, Why don't you come back some Friday because the lady who saw your mother, well she's retired now, but she works here on a Friday. Just to give me a bit of assistance, you know, Mr Dickens. Let's me get up-to-date with everything.'

'And did she, that lady, the retired lady, did she have any extra information?' I could hardly get the words out. Perhaps the mystery of poor Isabella's death might be solved.

'I couldn't say, to be sure.' She turned her attention to me for a second and then went back to admiring Dickens' signature and his carefully penned inscription *To Pauline by the Thames from her friend, Charles Dickens*.

'But the other lady, the one that had seen Isabella's mother when the baby was left here

170

at Greenwich Workhouse.' I interrupted her protestations that she would cherish that booklet for all of her life and she reluctantly dragged her eyes away from the words and turned to my companion.

'You could go and see her if you liked, Mr Dickens. Mrs Peters is her name. She lives in a nice little cottage just down by the river, damp, I suppose, but she likes the view, got two holly bushes, one on each side of the gate, small, they are, the winds don't suit them, but, God help her, she does the best with what she's got and that's all that any of us can do, isn't that right, Mr Dickens?'

After Dickens had gravely assured her that she was right and had promised to drop in the next time that he was in Greenwich by which time she would have all his books piled up on the counter ready for him to sign, we got away from Pauline and made our way back down to the river. Eventually we found the cottage and I knocked at the door, my heart pounding in unison to my taps on the knocker. The dark, angry face of the schoolmaster, Mr Cartwright, was before my eyes. I wondered whether he knew that we were on his tracks.

'I've got the kettle on and waiting for you, Mr Dickens and Mr Collins,' were the words that we were greeted with and when we looked puzzled the elderly lady laughed.

'Pauline sent Mary Ann down by the back lane to warn me,' she said. 'Sent a little note, too, about your business and I've been racking my brains to see if I can help you.' She dished up the tea and a couple of slices of homemade cake, told us, without referring to a timetable on the wall, that we had fifteen minutes before the steamboat arrived on the return journey to Westminster.

'I've sent Mary Ann to tell them to wait for you,' she said in a businesslike way. 'Now you drink your tea, Mr Collins and Mr Dickens and while you are doing that, I'll tell you what I told that poor girl. Tell me first of all, how is she?'

Her face grew grave when Dickens told her what had happened.

'I'm very sad,' she said after a moment. 'She was a girl of character. You knew her, did you?' Her glance went from one to another.

'She was in a home that Miss Coutts set up for homeless girls. I was associated with it,' said Dickens. He always, I had noticed, underplayed the role he had in Urania Cottage, rarely mentioned the amount of time that he spent there: the twice weekly visits, the visits to gaols and in police offices checking histories of potential new inmates, and of course, the hours spent talking to the staff and to the girls themselves. 'But I'm afraid that she wasn't right for us,' he concluded.

'Full of anger,' said Mrs Peters unexpectedly. And then when he looked at her in surprise, she nodded at him. 'That's right, Mr Dickens. They mostly are. They know; even as small children, they know that life has dealt them a bad hand. I used to watch them sometimes in the small time that they got for play. There was a little girl who liked to pretend to be a teacher, to have a school. That's what she called it when I asked her what

172

she was doing. She would take some stones from the path, arrange them in lines and then go along hitting them with a stick from the hedge and shouting at them. That was her way of playing at school, Mr Dickens. Some of them get adopted, or more likely taken on as cheap servants, but they mostly get sent back to us if they are young enough, or turned out on the streets if they are not. Bad temper; that's what people say. Ungrateful, too! That's what people say. They can't be grateful, you see, Mr Dickens. In a book they could be; like your little Oliver Twist; he was so grateful and so well-spoken, wasn't he? Nice to read about, but nonsense really. I'm afraid that they're seldom grateful, not in real life. The iron has entered into their soul.' And this surprising old lady nodded at us both and added some more hot water to the teapot. Dickens, for once, was speechless and I kept my eyes fixed on my teacup.

'And now about Isabella Gordon,' she said. 'Pretty name, pretty girl. She didn't remember the place too clearly, blotted it all out, I suppose, poor thing, but she remembered the boats and ships on the river. Pauline had told me that she might be coming back to see me when she had her day off in a month's time so I had a chance to do a little browsing in the register. Easy enough, not a local name, Gordon, not too common in London either, sounds Scottish to me. So there she was.' Now for the first time, Mrs Peters hesitated, gave the pot another stir and then a penetrating look at the two of us, as though endeavouring to size us up.

'And the entry, did it give any details about

Isabella?' asked Dickens. He spoke rather coldly, upset about her criticism of the book that had made a fortune for him.

'Well, there was something,' Mrs Peters now spoke in quite a slow and hesitant fashion, unlike her previous crisp delivery. I got the impression that she was weighing up her words as she uttered them. 'There was something else, written in my handwriting, something that Pauline hadn't noticed, the words "drawer 786". The mother had left something. We have all those drawers, a roomful of them, most of them never opened, I must say. Anyway, I found the package. "Deposited by mother who said that she wanted to come back for her baby"; these were the words,' said Mrs Peters briefly. 'Lots of them say that, and when they do, we ask that they leave some article that they can mention when they return – in case we give the wrong child, you see, Mr Collins,' she said, politely including me in the conversation, or perhaps she thought that I looked surprised. It wasn't surprise, though, but pleasure. An article might help to solve Isabella's quest.

'In this case, two articles were left instead of one, and that was a little unusual in itself. One was a little cheap bead necklace, but the other, the surprising one, was a man's knife. The blade was broken so it was useless, but I thought that it had been a good knife once. And another thing, it was scorched as if it had been in a fire.'

'You have a very good memory, ma'am,' I said politely, while Dickens knitted his brows over this.

'I saw it again only a few weeks ago when I

174

got them out and gave them to Isabella.' There was, once again, a slight hesitation in her manner. I wondered whether Dickens noticed it, or whether I was imagining it. I glanced across at him but he was still frowning at the lacy tea cloth. Mrs Peters looked at him also. Our glances met for a second then we both looked away and she continued rather hurriedly. 'And I remembered then all about it,' she said. 'You see, Mr Dickens, it's our rule that we only take children if there is no man to support them so the knife made me a bit suspicious. I see I have a note here stating that the baby looked well cared for and well fed, not at all like most of the little mites who are given up to the poorhouse. I asked the woman if she were married and she said, no, no, that she had never been married. She came out with the usual story that they had planned to marry, but then the father of the baby had been blown up in an accident in the gunpowder mills and she had been left on her own to care for the child. Well, that was plausible enough. There were always accidents happening in these places, but I had a quick look at her hand. You see, Mr Dickens, here in Greenwich we get the fog that you get in London, but we get a bit of sea air, too, and most people get brown in the summer. This was December, so there wasn't much of the summer tan left, and that girl was pale, after having the baby, I suppose. But her hands, well, they were still quite brown. And there on the girl's left hand, on her ring finger, was a broad white band. I could have sworn that she had been wearing a wedding ring for a year at least.'

'So what did you do?'

'None of my business. I was only the clerk,' said Mrs Peters briskly. 'If the beadle wanted to make a fuss about it then he could, but I wasn't going to say anything. If a mother is determined to leave her baby, then it's best to take the little mite with no unnecessary questions asked. I had done my duty, done what I was paid to do and I wasn't going to do any more. I wrote down "unmarried", and that the child's name was Isabella Gordon and the mother's name was Annie Gordon. But I had my doubts. Not a local name, Gordon. Sounds Scottish, but this girl was local, I would have guessed, by the way that she talked. She had a Greenwich accent. She wasn't Scottish, anyway. There were Scots who worked in the gunpowder mill. I used to hear them sometimes when I was on my way home. Hard to make out a word of what they were saying.'

'So you think that the father could have been Scottish, is that right, ma'am?'

'That's what I thought, Mr Dickens.'

'And you may well be right, Mrs Peters. There was a mill blown up in Scotland when I was a young lad, completely destroyed. Could never be rebuilt. Blew up a mountain face behind it, broken rocks strewn all over the site. I remember the newspaper where I was working had a feature about it. This fellow, Gordon, might have travelled south for a job in another gunpowder mill.'

'Well, that band of white on her ring finger made me think that Annie Gordon had been married, for nine months or so at least and that's what I told this girl, Isabella, when I talked with

176

her. We had a nice chat. Not too busy that day. I gave her the knife and the string of beads and she went off with them. And that's the last that I saw of her, poor child.' There was a note of regret in the old lady's voice, but something else, also. Something that I noted. That slight hesitation.

'And that was all that was left for her, the knife and the string of beads. Nothing else, was there?' I asked the question to fill an awkward moment as Dickens seemed lost in his thoughts.

'As I told you, Mr Collins, that was what I gave to her,' said the old lady drily.

Not a real answer, I thought, but perhaps it was just her manner.

'Isabella spoke of a brother,' said Dickens. 'The other maidservant in the house where she worked told us of that. Did she have a brother?'

'Not here,' said Mrs Peters. 'If she had, it would have been on the same page. No, she was eight months old, according to her mother and weaned. I remember that was in the book. We sent her off to Mrs Dawson's baby farm.'

I saw Dickens look at me and I looked at him. We were both startled. Not a terribly unusual name, but not a very common one, either. Could Mrs Dawson of the baby farm be the same Mrs Dawson who worked as a housekeeper in the lodging house?

Dickens got to his feet and held out his hand. 'You've been very kind, Mrs Peters, giving us your time like that. Now we must go and relieve Mary Ann of her wait.' He half-hesitated. Now would be the moment when Mrs Peters would

177

produce a shilling booklet of one of his books, or even a piece of paper for the famous signature, and my friend Dickens was a generous man, generous with his time, and generous in acknowledgement of a debt. We'd partaken of tea and cake, had received the information that we had been seeking. He waited expectantly.

Mrs Peters, however, just rose to her feet and prepared to accompany us out. No books appeared, no requests were made. When we reached the door, Dickens hesitated again, but then contented himself with repeating our thanks. We were halfway down the path, facing the two inadequate holly bushes, when she spoke once more, her voice crisp and assured.

'Why don't you write about any nice sensible women who do a job of work in your books, Mr Dickens? After all, women can manage to write and to keep ledgers just as well as men. Not all of us want to spend our days cooking and cleaning and running houses for men, like your heroines seem to love to do.'

There was a moment's silence. An abrupt pause. Dickens, hat still in hand, looking back at this intrepid lady with a startled look on his face.

I jumped into the breach. Dickens, I guessed, would be flabbergasted and furious. 'I'm writing a book about a working girl, Mrs Peters,' I said hastily. 'I'll send you a copy if I ever manage to get it published.' I put my hat back on, raised an umbrella in salute and ushered my friend out through the holly bushes and hurried him down the hill before he exploded.

He didn't though. Forgot it immediately, which

wasn't like him. He had something else on his mind. He walked ahead of me, very rapidly, as was his way when he was thinking hard and he did not speak until we had stopped before a church, St Alphege's Church, rebuilt by Nicholas Hawksmoor a hundred years ago according to the board in front of it. 'We might get an answer to the puzzle here,' he said to me in a low voice. 'And, if I'm not wrong, this might be the man to help us.' An elderly clergyman was strolling through the graves and now he came up to us, his friendly smile turning to a broad beam.

'Do my eyes deceive me,' he said ecstatically. 'Is it really Mr Dickens? Do come and look over our beautiful church, Mr Dickens. It would do me the greatest honour to allow me to show you around. And if you have a moment to spare I have a twenty-shilling copy of *David Copperfield* back in my house – a work of pure genius, sir – never enjoyed anything in my life so much – laughed and cried over it, sir, I do assure you! It would only take a minute to fetch it. And I would be so delighted if you would sign it.'

That's more like it, I thought with a flash of amusement and wasn't surprised when Dickens whispered in my ear, 'Pop down and tell Mary Ann to get in out of the cold, Wilkie, there's a good fellow. We'll get the next boat, tell her. Give her a sixpence, will you, like a good chap.'

And then he was off, removing his hat politely and admiring the smoke-laden gloomy walls and listening attentively to the tale of the rebuilding of the old medieval church. When I looked back, I saw that they were both headed towards the presbytery, where, no doubt, the cherished *David Copperfield* would be produced.

But by the time that I returned, after releasing the obliging Mary Ann, and checking the times of the Greenwich to London steamers, they were both back inside the church, looking through the old registers. Dickens, I noticed, had a finger marking a spot halfway down a page that started in January of the year 1828.

'Bless my soul, I was only four years old in that year,' I said. Dickens, however, was not interested in reminiscences of my past.

'Make a lovely place for a wedding, Wilkie, wouldn't it,' he said, looking around him casually. 'Must get a couple of my characters married here. Did you know that King Henry the Eighth, the old tyrant, himself, was baptized here? What a historic spot!' And, still casual and unconcerned, his eye passed down the line of weddings and even more casually he turned back the page.

'Married in 1827, Wilkie,' he said when eventually we parted from the friendly vicar after an examination of the baptismal registers dating back to the mid-sixteenth century. 'Married in 1827, Annie Brown and Andrew Gordon. Occupation: *Refiner of Brimstone at Greenwich Powder Mill.*' He said no more until we boarded the steamer and made our way to the bows.

'So the woman, Annie Brown, was married in 1827, to a man with a good job, had a baby in 1828, not an illegitimate baby, you note, Wilkie. Born a respectable year after marriage. So what happened in the eight months after the baby's birth? She had cared well for the little mite. Mrs Peters told us that. She made a note that the baby was well cared for and looked well-fed. And then this Annie Gordon appeared at the workhouse, having taken off her wedding ring, left the baby to be called for, left her own string of beads, and her husband's knife – a damaged knife, no good to him, but it could be described and identified very quickly when they came back to claim the child. But why did she want to leave the child in a workhouse? Most people knew what a place like that would be like. Why leave a well-cared-for, and probably well-loved child in a workhouse?'

'She was a widow; she was destitute; she couldn't care for the baby. Wouldn't that be the solution?'

Dickens shook his head. 'Well, why not say so? A widow would be able to leave a baby if she could not care for it. She wouldn't have had to take off her wedding ring if that was the way. She could have been a respectable widow, much better than an unmarried mother. She could even have shown the death certificate if she had buried her husband down there at St Alphege's Church. I had a look at the death registers but nothing for that year, so there we have a husband with a well-paid job and a wife with a well-cared-for baby. Wouldn't have been too badly off, either. They probably had one of those cottages by the powder mills. Might even have owned it. And if he died in an accident, the company might have given her something. Why dump her baby and go off to a strange place?'

181

I thought about this for a while. 'Perhaps he wasn't dead; perhaps he had left her.'

Dickens shook his head. Still doesn't make sense. She would be able to prove that he had left her. They'd probably have admitted her, as well. She could have stayed with her baby. *Refiner of Brimstone at Greenwich Powder Mill*. That was a good job, a skilled job. A man doesn't leave a job like that very easily.'

'I'm not sure that this is anything to do with the mystery of Isabella's death,' I pointed out. 'And there doesn't seem to have been a brother, so why was the girl so anxious to get information about that brute of a fellow, Frederick Cartwright?'

'He couldn't have been the father, could he? How old would you put him?'

'Forty? Fifty? Not any younger than forty,' I said. I was thinking hard. I had a quick look around to make sure that no one was listening. But there was nobody near to us. Most people on the boat sat in the cabin. Dickens and I had the bows to ourselves. We could talk openly. 'But the husband of Annie Gordon was Andrew Gordon,' I said. 'It seems almost certain, doesn't it, that Isabella's father was Andrew Gordon and for some reason, the baby was put in the poorhouse. A well-cared-for and well-nourished baby, with a mother who loved it enough to leave that string of beads and the knife so as to be sure to recover the right baby when she came back. But why did she leave it in the first place?'

'I think,' said Dickens, 'I might go and have a word with the canon at St Bartholomew's Church.

182

But, first of all, perhaps, we should have a chat with my American friend about references for his housekeeper. I wonder what her past might hold. But now, what about dinner at Rules? That suit you, my dear old chap? Seven o'clock? And I know a man who would enjoy their game pie! We'll ask our friendly landlord to join us and pump him for information.'

Thirteen

Charles Dickens; *Household Words*:

> . . . a middle-aged man of a portly
> presence, with a large, moist, knowing
> eye, a husky voice, and a habit of
> emphasising his conversation by the air
> of a corpulent fore-finger, which is
> constantly in juxta-position with his
> eyes or nose.

Dickens' rich American friend wasn't the only guest at dinner, as I saw when I joined them at Rules, punctually at seven o'clock in the evening. Inspector Field was also invited and he, also, dug into the game pie with great relish. My friend had a quick word with the head waiter when we arrived and he had placed us at a small square table to the rear of the restaurant. No one to our backs, no table on either side. No possibility of being overheard if we wanted to discuss private matters. Dickens allocated places with his usual boisterous good humour, something that, I was learning, often overlaid meticulous planning and foresight. He himself sat with his back to the wall, his dark, bird-like eyes surveying the restaurant. Inspector Field sat at his right hand – another man who liked to be sure that nobody was to his back – and I was on Dickens' left side.

184

The easy-going landlord sat on the fourth side of the table with his back to the restaurant.

Dickens was always a great host, quick-witted, entertaining and interested in everyone. Once the second bottle of excellent claret had been swallowed, he invited Inspector Field to talk about his work, and about this new profession of detective.

'I've been doing a little detection of my own,' he said coolly when the man had finished. 'You remember that girl that you showed to us, when she was dragged out of the river, the girl in the red and green dress? Well,' he continued, 'I know who that girl was and I know who employed her and he is sitting here beside you tonight.' Dickens nodded to Don Diamond, then took a sip from his claret with an air of enormous enjoyment.

'Girl?' A momentary pause and a quick recovery on the part of the inspector. 'I knew it, I knew it, Mr Dickens. Knew that would interest you. Making a story out of it, aren't you?'

'Quick, isn't he, Wilkie,' said Dickens with a smile at me. 'Yes, I always think that servants might be the most interesting part of any household. They know what's going on. I suppose it was a servant, Mr Pickwick's servant, Sam Weller, who first showed me that I could write books. Once Mr Pickwick took him on, well, I never hesitated for a moment after that. The story rolled out. I saw Mr Pickwick through Sam's eyes.'

'Great man, ain't he, Mr Diamond?' said Inspector Field, as the waiter cleared away the remnants of the game pie and produced the cheese boards and the port. 'We're all very proud of him here in London. You wouldn't have anything as famous as that in America, would you?'

Don Diamond immediately disclaimed any pretentions of America to have a novelist like Mr Dickens and helped himself to a handful of crackers. He seemed interested and amused by the inspector and invited him to tell about his work as one of London's newly formed detective force.

'You'd be kept pretty hard at it, just keeping peace on the streets and allowing the citizens to go about their lawful business, I suppose, Inspector,' he said with a good-natured appreciation of a subject which was guaranteed to make the inspector the centre of attention at our little table.

'Tell Mr Diamond about that time when you found the fellow, by the name of Bark hiding out in the hall just next to the Egyptian mummy, side by side, the two of them. Oh, and how you tracked down the man who stole the silver cup made especially for the Queen,' I said.

The story of that spectacular theft from the Great Exhibition of London got so exciting that the inspector spilled some of his port while demonstrating how he set a trap for the thief.

'I suppose, Inspector,' said Dickens idly, as he waved the waiter away and personally refilled the inspector's port glass, 'I suppose that in the case of, for instance, this murder of a housemaid employed by my friend, here, Mr Diamond, you would follow the procedure of saying very little and keeping as quiet as possible while you followed up various possibilities and suspicions.'

Inspector Field blinked a little at this description of his activities during the days since the discovery of Isabella's body. 'That's right, Mr Dickens,' he said huskily.

'It does seem, from what the other housemaid said about the basement door being locked, that this might be not an affair of a man of the streets, but perhaps there might be some connection to one of the lodgers,' said Dickens. As usual, while praising all the food and wine to the heights, he had eaten very little himself and had drunk a bare half measure of the very excellent port. I helped myself to another glass and sat back to enjoy the play.

'It does, indeed,' said Inspector Field, tossing off the remains of his wine and taking out his notebook and a small, thick pencil.

'You know what these servant girls are like; they will snoop around bedrooms and they find out things that the owners would think as safe secrets.' Dickens nodded his admiration of the inspector's knowledge of the servant class.

'They do, indeed.' Inspector Field looked wisely through the pages of his notebook.

'But you would wait until all the evidence is complete before you pounce. That's the way that you work, Inspector, isn't it?'

'Lull them, that's what I reckon on doing, Mr Dickens. Lull them. Don't let them know that they're being watched.' Inspector Field's husky voice was full of passionate conviction. I laid a small bet, deep in my mind, that he had never even bothered to go around to the house where Isabella had spent the last couple of years. He would now, though. I was sure of that. It would be enough for him to know that the greatly admired Dickens was taking an interest in the matter. I wondered whether the American might think of offering a reward, but Mr Diamond had seemed to lose interest or else because Dickens, determined that his little party would be a success, had now turned the conversation to the exciting story of the gold rush where Mr Diamond had made a fortune. The landlord made a better story of it tonight than he had done at the dinner in Adelphi Terrace where he laid so much emphasis on his own cleverness of setting up boarding houses and public bars for the miners rather than going out with shovel and pickaxe. Now he told the story of the gold rush from the eyes of the miners, describing the veins of gold sparkling in the grey rock. 'It's not yellow, you know, gold is not yellow,' he explained, 'gold is very pale, more a sort of white with a bit of a sparkle in it when you see the veins of it glistening out of the rocks. Miners used to get up early in the morning, when the sun was low and would strike the side of the rock and then you might be lucky and you might find some. I did hear tell about how one man stared so hard at the bare side of the mountain that his eyes started to water and to rest them he turned and looked at a tree, an uprooted tree, half out of the mountain, it was; blown by the wind, its roots sticking in the air, still alive and green, though.' Don Diamond popped a piece of cheese into his mouth, chewed it and swallowed

188

it, washing it down with a mouthful of port. 'And then he looked down at the roots, sticking out like the claws of a giant crab. And he thought that he saw something there and gee whiz, what do you know, there was a sparkle.' He looked around at us all: Inspector Field, with his eyes popping; me with a germ of a story germinating in the back of my mind; Dickens smiling gently. And then he finished: 'Well, he filled a bag with the stuff, took the road to Philadelphia and was never seen again.'

'But you were never tempted to go back to digging, yourself?' I asked the question because Inspector Fields' protruding eyes looked in danger of popping out from his skull.

'Nah, I'd had enough of that. Me and another fellow and his wife. We thought that we'd chuck it in. Saw too many people lose their shirts on that tomfoolery. Like playing a lottery, Inspector, you could get lucky, you hear stories of the few people who won fortunes, but probably you won't hear the stories of the many that ended shooting themselves, or walking the whole way back to civilization, hoping to get a job on the roads. Naw, naw, Inspector, best to earn your money with a lot of hard work and common sense. Easy come, easy go, that's the way money is. I worked for my money and now I make my money work for me. You'd be surprised to hear how much property that I own in London. Find some good houses, do them up, turn them into lodgings, pop a housekeeper in, charge a fair rent and hey presto, as the Italians say!'

The inspector began to lose interest when gold

didn't come into the story any longer so he was on his feet, making his excuses. He had to go on duty 'down by Seven Dials', he told his host and there was a look in his eye that seemed to be hoping that Dickens might accompany him.

But he didn't. Dickens waved him an affable farewell, but sat on in the restaurant, idly toying with his glass. The article about Seven Dials at night time, and about Inspector Fields among the poor, the destitute, the criminals; well, that article had been written, and Inspector Fields had been immortalized in *Bleak House* as Inspector Bucket searching through the back lanes and the festering graveyards for the fugitive Lady Dedlock. Now Dickens' mind was on another story, the story of Isabella Gordon, who had begun life in Greenwich, had been taken in by an orphanage, farmed out to a baby farmer, named Mrs Dawson.

And then had gone back to Greenwich in order to dig through what remained of her past.

'Don, what do you know about Mrs Dawson?' he said in a low tone, once the inspector had left and the other three of us were walking down through Covent Garden. I remembered the matron of the workhouse in *Oliver Twist* and how she held the secret of Oliver's parentage. Perhaps we would uncover the mystery of Isabella Gordon's brutal murder.

'Who?' The man was startled.

'Mrs Dawson, your housekeeper, your housekeeper in number five Adelphi Terrace, the place where the dead girl worked before she was murdered.' Dickens sounded affable, but I knew that he was impatient. He had a very one-track mind. Once he bent his attention on anything, it became an all-consuming interest.

'Ah, now, I know who you're talking about. For land's sake, man, you haven't got enough fingers and toes to count the number of housekeepers that I employ. Yes, I suppose that there were references. I've an agent who finds housekeepers and they find their own housemaids and that's the way that it goes. Why? Is there anything wrong with her?'

I could see that Dickens was turning over the matter in his mind. But after all, what was wrong with being a 'baby farmer'? Yes, some of them had been evil, heartless women; he had publicized their cruelty and neglect in his book *Oliver Twist*, but that was not to say that all were like that. He would not condemn a woman unheard and perhaps risk her losing her job.

'No, nothing,' he said briefly. 'Just wondered how you engage all of your staff, that's all.'

'That lawyer fellow complained to me that his gin bottle had been interfered with; thought that someone had been fiddling through his belongings.' Don Diamond was obviously still worried by Dickens' words. 'Well, that's as maybe, but I didn't give him much sympathy. Just told him that cupboards with locks were provided in each room. Look it up, man, lock it up, that's what I said to him. He should have been in some of the places I've been in! Men slept in their trousers for fear that they'd be stolen during the night!'

And with those words, our American friend waved his stick and left us. We dawdled for a while, allowing him to get well ahead of us and then went towards the city. The bells of St Pauls sounded.

'End of vespers,' said Dickens. 'Not a good time to see a parson, Wilkie, don't you think? After prayer, his soul uplifted to the lord and his body looking forward to a hot whisky by his fireside! Let's go and visit the canon of St Bartholomew's tomorrow morning and find out what he knows about the teachers that he employs in his grammar school. I can't quite work this Mr Frederick Cartwright into the business at Greenwich, can you, Wilkie, but, do you know, I have a strong feeling that the man is somehow implicated in the murder of that poor girl. And when I get those strong feelings,' added Dickens with a flourish of his umbrella, 'then I am usually, not to say, always, right.'

Fourteen

'What you need, missus, is a good steak. You're looking ever so tired and washed-out like. I'm worried about you.' The morning's work was done and Sesina was bored after all the excitement of the day before. More than ever it looked to her as though that schoolmaster had something to hide. She needed to get out and investigate him, see if there was anything to be found out at that school of his. She looked solemnly at Mrs Dawson. *Can nearly smell her mouth water at the thought of a steak*, she said to herself. 'Ever such cheap, good steaks in Smithfield,' she added coaxingly. 'You wouldn't believe it, missus.'

That should fetch her in. The butcher, baker and chandler accounts were sent to the landlord at the end of each month. Wouldn't want no steaks appearing on the bill for a house where no dinners were served for the lodgers.

'I do believe that you're right, Sesina. I've heard tell about the steaks at Smithfield.' Mrs Dawson seemed to be turning the matter over in her mind. Almost tasting the steak. 'Now make sure that you get a good-sized one and then, I'll tell you what, you can have the trimmings, Sesina.' Mrs Dawson was up out of her chair and crossing the room, key in hand, making for the cash box.

'Thank you, ma'am. I'll just run and fetch my bonnet and shawl.'

193

Sesina was off as soon as she got the money in her hand. Didn't want any more errands. Lucky the woman was half sozzled and at best of times, Mrs Dawson wasn't too quick on thinking up ideas.

Great place, Smithfield. She always enjoyed it. Isabella and herself had done a lot of 'lifting' there, as Isabella always called it – *lifting* wallets and purses, of course. There was always a bullock or two, or even a goose, getting loose and causing chaos and it was easy to snatch something while everyone was pushing and shoving to get into doorways and side lanes.

Sesina made her plans as she went at top speed down the Strand. It was a quarter to four as she passed St Paul's and she broke into a run. By the time that she reached St Bartholomew's, the smaller boys were coming out of the school and the nursemaids were lined up at the gate to meet them. Sesina pulled her shawl well around her and came up to them.

'That's a terrible place, that school in there,' she said with casual confidence to the group of nurse-maids, huddled together beside the gateposts. 'Family I worked for, well, poor little Master Jimmy was in bed for a week after the beating he got from that schoolmaster, what was his name? Fellow with orange hair. Master Jimmy goes to St Paul's now. Happy as anything there. His mother said that she'd never let him inside the doors of St Bartholomew's again, not ever. Not after seeing the bruises on him. Black and blue, he was, from head to toe. I misremember the name of the school-master, but he was an ugly-looking brute. Some

194

poor boy; I knew his poor sister, well, poor fellow, he's no more . . .' She stopped and waited, pretending to be scouring her memory, but crossing her fingers as she clenched her shawl around her head, but no one finished the story for her. There were several teachers in the background ushering the children out of the school. One of them lifted a cane, a thin, black, walking cane and swished it through the air. A child cried out, bent down, doubled up with pain.

'That would be the one, that fellow there. That fellow with the orange hair sticking out under that mortar board of his.' She kept her voice down to a whisper, but pointed at the familiar figure.

'I know him! Got a terrible scar. Looks like a second mouth on his face. I did hear tell that he did something bad to a boy up north somewhere. Someone told me that.' The nursemaid's voice was shrill and Sesina saw Mr Cartwright turn his head. She turned her back on him, pulling her shawl a bit further over her head so that it made a deep frame for her face.

'Wait till I tell you what I heard . . .' And then the girl stopped. Her head swivelled and in a moment she was off, dragging the small boy by the hand. Another boy, howling miserably, was quickly taken off by his nursemaid. There was a general scattering. And the tread of heavy footsteps.

'What are you doing here?' The harsh voice was unmistakable. He had recognized her. Being so dratted small, that's what had got her into trouble. Sesina swore silently. He was in front of her now, staring down at her.

195

'Nothing sir, just stopped to give a piece of liquorice to that little boy that was crying.' She watched his angry face and tried to cling on to her courage. *You're not my employer, Mr Nasty-Face Cartwright. Nothing at all to do with you where I go, who I talk to, and where I stop.* The words, as they passed through her mind gave her courage and she looked up at him. Aloud, she said obsequiously, 'Mrs Dawson sent me on an errand to Smithfield, sir.'

'Well, be off with you, then. Don't loiter around here. Go on, girl. Do your business. That's the way to Smithfield.'

By now his presence had cleared all of the nursemaids and servants. They grabbed the hands of their charges and pulled them away, looking furtively over their shoulders at the repulsively scarred face that glared after them. The older boys were coming out now, shouting, whooping, hitting each other with horse chestnuts threaded on to pieces of string, but when they saw Mr Cartwright they became very quiet, very subdued and slid past him with sidelong glances. Sesina said no more and she, too, sidled past the school-master and went briskly down the road. When she got to the corner, she turned back. He was still standing there. He had taken off his mortar board, and his orange hair blew up from his head and made him look more like that orangutan than ever. And the next time that she looked, he had disappeared. Gone back to Adelphi Terrace, no doubt.

Well, she had got away from him, and had her suspicions confirmed!

It was market day at Smithfield. She had forgotten that. Not a good day to come. The ground was covered, nearly ankle-deep, with filth and mire; a thick steam of mist was perpetually rising from the reeking bodies of the cattle and it mingled with the fog, which seemed to rest upon the chimney tops. All the pens in the centre of the large area, and as many temporary pens as could be crowded into the vacant space, were filled with sheep, tied up to posts. By the gutter side were long lines of beasts and oxen, three or four deep. Countrymen, butchers, drovers, hawkers, boys and thieves were mingled together in a mass. The whistling of drovers, the barking dogs, the bellowing and plunging of the oxen, the bleating of sheep, the grunting and squeaking of pigs, the cries of hawkers, the shouts, oaths, and quarrelling on all sides; the ringing of bells and roar of voices, that issued from every public house; the crowding, pushing, driving, beating, whooping and yelling; the hideous and discordant din that resounded from every corner of the market; and the unwashed, unshaven, squalid, and dirty figures constantly running to and fro made it look a scene from hell.

Sesina hesitated. It had not been like this when she had come before. So this was market day. Everything was wild and savage. She could not even see the butcher that she and Isabella had wrangled with on her last visit. She moved a little back, looking around her for a safe haven.

And then it happened.

Sesina saw it all. She had turned around, trying to get her bearings in this scene of confusion. A

197

herd of bullocks were being driven towards where she stood. They were running along, controlled by two men and a pair of efficient cattle dogs that kept the animals in a tight pack.

And then a long, thin, black stick, or was it a cane, came out from a doorway. Even through the noise of the animals, Sesina heard the swish that came down and landed on the leading bullock's neck. It seemed to her as if all hell broke loose then. Deep-throated bellowing from the angry animals, high, excited barking from the dogs and hoarse shouts from the men. She stared, mesmerized for a few long moments, and then turned to flee. Too late. Something stopped her abruptly; something hard, unyielding. A stick. Thrust between her legs. For a moment she thought that she would die, trampled to death beneath the hoofs of the maddened bullocks, but her courage rose up. He wasn't going to get away with this. Just as she lost her balance, her eye was caught by something red and white beside her shoulder. She grasped it with a feeling of desperation. A barber's pole. Only jutting out from a cart, but enough to steady her. The barber, himself, reached out an arm and pulled her back between the shafts of the cart and she stood panting and listening to the man's complaints about the drovers.

'Don't like this place,' she said, as soon as she could speak.

'Me neither,' he said, patting her on the shoulder. He was as old as the hills so she allowed him to go on patting while she was getting her breath back.

'Did you see him?' she said after a minute.

'Who?'

'The fellow that tried to trip me up.'

He was stroking her neck now and she took a few steps back from him, scanning the scene.

'Didn't see nobody,' he said, abandoning her and sticking his head inside his covered cart.

'Thanks, anyway.' Sesina moved away from the protection of the cart's shafts. The bullocks were well away now. A woman was picking up a few filthy cabbages from the roadway and everything was getting back to normal. There was no sign of a man with a cane, just drovers with heavy sticks.

'Did you see a gent walking along here with a cane in his hand, a black cane?' She asked the question of the cabbage seller, but the woman just shook her head. Had her own troubles.

I'm getting out of here, thought Sesina. Buy Mrs Dawson's steak on the Strand. Be a bit dearer, but she could make up a story about that. Anyway, she told herself, fish should be new-caught, but steak should be hung for a few days; Mrs Morson always said that when she was teaching the girls to cook and to give Urania Cottage its due, Mrs Morson could run rings around Mrs Dawson when it came to cooking. She walked briskly away from Smithfield, continually turning her head to look behind her and making sure to keep on the inside of the footpath. Her courage was rising. She knew how to take care of herself. Once she was sure; once she had real evidence, she'd make sure to talk to him inside the house. None of this business of meeting a man out there on Hungerford Stairs.

Fifteen

Wilkie Collins, *Dead Secret*:

There could not be the least doubt of
his identity; I should have known his
face again among a hundred. He looked
at me as I took my place by his side,
with one sharp searching glance—then
turned his head away toward the road.
Knowing that he had never set eyes on
my face (thanks to the convenient
peephole at the red-brick house), I
thought my meeting with him was
likely to be rather advantageous than
otherwise. I had now an opportunity of
watching the proceedings of one of our
pursuers, at any rate—and surely this
was something gained.

'There is a possible solution, Dick,' I said and I
could hear how eager and how loud my voice
sounded. Unlikely that anyone would be listening
to our conversation in the busy street, nevertheless I lowered it and seizing him by the arm,
made him stop his rapid progress and step aside
into an alleyway. 'I have an idea,' I said. 'How
about it if Annie Brown from the marriage
register, was not Annie Brown, but really Annie
Cartwright. She and her husband had parted.

Perhaps she ran away from him, taking the baby with her, but leaving the older boy with his father up in Yorkshire. Brown sounds as though it could be invented. Smith or Brown, both of them are the first names you would think of, wouldn't you? Well, you wouldn't, perhaps,' I said as I thought of the extraordinary surnames in Dickens' books, 'but lots of people with no imagination would. So Annie runs away from her cruel husband, leaving the older boy with him, perhaps he was good to the boy at that stage, proud of having a son and so she left the boy, came to Greenwich, perhaps she was originally from there, and she and Andrew Gordon got married.'

'Fraudulently,' put in Dickens.

'It happens,' I said with a shrug. There was a faint frown on his face.

'Why did she bother?' He started to walk again at his usual rapid pace.

'Gave her more security.' I struggled to keep up. I said no more but the ideas were flooding through my mind. Perhaps this Annie left her baby at the workhouse because she had determined on a journey to reclaim her older son. Perhaps this Andrew Gordon had gone with her. He may have lost his job, hoped to get a new one. Plenty of mills in Yorkshire. 'I've got it, Dick,' I said. 'Andrew Gordon lost his job at Greenwich. They decided to try their luck in Yorkshire. And Annie may have decided to reclaim her son from his brutal father. They had no money, would have to walk, perhaps, and so Annie left the baby, little Isabella, in the workhouse.' Dickens wasn't listening and so I

201

stopped. We were approaching the parish of St Bartholomew's and the church, with the school nestling beside it, loomed up, threateningly, in the foggy air.

'They say that this place is haunted,' said Dickens over his shoulder to me, but he led the way without hesitation towards the door. An elderly verger was standing, yawning, keys in hand and he looked at us severely.

'Vespers is finished, gentlemen,' he said and then his face changed as Dickens came towards the gas lamp outside the porch door. For a moment it crossed my mind to hope that one day my face would be as easily recognized as his, but then I banished the thought, feeling ashamed of myself. I should keep my mind concentrated on that poor young girl, Isabella Gordon, beaten and strangled to death. Nevertheless, I was conscious of a twinge of envy as the familiar words: 'Why, you must be Mr Dickens! Good evening, sir. I've been reading your *Bleak House*, wonderful work. That poor little Joe. Brought tears to my eyes, it did. Have you come to see our church?'

'We've come to see the canon,' said Dickens. 'What an interesting old church, you have here!'

'That is the canon, sir. The reverend gentleman up there by the altar, sir.'

He took us up and introduced us. The canon was a small man with a round head, side whiskers sprouting untidily from ear to jawline. Smaller even than myself. Short, rotund. He had changed from his vestments and was soberly dressed in the Church of England fashion, wearing gaiters and a frock coat. He came rapidly towards us with a slightly stiff walk, legs wide apart. A beaming smile. A nice man; I decided immediately. His opinion on Mr Frederick Cartwright would be worth having.

'Don't be surprised if a church plays a major part in my next book, Wilkie; I think that churches will haunt my dreams tonight,' Dickens murmured in my ear as the canon rushed away to find the key to a cupboard where a Queen Elizabeth communion service was stored. We both admired it and consented to see around the outside of the church and have its Norman features pointed out to us. Our host put on a low-crowned, wide-brimmed clerical black hat and escorted us outside where we were shown the ancient features of the church. An adroit question about the choir, though, soon turned the conversation to the school next door.

'We met one of your teachers recently at a dinner held by his landlord, an American friend of mine. A man with red hair, if I remember rightly.' Dickens managed to introduce the matter in a careless fashion, turning to me to supply the name of the teacher.

'Ah, yes, that was it, Mr Cartwright. A Mr Frederick Cartwright. He teaches here, does he not?'

A visible shade passed over the old man's face. Absent-mindedly, he hauled on a gold chain, bringing a handsome gold watch to the surface of his waistcoat pocket. He looked at it as though in hope of being reminded of an urgent appointment, but it disappointed him and so he replaced it and turned to face us bravely.

'Yes, well, yes, Mr Frederick Cartwright does teach here.'

'Been here for a long time, has he?' I asked the question in an idle fashion, reaching out to run my fingers over a Norman buttress.

'No, no!' He was quite startled. The words came out with a slight squeak. He looked distressed beyond measure as though the long-term presence of Mr Cartwright in the school for which he bore responsibility would have been a sin beyond forgiveness. He wore a plain gold ring on his fourth finger, slightly too loose for him, and as he mused on this, he moved it rapidly up and down, sliding it nervously over the central joint of his finger.

'That's right, don't you remember, Collins? Didn't Mr Cartwright say that he came from Yorkshire?' Dickens had a reproachful note in his voice and I bit back a smile. Dickens and I had first met when I had played a small part in a play that he was putting on and now I felt almost as though we were both taking our parts in another play. The elderly canon looked from one to the other of us with a puzzled expression on his face. The gas lamp flashed a ghostly reflection from the glass of his gold-rimmed spectacles.

'From Yorkshire,' he murmured in a perplexed fashion. 'Well, you may be right, gentlemen, but I had not heard that.'

'He had been previously in another London school, then, perhaps,' I hinted. Surely the man would have had to give references. You needed references for every job of work in the country. My mother always complained of being pestered

204

for references for former scullery maids when she hadn't the slightest recollection of their names. 'You would have had a reference with him, wouldn't you, sir?'

I hoped that he would not be offended, but, on the contrary, his face cleared. 'You're right, Mr Collins, yes, of course, I had a reference for him.' He compressed his lips together and behind his gold-rimmed spectacles his eyes grew large with the effort to remember.

'I know,' he said triumphantly. 'I just couldn't think for the moment. When you get to my age, gentlemen, the memory begins to fade. Words come to the tip of the tongue and then they vanish into the thin air. I knew it was by the river. Greenwich,' he said triumphantly, 'that's where it was, Greenwich. He taught at the Royal Navy College in Greenwich previously. And that accounts for it, I suppose.' He said the last words more to himself than to us, muttering them in an undertone, his fingers fidgeting with his ring, his eyes bent upon the ancient cobbled path at our feet.

'Strict disciplinarian, isn't he,' said Dickens quickly. 'I got a flavour of it when he was talking about boys when we were drinking our port. Yes, a very strict disciplinarian!' I could see that the old canon lifted his head very quickly, focusing on Dickens who was not looking at him, but at a Norman buttress. 'I remember my old school-master,' went on Dickens cheerfully, 'would flog you as soon as look at you. Well, they say that boys are all the better for it, don't they?'

'No, no, you're quite wrong there, Mr Dickens.

I don't think that it does any good. Just fills the boys with resentment. We should lead by example or else we raise young savages.' The elderly clergyman looked the famous author in the face and spoke to him as sternly as any schoolmaster.

'I'm so very glad to hear you say these words,' said Dickens earnestly. He paused for a moment and then said, 'But surely Mr Cartwright didn't come straight here from Greenwich, did he? I understood that he had been up in the north of England for some time. Isn't that right, Collins?'

'That's right,' I confirmed without a blush. 'I, like you, had Yorkshire in mind.'

'It may be, it may be.' The canon was lapsing back into the vagueness of old age. 'I seem to remember him telling me that he had not taught for some time. Some illness, no doubt. And, they do say that the air in Yorkshire is very bracing. I knew a bishop who would swear by sea-bathing in Scarborough. Wouldn't care for it myself, but there is no accounting for tastes. Now, myself, I don't like Norman architecture,' he confided with the air of one confessing to a grave sin, 'but there you are, the world is full of clever people who come here to look at the Norman section of our ancient church. We can't all think the same way, can we, Mr Dickens?'

'Except in the treatment of children,' said Dickens gently and the old man's face brightened.

'God bless you,' he said. 'God bless you for what you said there. I heard you speak at the dinner for Great Ormond Street and I'll never forget the little story you told about the sick poor child lying in an old egg box.' The kind old man wiped his eyes. 'God bless you for the way you open men's hearts,' he said as he turned away.

'I usually aim to open their purses,' said Dickens in my ear on our way to the gate, but I was not fooled by the cynical words. We had both been touched by the canon of St Bartholomew. 'Not a man to like brutality,' he said after a minute, watching the disappearance of the kindly old man. 'I think that if my little friend Isabella had threatened to tell the holy man, the canon of St Bartholomew's, about the past history of Frederick Cartwright, she would have put herself in considerable danger from that amiable school teacher.'

'Interesting that he, that Cartwright, I mean, came from Greenwich, isn't it? I wonder how Isabella found that out.'

'From one of those young chaps in the top storey of the house. I'd be willing to lay a small bet on that. Journalists pick up odd facts about people. The pair of them seemed to have been very friendly with the two girls. It always happens. These young fellows always flirt with the house-maids. And, of course, Cartwright would have no reason to keep Greenwich a secret. He was probably a good enough teacher for the Royal Navy School. They expect brutality there. But he might have gone a step too far in Yorkshire, though. D'you know, Wilkie, I'd give a lot to find out what the truth is about this story of a brother.'

'Well, even if Cartwright had nothing to do

with Isabella's mother that does not mean that she did not have a son. Annie Brown might have been a married name. She could have been a young widow with a son who was old enough to be of use to them if they went off to a new life. That would fit in with this plan of coming back for the baby when she was a bit older.'

'That story about an illness, that was to cover up the man's time in Yorkshire. If he beat a boy to death while he was up there, they may not have been willing to have given him a reference. So our friend Cartwright has erased that from his professional life.' Dickens gave a short laugh. The Yorkshire thing interested him.

'Don't you think that we should make a thorough search of that room, of Isabella's room, in Adelphi Terrace, Dick? You're friendly with the landlord. Can't you get him interested? Ask his permission. We can't keep relying on Sesina. She has her own work to do. I wouldn't like to get her into trouble either, poor little thing.'

'Don't you worry about Sesina, Wilkie,' said Dickens as we paused outside my lodgings at the Temple Inn. 'She's smart enough to run rings around Mrs Dawson, you know. She'll come up with an explanation for anything that she's doing. "Just thought I'd give the place a clean out. Heard mice in there, missus." He mimicked Sesina's high-pitched voice with great accuracy. 'You know, Wilkie,' he said, 'I've had a few sessions with our friend Sesina in the past. She tried to run rings around me on one occasion, persuading me to restore marks that she had lost by a fit of temper: "Can't do my work agreeable to myself,

Mr Dickens, without having my marks put back into my book." Quite a girl, our little Sesina.'
Dickens laughed heartily and I said no more, but my anxiety about the girl wasn't so much the fear of a scolding from Mrs Dawson, but that she might be putting herself into grave danger from a murderer who might be lurking in that house.

And what about Mrs Dawson, I thought, as I made my way up to my rooms. We had not really discussed this matter; by now, Dickens had probably brushed the matter aside as a coincidence of name, but what if Mrs Dawson had been the woman who had the baby farm, like the woman in Dickens' book, *Oliver Twist*? What if Mrs Dawson was the woman who had raised Isabella? I imagined from all that I heard from Dickens that Isabella had been a smart, intelligent girl – the handwriting on those cards was fluent and well-educated. What if she had a childhood memory of some scandal, some piece of brutality; a memory that had suddenly come to the fore when Mrs Dawson had said or done something? That could happen with childhood memories; my mother was a great believer in things like that.

And now that little housemaid, Sesina, if she went on prowling for clues, might well be in danger of the same fate as her friend. I felt worried about her. Wondered whether I could get her to confide in me.

Sixteen

Sesina was exhausted when the door knocker sounded in the mid-afternoon.

Today was washing day and on washing day mornings, she and Isabella had always got up at five o'clock in the morning. The fire in the wash-house in the lower basement had to be lit to heat up the water to boiling point. Later it would help to dry the clothes so that they could be ironed. There was no place at Adelphi Terrace to dry clothes out-of-doors, like the garden they had at Urania Cottage where the girls had all learned how to wash clothes, how to take out stains, and which materials could be boiled and which had to be carefully washed by hand. All about starches, too and how to iron the clothes, how to make sure that the flatirons' temperature was right for the cloth. She remembered windy days when white petticoats blew like sails from the washing lines and those competitions they had, watching balls of spit bubbling on the hot surface of the irons and betting whose spit would last the longest. Washday had sometimes been fun in Urania Cottage. She had to admit that. And the girls all had a little rest in the afternoon after washday and something special for supper.

Not here, though. Too much work for two people, well, one and a half, really. Sesina looked across at the young girl that Mrs Dawson had imported to help her. Crying, poor little thing. Her hands were a mess. Big chilblains swelling out making her fingers look like sausages. One of them bleeding too. That mixture of lye and ashes was bad for the hands, cracked the skin something terrible. She felt a bit ashamed that she had forgotten to tell her to put goose grease on before she started to scrub. Now she decided to ignore the knocker for a moment while she took the bowl from the netted safe in the pantry.

'Here, rub some of that on your hands. Makes them feel ever so soft. You'll be a lady in five minutes.' That got a smile from her. Thirteen years old. Still growing by the look of her. Sesina ignored the knocker once more and fetched a slice of bread from the bin and slapped some of the grease on with an old broken knife.

'You eat that up, get it inside you. Inside and out, that's the trick with goose grease.' She gave the girl a wink and began to climb the two flights of stairs up from the kitchen.

'So there you are; I thought that I was going to have to answer that door myself.' Mrs Dawson had a head outside her parlour when Sesina opened the door to the back stairs.

That would be terrible, missus, wouldn't it? After all, I've only spent the last eight hours on my feet, scrubbing, banging, lugging pots of boiling water, busting my guts with that mangle, taking the skin off my hands with that lye soap and my legs on fire with bending over that tub. It would be a dreadful thing if you had to cross the hall to open the front door. Sesina bit her lips to keep back the words. After all, except for

211

Mondays, the work was easy here. The kitchen was warm and the food was plentiful. *Wait until I make my fortune and then I'll tell you what I think of you.* That was what Isabella used to say.

And, surprise, it was him again. But not just him and his friend. This time there were three of them. Sesina had seen Mr Dickens' head first, his friend at his shoulder, but one more behind them. Big, heavy man. Bringing all his friends along to see the place where the murdered girl used to live. Making a show of them. Soon they'd be like Aspley's on the Strand where they showed the wild beasts to people who had the money to pay for the sight.

'Ah, Sesina.' Mr Dickens on the look-out as usual, with one of his quick looks around the hall as if he was doing a spot check to see if there was a speck of dust anywhere to be seen; the girls of Urania Cottage used to giggle behind his back when they saw him doing this and Sesina had to tighten her lips to keep a smirk back. That nice Mr Collins gave her one of his little smiles. The hall had passed muster. Mr Dickens' head bobbed a quick nod and then turned to one of the other men.

'This girl was a friend of the dead girl, Inspector Field. Her name is Sesina. A clever girl. I'm sure she will be a great help to you, Inspector.'

Inspector – from a prison? Inspecting what? Who was he? Wearing a top hat and a black coat. Fat. Huge stomach. Not interested in her. Sesina took Mr Collins' hat before she took his. She'd give that hat a brush before she handed it back to him. Inspector Field's hat was better brushed, but the leather lining was slimy with sweat.

'Inspector Field is the policeman in charge of poor Isabella's murder, Sesina.' Mr Collins gave her a nice smile as though he could read her good intentions towards his hat.

'Would you like to see Mrs Dawson, sir?' Sesina did her best to make her voice sound polite and helpful. The missus wouldn't like the police wandering around the place. Goodness knows what they'd find. Though a policeman is only a man when all is said and done. There was a girl in Urania Cottage who had started to go out with a policeman. Kept it a secret for ever so long. Even Mrs Morson thought nothing of a policeman walking past every day and never wondered why Hannah was spending such a time in the garden, not until the night when poor old Hannah became stone drunk from the bottle of whisky that she and the policeman had been drinking in the garden shed. Great fuss about that, of course. Mrs Morson sent a note by a fly across London for Mr Dickens to come and deal with Hannah. But before he could arrive, Hannah just crashed out of the place, breaking down the fence as she did so. *Couldn't leave by the gate, like any normal human being, had to make a theatre out of the whole business.* That was Mr Big-Headed Dickens! Always going to the theatre himself. Or going off to France when he felt bored and stale. Sesina had heard him telling Mrs Morson how he really needed a break. What did he think that *his* girls, as he called them, would do when they felt bored and stale and really needed a break? She and Isabella had a good laugh over that. 'Hannah just needed a break,' whispered Isabella, while they were eating their dinner, listening to a carpenter mending the broken fence. Mrs Morson, at the head of the table, had looked puzzled when all the girls choked over their soup; they were laughing so much at the notion of Hannah and her idea of 'a break'.

Ah, well!

'In here, sir,' she said demurely, addressing her words to Inspector Field and tapping politely on the door of Mrs Dawson's sitting room. She dropped one of her curtsies and left them to it.

They took quite a while before they came down to the kitchen. She had time to ease the ache in her calves by putting her feet on the stove and, feeling a bit sorry for the poor little thing, she told Becky to do the same.

'Keep on rubbing that stuff into your hands, though,' she advised. 'I'll give you a bit to take home with you in a jar. Washday comes around quicker than you think. Those little hands of yours will split and crack tonight if you don't keep them blisters well greased.'

Sesina was almost half asleep before she heard the creak of the backstairs door. In a flash she was out of her seat and in the washhouse, testing the iron by spitting on it. The sheets, dangling down from the clothes horse, were still too wet for ironing, even though they had put them through the mangle twice and had stoked up the fire as high as possible. The window to the yard was open, too, but there was a heavy fog outside so the steam had nowhere to go. She let the men stand around there for a couple of minutes, though, as she busily raked the embers and turned up the damper a bit more. Do them good to breathe in a bit of the atmosphere. Not a nice smell, that lye. *If I ever get my money, I'll send all of my washing out; sheets, everything*, she decided keeping her back turned on them and noisily riddling the embers. When she turned around eventually, Mr Dickens wasn't looking at her, but was absent-mindedly turning the handle of the mangle.

'Someone should invent a machine to do all this washing, shouldn't they, Wilkie. Bless my soul, we have trains tearing through the length and breadth of the country, their wheels turned by steam. Why doesn't someone invent a steam-powered washing machine, Sesina?'

'I don't know, sir,' said Sesina. She did, though. Why bother when you can get girls to do it for ten pounds a year? And scrub floors, dust walls and ceilings, haul carpets down stairs, wash dishes, carry slop pails, clean fireplaces, rake out the coal, open doors to visitors and answer their stupid questions. She put back the iron on top of the stove in a businesslike way and moved towards the door.

'It's not so steamy in the kitchen, sir.' She held the door open for them.

He gave her a stern glance that seemed to mean: I'll decide for myself, young woman, but when they came in to the warm kitchen, he stopped at the sight of poor little Becky holding out her sore and bleeding hands in the air. When she stood up, he went over and silently tucked a coin that looked like half a crown into the poor little thing's

215

apron. Not bad at times, Mr Dickens. Bark worse than his bite, she thought.

But then he turned back to Sesina. He had a determined look on his face, she thought.

'This business of Isabella has to be sorted out, Sesina. You do see that, don't you?'

'Yes, I do, sir.' She thought that the words sounded a strong note and goodness knows she hoped that it was a true note. Why should Isabella die like an unwanted dog with a cruel master? Why should any man do that to her? Beat her, strangle her and throw her in the river? Men like that, she thought viciously, should be hanged.

'I want the man who was responsible for killing Isabella to be caught, sir,' she said to him and she heard a note of sincerity in her voice. He heard it also and she saw him nod his head. He lowered his voice so that he just spoke to her.

'We want to have a good search of that room next to the kitchen, Sesina. That's the first thing to do, don't you think? We'll see if Isabella has left us any more clues; that's what I'm hoping for.'

'We know that you had a good look, Sesina, but you don't have much time, do you? You've got too much to do and not much help to do it.' Mr Collins, too, cast a pitying look at poor Becky and her poor hands and then patted Sesina on the shoulder as he whispered the words in her ear.

'I'm sure that you are right, Mr Dickens.' Sesina hoped that her voice sounded humble. Always liked to be right, did Mr Dickens. Nice as pie once you told him that he was right. 'I don't get the time for anything but work.' That was true, anyway. What with doing Isabella's work as well as her own, there was not much time left in the day.

He gave her a nod and walked out after the other two. She could hear them moving around, shifting the bed, taking all the drawers out of the chest, and then the creaking of a chair, probably holding up the weight of that police inspector as he climbed on it to see the top of the press. And then the chair was moved and there was more creaking. She would have liked to have a look, to see if they discovered any new hiding places, but she stayed where she was. Might as well rest her legs. And rest her tongue. All this 'yes, sir; no sir' business was tiring. Just as if she wasn't as good as any of them. A couple of years ago she would have said it out loud. That's what had made her leave Urania Cottage. She couldn't keep her temper. And the more marks she lost, the more her feelings boiled over. Couldn't stand the sight of that silly book. She might be different now, she thought. She was older and a bit more sensible. But there was never any use in looking back. Best to concentrate on getting her money out of that man. Safely, she reminded herself. And then clearing out of Adelphi Terrace.

'What are they looking for?' asked Becky, flexing her fingers. They glistened with goose grease in the firelight. That way they wouldn't crack and bleed too much. Sesina and Isabella had learned that early in their time as housemaids. It eased the pain and the sting, also. The little girl was looking brighter – a bit happier.

217

'Where do you sleep at nights, Becky?' she asked in order to change the subject. Becky wouldn't really understand even if Sesina explained what was going on. The girl wasn't too bright. Couldn't read or write, poor thing. I miss Isabella, thought Sesina.

'Covent Garden,' said Becky. 'The apple woman lets me sleep in her stall.'

'Do you like it, Becky? Isn't it very cold?' There was a strange scratching noise from the small bedroom beside the kitchen. Raking the top of the water tank with the handle of an umbrella, she guessed after a minute. That would be worth doing. She, herself, had stood on a chair and felt back as far as she could, but she had not been able to reach right to the back of it. An umbrella was a good idea.

'It's scary there at night,' said Becky. She sounded dreary. Used to it, thought Sesina. Things never seemed so bad when you got used to them. You just had to keep going. That was her experience, anyway.

'You got a mother or anything?' she asked and Becky shook her head. Didn't want to talk about it. Mothers weren't much use in Sesina's experience, probably not in Becky's, neither. Wanted to go on about Covent Garden.

'It's really, really scary, Sesina. You wouldn't like it a bit. When the traders go, the rats come. Ever so big some of them. I bet you've never seen such big rats. Size of cats, you've never seen such a thing.'

Bet I have, thought Sesina and then she pushed the thought of the past from her head. Look forward. Don't look back. That was her motto. She sat very still, gazing into the fire. Money, she thought. That's what I need. Money. A nice place of my own. Becky had fallen asleep by the time that she looked across at her again, and so she went back to her little daydream. Money enough for a coffee stall. She imagined it. Nice little stall. Cover over the top so that the rain didn't come on to the cups and the food. Coffee, tea, buns. Loads of people queuing up. Herself in a nice white apron. She could pinch a few from the linen cupboard here in Adelphi Terrace before she left. Plenty of them there. Take a few tablecloths, too, while she was at it. Would give a bit of class to the place. Dead clean, white tablecloth spread out under the cups and saucers. She'd keep it clean and starched. Send out her washing, too. Never no more wash days, she swore under her breath with a glance across at the sleeping child opposite. *Money!* She said the two syllables softly beneath her breath. She liked the sound of the word. How much should she ask him for? What would her silence be worth to him? Twenty pounds or perhaps it should be ten pounds. Isabella might have been asking too much, asking for a meal ticket for life, and look where that got her. She glanced across at the door and, as the handle turned, for a second she almost expected to see Isabella. She stayed watching it, wide-eyed, for a second and then gave a terrible start as it opened slowly.

'God, Mrs Dawson, I thought that you were Isabella's ghost, coming in so quiet-like.' Not like the missus to steal down so quietly. What was she after? Sneaking around to see what they were up to in the next room? Listening to what they were saying. Sesina looked at her with interest.

'Don't be stupid, Sesina,' snapped Mrs Dawson. 'No such thing as ghosts.'

'Easy to say when you don't sleep down here in the lower basement, missus. There's something moves around at night this last week. I'm not sure if I can stay here on my own much longer to tell you the truth.'

That gave the missus something to think about. Sesina could see the old fat face tightening up. Lazy old cow. Wouldn't like to lose Sesina now as well as Isabella. Might have to do some work herself. The great Mrs Dawson cleaning out fireplaces, carrying slop pails, turning a mangle over dripping sheets, scrubbing floors! Sesina left a silence long enough for the woman to think about these things. And it worked. Mrs Dawson looked across at the sleeping child.

'We could keep that little one, Sesina, what do you think? Be company for you, wouldn't she? Nice little thing. You could train her up to be useful, couldn't you, Sesina? I'm sure the landlord wouldn't grudge the money that she'd cost, even if we do get another housemaid in a while.'

You might find yourself doing the work, if you don't hurry up about getting another housemaid. I'll be off once I have the twenty pounds in my pocket, thought Sesina, but aloud, she said, 'Well, what about popping down to see the landlord, now, missus. Get it fixed up and then we can tell Becky when she wakes up. And while you are at it, missus, see if the greengrocer can give you another cat. I'd swear I heard mice last night. Never did hear them before that butcher ran over our cat.'

That got rid of you, thought Sesina as soon as Mrs Dawson hurried upstairs to put on her bonnet. Never did like mice. Couldn't stand up to men, either. Didn't want to have any argument with the butcher when he ran over that poor cat – on purpose, too. Left Isabella to deal with him. Did it, too. Poor old Isabella! Afraid of no one. Could stand up to Mr Dickens himself. Never forget the day that she defied him. The sight of her deliberately turning her back on him, going up the stairs, holding out her skirts like a lady, had made every girl in the place double up, laughing inside themselves. Sesina smiled a bit at the memory of that day and then stood up when she heard the sound of a door opening. Let the poor little mite sleep, she thought, as she went towards the kitchen door, seizing a mop and pail and carrying them in a busy manner.

'Ah, Sesina, just come in here for a moment. We want to show you something.'

So they had found something else. The policeman, this Inspector Field, he didn't care for her being brought into the room. His big thick lips were pouting a bit and he pulled at his ear. Didn't dare say a word, though. Mr Dickens probably wouldn't let him. Bossed everyone, so he did.

'Did you find something else, sir?' She dumped the bucket and mop and followed them in. Freezing cold that place. If Becky did stay, then she'd have to share her room upstairs, have Isabella's bed. Couldn't have the child sleeping in that cold, damp place on her own. Not that I'll be here for too long, I'd say, she thought as the picture of her coffee stall with its starched white tablecloth came to her mind and brought a smile to her face.

'Look at this. Inspector Field found it.' Mr Dickens, of course, was as triumphant as if he had found it himself. All excited he was. And the other little fellow, Mr Collins, eyes sparkling away behind his gold-rimmed spectacles as he held out a cotton handkerchief to her.

'Do you recognize this, Sesina?' he said and he sounded like a little boy, all excited.

'Yes, sir. That was belonging to Isabella.' To Mrs Dawson, actually, but Isabella had unpicked the initials, S.D. And then she had boiled it for so long that the pale pink colour had faded to a dingy white. 'Yes, that was belonging to Isabella.' She heard her voice shake a little and that nice Mr Collins patted her on the arm. She would give him a free cup of coffee if he ever passed by her stall in the early morning at Covent Garden.

'Do you recognize the handwriting?' This Inspector Field had a hoarse voice and a disgusting habit of clearing his throat before everything that he said. He had taken the handkerchief off the little bundle of calling cards and he was peering at her suspiciously, but then policemen were all the same. Put you in prison at the stroke of a pen if you said a cross word to them.

'Yes, sir.' She dropped him a curtsy. Wouldn't hurt. Men liked that sort of thing. 'Yes, that's

222

Isabella's handwriting. She always made the letter C like that, all curly.' Sesina frowned a little at the cards. 'The mice have been at those cards, sir. I told Mrs Dawson that we should get a new cat. The butcher killed our nice old fellow. Isabella went out and give him a piece of her mind. Ever so nasty he was to her, too.'

That would give Mr Dickens something to think of. Fond of animals, he was. She'd seen him stroke a stray dog and come back to the kitchen to find something to eat for it. And the cat at Urania Cottage always made a beeline towards him the minute that he sat down.

'I met that butcher, I think,' said Mr Collins in a low voice. 'So Isabella gave him a piece of her mind, did she? Brave girl!' And he looked at Mr Dickens and the pair of them seemed to be thinking hard about the butcher. And why not. Good for that fella if the police hauled him into one of their stations and shut him in a cell before questioning him. That Inspector Field wasn't taking much notice though. He was holding out one of the cards to her.

'What do you think this means, my dear?'

Sesina frowned over the cards. What could Isabella be thinking of?

'"Booklet One", it's like she was thinking of a book. What do you think?' She turned towards Mr Collins.

'That's what we were thinking of, Sesina. That's just the way I go about writing a book.' Mr Collins sounded all excited. He started telling Mr Field all about it, all about how he writes his books. Thought she'd be too stupid to understand, she supposed. 'I get a pack of cards, Inspector,' he was saying. 'I buy them from the stationer, and I write across the top of each one the number of the booklet: booklet one, booklet two and so on until I reach at least thirty and then I go back and put ideas on the cards as I think of them. I do that for a few weeks or a few months until I have my mind full of ideas and then I write the book.'

'You're a planner and plotter, then, Mr Collins.' Inspector Field gave a great laugh that ended in another one of those throat-clearing businesses. He wagged his finger, silly old foozler. 'I know some men like you down at Seven Dials, Mr Collins,' he said. Thought he was very amusing, of course. 'But it isn't books that they are planning and plotting. Not them. A different story entirely. That's what they are after.' And Inspector Field had another good laugh at his own little joke.

Plenty of people that I knew used to have a laugh at you and your big notions of yourself, Mr Inspector Field, thought Sesina, but she kept her eyes fixed on the cards and then, aloud, read them one by one.

Booklet 1: A picture of a murderer. The murderer walks the dark streets of London at night. He has a terrible scar on his face. People run away from him. He has a look of death in his eyes. He walks the streets, trying to forget the dead boy. Trying to forget the lifeless body at his feet.

Booklet 2: The murderer finds a new job. He has to hide the past. He lies about his past. Pretends to be what he is not. Pretends to be kind and caring, but the scar tells a different story. It speaks out like a mouth.

Booklet 3: The murderer must hide his past. No clue must be left. No trace in his room. He must check through all of his belongings. No one must know where he comes from. He does not know that it is too late!

'His room,' said Sesina thoughtfully. '"No trace left in his room."' She saw Mr Dickens look at that Inspector Field and the policeman returned the look, nodding his head and touching his nose with his forefinger, trying to make himself look very wise.

'Tell us, my dear, would this Isabella have searched a room in this house?' asked Inspector Field looking at her very intently, trying to see into my mind, thought Sesina.

'Oh, no, sir, we wouldn't do things like that. Just dusting and cleaning and tidying up after the gentlemen.' *Leaving their wet towels and their disgusting, dirty underclothes lying all over the floor and expecting us to pick them up and put them in the laundry basket.*

'The scar,' said Mr Collins, raising his eyebrows at the two men.

'"The scar tells a different story", that's what it said, didn't it, sir?' She said the words to him in a low and confidential tone of voice. It was nice to give a bit of encouragement to Mr Collins. The other two would talk over him. He should stand up for himself, she thought and wished, once again, that she was a housemaid in his place. She wouldn't send him out in the morning with a hat like that. There were even cat hairs all over it today. And creases in his coat as well.

'So my little friend Isabella was planning to write a book, well, well, well.' Mr Dickens sounded quite sentimental. Could be as hard as nails, of course, but he could be handled. Looking back on it, some of the girls at Urania Cottage could handle him, could always get around him. Still, who wanted to be shipped off to Tasmania, across the world in one of them ships? *London is the place for me*; Isabella used to say that and Sesina agreed with her.

'Who do you think that Isabella is talking about, Sesina?' Mr Dickens was watching her very carefully. *Trying to see into our heads,* that was what the girls in Urania Cottage used to say about him. He was a contrary man, too. You'd say one thing and he'd say the opposite. She'd try that.

'I suppose she just made it up, sir. It's a story, ain't it? Ain't a story made up, sir?' Sesina said the words quietly and waited for him to contradict her. And, of course, he did. She knew that he would.

'Well, you know, Sesina, I wonder whether she did make it up; whether she had someone in mind. And, of course, there is only one person in this house with a scar. You'd agree to that, wouldn't you? Do you think that your friend

Isabella was thinking of Mr Cartwright when she wrote that?'

'Searched his room, too, I'll be bound,' said Inspector Field, holding his pudgy hand against the side of his red nose and speaking to Mr Dickens behind it, pushing out his fat lips. *Must think her dead stupid. Or blind and deaf. That was the police for you. Dead stupid, the lot of them.*

With a slight shrug of her shoulders, Sesina left them to it, to their low-voiced conversation, to their brooding looks at the mice-nibbled cards which could lead to the uncovering of the murderer of poor Isabella. There should be another card to find. There had been eight cards missing, only twelve were left from the original pack of twenty. She wondered whether they had remembered that as she went out to the coal cellar. Or perhaps they were all too stupid to subtract twelve from twenty. She had a little giggle at that. Funny how it warmed you up and made you feel good to have that little giggle. Poor old Isabella. She did miss her. Hopefully that brute would soon be locked up. Sesina went out to the coal store and filled a pail with small, dusty nuggets, brought them back into the kitchen and then added a few sticks from the basket by the fire. While she was tearing up some old newspapers, reducing them to some puffed-out balls, her mind was working rapidly.

Surely it was as obvious to them as it was to her, where those notes were leading. Surely they couldn't be so stupid. All three of them. Two famous writers of books and one police inspector.

227

Still the chances were that she was as clever as any one of them. No harm in being ahead of them, anyway.

She went silently past the kitchen maid's bedroom, as she went towards the stairs. The voices were very low now. That was good. *So you're beginning to catch on!* She wished that she could say the words aloud and watch their surprised faces. But no point in dreaming for the moon, be content with what you can get without too much danger. Ten pounds, she thought, reluctantly. That was probably all that she should ask for. That was reasonable. He could afford that. Meet him indoors, in the house. Easy enough to do that. And then she'd vanish from the scene, wouldn't say another word to nobody, just clear off and let that fat policeman and Mr Dickens, of course, get on with putting him in gaol and hanging him for what he did to Isabella. That's if they had the brains to do that. In any case, she should be safe enough, she thought confidently, as she went quietly up the stairs towards the hallway. They were well on the trail, now. The bell from St Martin in the Fields Church on Trafalgar Square sounded the hour, as she opened the door into the hall, just before the hall clock chimed its four silvery strokes. Four o'clock, Mr Cartwright would be home soon.

No sound from the lawyer's rooms; he was still out. She passed by quickly, clambering swiftly up to the next storey. She set the schoolmaster's fire, expertly layering the sticks above and below the balls of newspaper and then she struck the match. The tenants were supposed to ring when

228

they wanted a fire, but you could set a clock by the schoolmaster's arrival home. It was easier to do it without his eyes on her backside. Sesina puffed the bellows vigorously. He'd be back in about ten or fifteen minutes. There was a good draught on this fire. By then the room would be warm. The three gentlemen, cudgelling their brains downstairs, would have a nice comfortable time interviewing. Hopefully, they would frighten the life out of him. Tighten the noose around his neck. Sesina gave a little giggle. She'd pick her time, just hand him a letter and wait for him to summon her. After the police questioning he'd be shaking in his shoes and willing to buy her silence at any price. About seven o'clock in the evening, she decided. That would be the best time. The two lads upstairs would have gone out, out on the tiles like a pair of tom cats. The lawyer would be out, too, going wherever he went of evenings. Mrs Dawson would be sipping her gin and dozing by the fire. No one to interrupt.

In about half an hour, she decided, yes, in half an hour a conscientious and hardworking housemaid would be perfectly justified in appearing with a fresh pail of coal. And by then the conversation should be getting interesting. Listen at the door for as long as it was safe and then a knock if anyone was coming up the stairs, or if the conversation got boring. The important thing would be for her to pretend she knew all about everything. Get him rattled.

That was him now. What would he say? She waited until his key turned the door lock and he had one foot in the door.

'The police are down in the basement, now, Mrs Dawson,' she said, calling words up the stairs as clearly and as loudly as she dared. And then she pretended to notice him. 'Good afternoon, Mr Cartwright.' She even dropped him a curtsy as he came up from the hallway; pounding his weight down on each step and gripping the banisters, white-knuckled, like a man who is just about holding on to his temper. Nasty-looking fellow, she thought, watching him as he passed her with a glare. Heavy face, side whiskers, round eyes, bottom teeth sticking out nearly covering his top lip. Made him look like a snarling dog, Isabella used to say. That scar of his. Looked like another mouth, stretching from cheek bone to chin. Eyes glittering and darting from side to side. Wide-legged stride. Chin lowered on chest. He had a very high colour, too. Didn't suit him. Wasn't healthy. More purple than red. He'd be even more purple-faced soon, she reckoned. Her quick ear had caught the sound of footsteps on the basement stairs.

They reached the hall as soon as she did. The three of them. The inspector looking pompous and knowing. Mr Collins looking a bit sheepish. Half wishing that he could keep out of it, poor fellow, but sorry about Isabella. Mr Dickens, though; well, he was just calm and determined. She had to give him credit. As keen to revenge Isabella's horrible death as she was, that's what the two of them were. Spending time looking for clues, talking to the people in the house. And she'd be willing to bet that Inspector Field would not have been bothered about the death of a servant girl if Mr Dickens hadn't chivvied him along. *Very powerful man, Mr Dickens*. She'd overheard Mrs Morson at Urania Cottage say that once. Well, let him use that power now. Get vengeance for poor Isabella and do a good turn to little Sesina while he was at it.

'Was that Mr Cartwright who came home just now, Sesina?' he asked now.

'That's right, sir,' she said obligingly. 'Do you wish to see him?' She turned as if to go and summon the schoolteacher, but he stopped her with a hand on her arm.

'You go back downstairs and have a rest, Sesina,' he said in a surprisingly kind tone of voice. 'We'll announce ourselves.'

'Thank you, sir,' she said. She stood in the hall and watched them climb the first flight of stairs. They turned the corner and did not slacken pace. Three sets of footsteps climbing steadily. On the first-floor landing, now. Then the two next flights.

And then a sharp knock, a heavy knock, sounded right through the house. The inspector's husky voice. 'Mr Cartwright. We'd like a little word with you, if you please. Inspector Field from Scotland Yard.'

She wished that she could see his face. Well, he'd have to let a police inspector into his room and, of course, once the door was opened, the other two would pop in.

Bit of a cheek, really, Mr Dickens and his friend butting in on police business. He'd make up something, though. She knew *him*. Always sure that he was right. Always had a smart

231

explanation for everything. Look at the way he was in Urania Cottage! It was that rich lady, Miss Coutts, who was really in charge. Miss Coutts who paid all the bills. Everyone knew that. Mr Dickens, himself, always spoke of Miss Coutts as being the one that they all had to be so grateful to. But he was the one who was in and out of the place two or three times a week, he was the one with the power, the one that everyone was a bit afraid of, the one that some of those girls would do anything to get a word of praise out of. She smiled a little to herself as she waited in the hallway. She could just imagine him explaining to Mr Cartwright all about how fond he was of Isabella Gordon, how he felt responsible for her, how he brought along Inspector Field to try to find any clue as to her death, how they knew that everyone in the household would do their best to catch the murderer.

But then the doorknocker sounded again, a smart rat-tat-tat. A tall figure. The landlord. Must have misplaced his key. Now Mrs Dawson could have no more peace. Surprising that she wasn't out already with all the voices in the hall. Asleep, drunk, most like. Well, she might as well do her a good turn. Ignoring the front-door knocker, she went quietly to the parlour door and knocked smartly on it. No answer. Sesina opened it and went in. Mrs Dawson was so fast asleep that she had to put a hand on her to wake her up. Impatiently she shook the fat shoulder.

Mrs Dawson woke with a start, just as the hall doorknocker sounded even more loudly. The landlord was getting impatient.

'Goodness, gracious, Sesina, what are you about? Open that door immediately, girl.'

'Yes, missus,' said Sesina obediently. 'I think it is the landlord, missus.' She thought of offering to put away the glass and the bottle, but Mrs Dawson was well and truly awake now, getting to her feet immediately, looking in the looking-glass and patting her hair. By the time that Sesina had reached the door, the bottle and the glass had been rapidly tidied away.

'Sorry to keep you waiting, sir,' Sesina said when she opened the door. Two of them there. Mr Doyle was a bit further down the steps, looking across at the river and so she had not seen him through the glass. She kept her attention on the landlord, though. 'We are all in a heap today, sir,' she said, dropping a curtsy. 'What being short-handed and washday in the morning and now, this afternoon, we have the police in the house.'

'The police!' That gave him a bit of a shock. Gave Mr Doyle a shock too. He had turned to come up the steps, but now he turned back towards the river again. She raised her eyes to look after him. Going towards Adam Street. Walking at a fair old pace. Well, none of her business. She turned back to the landlord.

'Yes, sir, they are up with Mr Cartwright, now, sir.'

'And Mrs Dawson?'

'In her parlour, sir.'

He frowned a little over that. She could see him thinking about it. And then, unexpectedly he smiled at her. 'You're enjoying all of this, aren't you, little girl,' he said in a teasing manner. Rich as anything, so they'd heard, but very friendly. Americans were so different to the English, she thought. No English landlord would bother about someone like herself. They would just despise her. Call her a skivvy. Never think of her as having opinions, having a laugh at them behind their backs.

'I'm very upset about Isabella, sir,' she said and she knew from the change in his expression that he recognized the note of sincerity in her voice. 'I would do anything to help the gentlemen to bring that murderer to justice.'

'Good girl, good girl,' he said heartily and then gave her half a crown.

Nothing like the Americans for generosity, she thought. And then she wondered whether she could make use of him. 'Isabella has been writing down her suspicions about someone, sir,' she said in a whisper. 'I think that's why the police are here. They're upstairs in Mr Cartwright's room, second-floor tenant, sir.'

That interested him. She could see it in his eyes. For a moment he looked towards the stairs, just as though he was tempted to go and join them, but then he said, 'Well, I won't disturb them. Mrs Dawson in, is she?'

'Yes, sir, in the parlour, sir.' Sesina showed him into the parlour. What did he want to see the old podge for? She went to listen at the door, but had to move away smartly when the handle turned.

'Just wondered if you needed some tea, missus,' she murmured. She didn't fool Mrs Dawson, who gave Sesina a nasty suspicious look, but the landlord gave her a nice smile through the opened door.

'Waal,' said the American landlord and Sesina liked the way that he said the word, drawing it out, his mouth smiling all the time. He patted her on the head, not something she liked, but always all right when a coin was popped into the apron pocket at the same time. 'You got yourself some darn good girl there, Mrs Dawson, but we can't have her worn out, can we? You fix up for the other girl to work fulltime with her and any extra help that you can get. Someone for washday, what do you think, Mrs Dawson?'

'That would be most convenient, sir. Thank you, sir.' Make a cat laugh, she would, with her curtsies and her genteel accent, mouth pursed like a lady. 'Oh, here come Mr Dickens and his friend,' she said, still in that prissy tone of voice, as if everyone couldn't hear the two of them coming down the stairs, talking so loud and that fat inspector pounding on the steps, make the stair rods pop out if he wasn't careful.

'Come in, Mr Dickens, come in, Inspector, Mr Collins, come in, won't you?' The American was taking charge now. Had a right to it, of course. Owned the place, didn't he? Ushering the other two into the room and then smiling at her. 'No, no tea, thank you, Sesina. Thank you, Mrs Dawson.'

And Mrs Dawson found herself on the other side of a closed door, staring angrily at Sesina.

Seventeen

Wilkie Collins, *Basil*:

I looked up at the sky. It was growing
very dark. The ragged black clouds,
fantastically parted from each other in
island shapes over the whole surface of
the heavens, were fast drawing together
into one huge, formless, lowering mass,
and had already hidden the moon for
good.

By God, it was a lie. That woman was lying!
And neither of us, neither Dickens nor myself
noticed it. I woke in the middle of the night with
the words on my lips and swore.

Every line on that elderly face was clear to me.
Every hesitation sounded in my ears. She had
misled us. Perhaps not wished us to trace the
girl's origin, the girl's mother and father. Not
wanting to incur blame. What could have been
the motive? I lit the candle beside my bed and
peered at my watch. Past midnight. I had a strong
impulse to get out of bed, to get dressed and to
walk the streets, just as Dickens so often did
when he brooded a clutch of ideas in preparation
for a new book. I got out of bed and walked
across to the window, opening the curtain. A fine
night. The moon would give me light and I would

walk from my rooms down to the Temple Steps and gaze at the river. We lacked a vital piece of evidence, I thought, as I knotted a belcher scarf around my neck and pulled on a pair of trousers over my nightgown. If Mr Cartwright were guilty of the murder of Isabella, what could have been his motive? He had been confident and dismissive about the prospect of uncovering any murder in his past. Had totally denied ever being a teacher in Yorkshire, had said that he had never even visited the place. And, somehow, as I thought the matter over in the dim light from my candle, his voice in my ear bore conviction. The man, I thought, was an unpleasant, unprepossessing fellow, may well have been accused of mistreating a boy, perhaps in Greenwich, but that was not to say that he was a murderer, or even a liar. As I laced up my boots, I went through the law cases that I had perused during my idle years of study, more for getting plots for stories than with any idea of passing examinations. Surely a motive was of importance. With no witnesses, with no evidence possible to be found at this stage – and the inspector had made a brief, but thorough search of the schoolmaster's two rooms, without finding a single spot of blood. Surely it would have been impossible for the man to murder a girl, to beat her and to carry her body to the riverside without leaving some trace, and without alerting someone within the house.

Without evidence like that, there was no possibility of accusing the man, I thought, as I pulled on a woolly cardigan, covered all with a warm overcoat and made for the door. Unless a strong motive could be found and then the means could be revaluated, the murder of Isabella will go unavenged, I said to myself as I went down the steps and out into the night air.

But the moon, in its capricious manner, had disappeared and everywhere was very dark. I paused for a moment outside the door. To go down to the river now would risk a broken ankle or worse. I turned and went towards the Fleet Street Gate, guiding myself by the dim light which glimmered from the watchman's lantern.

'Dark night, sir,' he said, holding the gate open for me to pass through.

'It is, indeed,' I said. *Dark night*, I repeated silently, as I went up the narrow passageway that led to Fleet Street. A night for a murder. I remembered poor Isabella's penned words about the murderer walking the dark streets of London at night. Did he? Or did he sleep peacefully in his bed, sure that no one could pin the evil deed on him? I turned my mind back to the thought that had woken me from my sleep.

Mrs Peters.

She had been eager, very prepared to help.

And then had come her unfortunate remark about the unreality of a 'grateful' Oliver Twist. I smiled to myself as I dodged a drunken man with his arm around a disreputable-looking girl. Dickens, the soul of generosity to friends and indeed, to the friendless, hated criticism of his creations. The atmosphere had stiffened.

The woman had hesitated, I remembered that well. She had hesitated, giving us a penetrating look, trying to size us up, trying to decide whether we were worthy of trust. Then she had gone on to relate the entry about the baby, Isabella, and had told us of the two articles left behind, the string of beads, and the tantalizing story of a broken knife that had been in the fire.

And then.

I cudgelled my brains in an effort to remember. There had been a hesitation in her manner. That I was certain of. And I remembered also that her glance had met mine, when Dickens was frowning at the tablecloth. I could visualize that glance. She had wondered whether she could trust me, or whether she should say nothing. And then she had hurriedly gone on to talk about the knife.

But what if there had been a third object there – what if Mrs Peters had been on the brink of telling us about it, but for some reason had mistrusted Dickens, had not wanted to reveal this third object for some reason. Perhaps even more definite evidence of a father which she, being sorry for the woman, Anne Gordon, had decided to suppress. She had deemed Dickens a man who had no esteem for women, had wronged him, I thought. It had taken me a year of close friendship before I realized that the great and the successful Mr Dickens had a gaping hollow of terrible insecurity within, cloaked by a joking, hail-fellow-well-met exterior. Money was of great importance to him. And in order to get money, then he had to please his readers. And in order to please his readers, he had to present a glorified view of women, present them as saintly

239

home-loving goddesses. But, of course, deep down, he did not believe in these creations, these perfect women. To hear him laugh admiringly about the spirit and the brazen self-confidence of the girls in Urania Cottage was to know that the women Mrs Peters objected to were a crowd-pleasing creation.

I stopped outside Al Tack's Opium Den and gazed at it meditatively. Perhaps I should try a pipe. It might open up the puzzle, give me insight. After all, laudanum was a mixture of opium and alcohol and I had found it of great assistance when I was troubled with pain from gout. Still not a good idea to take opium, I thought. Laudanum was different. Just one tenth of it was the deadly opium, the rest was made from health-giving herbs and sherry wine. As I hesitated at the door, I saw a familiar figure lying on a couch within. The lofty forehead and the bald head glistened in the light, and the pale blue eyes, turned towards the ceiling, were lacking all reason, all discrimination. The man was completely under the influence. A row of pipes, I counted seven, beside him showed that Mr Doyle had been there for most of the evening, if not for most of the day. I drew back hastily, filled with repugnance as I looked at the slack muscles of the drooling mouth, the stained coat, the spectacles askew upon his nose and the drooping eyelids. I thought I knew the secret now of why his rent was paid by a solicitor who managed a family estate, rather than by the man himself.

My momentary temptation had passed. I turned to go away from the opium den but then I paused.

An elderly Chinese woman, lying across a bed or sofa, sat up and began to blow down the pipe beside her. As she blew, shading it with her lean hand, she concentrated its red spark of light and it served in the dim light of the room as a lamp to illuminate the figure of the lawyer lying beside her. And to illuminate, in striking detail, the engraved gold watch that had slipped from his waistcoat pocket and now hung dangling from its gold chain. A beautiful watch, gleaming and without a scratch, brand new in appearance. On the other side of the room, a rough-looking sailor, less dazed than the others was sitting bolt upright, a knife in his hand and his eyes on the gold watch.

I didn't like Jeremiah Doyle; not at all, but I couldn't see him robbed or even murdered while I stood by and did nothing. I couldn't turn my back on him. Leaving the door to the street open, I strode in, crossed the floor, not looking from right to left, not allowing feelings of panic to overcome me, but trying to act as casually as if I had seen a friend in a restaurant.

'Mr Doyle,' I said, shaking him by the shoulder. 'Mr Doyle, it's Wilkie Collins, the friend of your landlord. Come with me, Mr Doyle.' I remembered the time when we had met and how I had disliked him for the sneering, supercilious glances that he gave over the top of his spectacles, but now the spectacles had fallen askew, lodged at a crazy angle by the tip of his nose, and the sneering mouth was slack, displaying some blackened teeth above a coated tongue. The pale blue eyes tried to focus on my face, but I could see from

241

the haze upon them that he could hardly see me. I hooked my arm under his shoulder and raised him. He was a tall man and I was a small one, but beneath the expensive broadcloth of his coat, he was skeleton-thin. I raised him without difficulty, tucked his expensive gold watch back into its pocket and moved him towards the door.

The old woman in the background said something, but I ignored her. My eye was on the sailor with a knife. He made a move as if to come towards us and I shouted out, 'Cabbie, Cabbie, come and lend me a hand.'

There was, of course, no cabman outside, but the unexpectedly loud voice in this roomful of dazed and zombie-like figures acted like a sudden shower of icy rain. Suddenly all muttering stopped. The sailor took a step backwards, retreated into the shadows, the old woman pulled a shawl over her head as though a bright light had shone in her face and the fat man desperately sucked at his pipe for reassurance. With strength that I didn't know I possessed, I hauled the sleep-walking form of the lawyer up to a standing position, tucked his cane over his arm, tugged him towards the door, opened it, thrust him outside, and then slammed it shut behind us.

There was a keen wind blowing down the alleyway and I propped Doyle against a wall, still keeping my arm below his armpit and my other hand flat against the breast of his starched shirt front. Oddly, he seemed aware of the cane and now held it firmly in one hand.

'All right, sir?' A policeman came down from Fleet Street, attracted by the two figures. He touched his hat, perhaps in recognition of a mistake.

'Thank you, Officer. My friend has had too much opium, I think.'

The policeman surveyed him with a knowledgeable eye. 'Takes them that way, best to get him some air. Walk him down to the river, sir. Fog's lifted at last. Lovely moon. Bright as day. Yes, take him down there. He'll be right as a trivet as soon as he gets the breeze in his face.'

I had planned on getting the man in a cab, but I thought it polite to murmur an acquiescence.

'It's Mr Collins, isn't it?' went on my new friend chattily.

'Yes, indeed.' I felt a slight thrill at being recognized here on the midnight streets of London. Perhaps the policeman had read *Basil*.

'Seen you around with Mr Dickens,' continued my new friend. 'Now you keep your hand on the gentleman's right arm and I'll take the other arm and we'll get him down to the river with no trouble. There's a bench down there, beside the Whitefriars Stairs, sir.'

'Collins, Collins,' muttered Mr Doyle. His voice was that of a drunk man, but his eyes as they turned towards me, seemed, beneath the gas lamp, to be regaining some sense. 'That girl, Collins' girl.'

'That's right sir, one foot in front of the other, that's the way.' The policeman, perhaps out of a feeling of tact, continued to make loud encouraging sounds, but beneath them, Doyle was still muttering to himself, repeating over and over again the two words: 'that girl'. He was walking more strongly, though, and I stopped when the Whitefriars Steps were in sight.

'Thank you, Officer, I think that we'll do very well now.' I gave him a coin and was glad to see the back of him. There was a bench there for waiting passengers and I thought that Doyle would come to his senses, sitting there in the cold damp air.

He was quite amenable, almost like a limp rag doll. I guided him over, pushed him gently, a hand on each shoulder, and he collapsed on to the bench. I sat beside him and looked across the river at the boats. A police launch passed, going at high speed down river, going towards Wapping. My eyes followed it. A horrible place, Wapping, a place where pirates and smugglers were executed, their bodies left in iron cages until a high tide put an end to their lives. I tried to distract my mind by scanning the river and then, with relief, noting that the ferry was pulling out from Blackfriars. It was just at that moment I felt a prod on my arm.

'Look at this, Collins.' The man had come to his senses. His eyes were still vague and cloudy, his words slurred, but he sat up straight and he had his cane in his hand.

'Yes.' I turned my attention on him.

'Wanna show . . . something.'

And then, to my horror, he slid open a centre portion of the cane that he carried, took from his pocket a cartridge and inserted it into the space. The cane was a disguised gun.

'Give me that!' To my alarm, my voice rose to a shriek. The man looked at me with his blurred eyes, looked startled. I tried to control my voice, to sound authoritative.

'Good man. Just you give that to me.'

'It shoots . . .' His voice trailed away.

'So it does,' I said, trying to make my voice sound unconcerned. 'But, I think that you've put the cartridge in upside down. Let me fix it for you.'

After a moment, I had shaken the cartridge loose and with a shaking hand, I pushed it deep down into my trouser pocket. Let him think that he lost it. He was on his feet now, aiming the cane at me and I had no intention of letting him have the cartridge back. He staggered and I held his upper arm firmly. A cloud came across the moon, but there was still light enough to see that a boat was coming towards the stairs and I hailed it with my umbrella while still supporting the drugged man with one arm.

'York Stairs,' I said as soon as we were seated. I had needed some assistance to get the man on board. The boatman had held the boat steady against the steps while his assistant hauled Doyle by one arm and I pushed. Soon we had him seated under the lantern in the prow of the boat. Both men recognized him and neither was surprised by his condition.

'The air will do him good, sir.' The boatman echoed the policeman's words. By the light of the lantern there I could see that Mr Doyle's face was beginning to look a little healthier. His eyes, though, were still vague and unfocused. A stream of words came from him, random and meaningless and then, quite suddenly, my name once again.

'Collins. The girl,' he said. 'The girl.'

'What did the girl say?' I asked the question in his ear, so quietly that the boatmen, who were singing softly together, had no chance of overhearing.

Doyle turned his face towards me. He seemed, at first, to be puzzled by my question, but then, quite unexpectedly, he gave me an answer.

'She wanted my opinion on her father's will.' The words were crisply spoken and quite unlike the meandering vague utterances so far. I drew in a breath.

'Her father's will,' I repeated. Was the man wandering, thinking perhaps of some case that he had worked on, something that he had studied. Or did his words concern Isabella?

He said no more for a moment, just sat and listened to the plash of the oars against the water and the soft song of the boatmen.

'Isabella,' I said, trying to jog his memory, but it was no good. He had lapsed into an opium dream, muttering to himself.

'Nearly there, now, sir,' called the boatman and his assistant took the grappling hook and a noose of rope from beneath the front seats. The freshening wind blew some of the ragged clouds away from the face of the moon and the sudden light seemed to startle my companion. He sat up very straight, looked all around him and then spoke in clear, precise tones, as though making a submission at the bar.

'Isabella Anne Gordon, daughter of Andrew and Anne Gordon.'

And then he began to groan a little and to shake.

246

By the time that the boat was moored beside York Stairs, he had lapsed into a state of tremors and total misery, weeping softly as I and the boatman dragged him out while the other man held the boat as steady as he could.

'Will you be all right, sir?' The boatman eyed the size of the tip that I had given and decided to be generous. 'Here, Jem, you help the gentleman get him up to the top of the steps.'

I got rid of Jem at the corner of Buckingham Street. I was bursting with excitement and impatience. *Isabella Anne Gordon, daughter of Andrew and Anne Gordon.* How on earth could the lawyer have known these details if Isabella had not told him?

Mr Doyle, however, said no more as I steered his footsteps towards Adelphi Terrace. When we reached Robert Street, though, he dismissed me with the haughtiness of a lord, thanked me for the pleasure of my company, but he would trouble me no more. I watched him go with regret. He was quite steady on his feet now and strode along with his head slightly tilted, nose in the air and one hand swinging the cane gun. I fingered the cartridge in my pocket and waited as he mounted the steps to number five. He found his key with ease, inserted it into the door and vanished within. How had he managed to sober up so quickly? Dickens, I thought ruefully, might have been more forceful with the man, would probably have insisted on his explaining how he knew these details about the murdered girl, but I couldn't quite see how I could do any more at this late hour of the night. My mind went to that other night, the time when I had spotted the watch and someone had taken a shot at me, had scared me off, and perhaps, coolly retrieved his watch.

But who had been that person?

It only now occurred to me to wonder why my unseen watcher carried a gun. Not a usual thing for a gentleman to do on the streets of London. A pistol, perhaps, but not a gun. My mind went through the other inhabitants of number five Adelphi Terrace. The schoolmaster, a brute of a man, educated, but from a low-class background, I would have guessed. Would a man like that even have learned how to shoot? And then there were the two young journalists. A gun was an expensive purchase. One of them had talked about a shooting gallery. But the guns in a shooting gallery were hired for the occasion.

But what about a man who had a gun slotted into his cane, always with him, always ready for use.

I shrugged my shoulders and walked back towards the Temple Inns at a smart pace. My mind had been made up. I would go back to my rooms, banish all thoughts, all wonderings from my mind, go to sleep and in the morning, I would get up with the lark and I would go back to Greenwich again. I would take the nine o'clock steamer, I decided. An unbelievably early hour for me, though I shamefacedly thought of how my industrious friend Dickens would already be at his desk, sharpening his quill pens at that hour. '*Can't bear those new-fangled steel pens, Wilkie,*' he used to say to me. '*A pen has to be moulded to my design before it can record my thoughts.*

There is something so unyielding, so alien about a steel pen.'

So, while Dickens' newly-made pen, dipping in and out of a pot of blue ink, was filling a long page with the words from his brain, I would be on my way down to Greenwich to find out some more details about Isabella Anne Gordon from Mrs Peters. I felt more capable of dealing with her than I did with cross-examining the lawyer, a man probably twice my age. Women, though, were different. I always got on well with women, liked them and enjoyed their company. I would bring Mrs Peters a gift of some chocolate drops, I thought sleepily.

Eighteen

Wilkie Collins, *The Moonstone*:

My aunt's room was in front. The
miniature of my late dear uncle, Sir
John, hung on the wall opposite the
bed. It seemed to smile at me; it
seemed to say, 'Drusilla! deposit a
book.' There were tables on either side
of my aunt's bed. She was a bad
sleeper, and wanted, or thought she
wanted, many things at night. I put a
book near the matches on one side, and
a book under the box of chocolate
drops on the other. Whether she wanted
a light, or whether she wanted a drop,
there was a precious publication to
meet her eye, or to meet her hand, and
to say with silent eloquence, in either
case, 'Come, try me! try me!'

Yes, a large box of chocolate drops, layer after
layer of them. That had been a good gift. I had
always a theory that a gift should be something
that both could enjoy and Mrs Peters and I sat
cosily by the fire and tempted each other and told
each other how beneficial they were for the health.
  'My friend is brooding on producing an intelligent woman clerk for you, Mrs Peters,' I said

jokingly. 'I left him hard at work. You were a bit unfair to him, you know. What about Sally Brass in the *The Old Curiosity Shop*? She was sharp as a needle, twice as sharp as her brother Sampson. And she never did housework, either, now did she?'

She laughed a little at that. 'I must say that I rather liked Sally Brass. I had forgotten about her. Still, no one could call her a heroine, could they, Mr Collins? And so I think we score evens.'

'Shake hands on it and do have another drop of your excellent sherry with your chocolate drop, Mrs Peters,' I said, filling both glasses to a generous measure, while she selected a sweet-meat and then pushed the box across to me. And then when she had relaxed over the soothing combination, I said tentatively, 'And now, Mrs Peters, are you going to tell me what you were going to say the other day? There was something, wasn't there?'

She didn't look surprised, just took another sip of her sherry while I bit into a chocolate drop.

'You see, I wouldn't want to get anyone into trouble, Mr Collins,' she said after a moment. 'That Mr Dickens, you'll excuse me for saying this, but I think he might be a bit of a stickler for rules and regulations, and after all, it was a very long time ago.'

'I'm sure that he wouldn't see it that way, Mrs Peters,' I said earnestly. 'You can rely on me to persuade him. I do give you my word that no one will get into trouble.' I wondered what was coming, but felt sure enough of Dickens to be able to make the promise.

'It was Pauline, you see,' she said unexpectedly. 'She was only a youngster at the time. A bit giddy, you know. But under me, my responsibility and so I wouldn't like her to be reprimanded for something that she did when I was supervising her.'

'No, indeed,' I said, wondering what was coming.

'Well, it was about eight or nine years after that girl Isabella had been left by her mother. She wasn't with us anymore. She had come back from the baby farm when she was seven and she would have been working with the other girls, picking oakum, would have been about nine years old, I'd say, and she just upped and went. Lots of them did, and still do, Mr Collins, and I have to say that not much effort is taken to try to trace them. Save the parish money, is the feeling, you know.'

'Did her mother came back for her?' I asked.

She sighed at my stupidity and ignorance, but then helped herself to another chocolate drop. 'No, Mr Collins, this is not a fairy tale, not one of your friend, Mr Dickens' novels. No, her mother did not come back for her, but there was a letter, addressed to her. Now, if young Pauline had done her job properly, seeing as the girl was no longer a resident of the workhouse, then the letter should have been sent back to sender.'

'But there was no name on the envelope, no return address,' I put forward the surmise instantly, hoping that she would be impressed by my quick wits.

'Wrong,' she said triumphantly. 'But I see that

252

'I'll have to tell you something about Pauline as a young girl. She used to collect stamps.'

I swallowed some more sherry in order to assist me in thought and it did not fail me. 'It was a letter from overseas,' I guessed. Suddenly everything was beginning to make sense.

She smiled with pleasure. 'How did you guess?'

'Well, a stamp from anywhere in England wouldn't be too valuable, but from overseas, well that would be exciting for a girl who collected stamps. She removed the stamp and then put the envelope with the other objects in Isabella's folder.' I took another chocolate drop and beamed at her. She lifted her sherry glass in tribute to my quickness and I thought, once again, how women were so much easier to deal with than men. I exerted my mind to win more approbation, as though she were my nursery governess, teaching me my letters.

'And then there is Greenwich,' I said with a wave towards the window. It was decorously clothed with a net curtain, but that was not enough to hide the stately ships, sailing ships, steamers, dredgers, pilot boats, and police boats that bobbed on the river outside. 'We were thinking, myself and Mr Dickens, about Anne Gordon and her husband going up to Yorkshire, perhaps to collect a boy from a previous marriage of hers, but, of course, now it makes sense to me. They were off to make their fortune. They put the baby in the workhouse, put her there because it would be no place for her until they had made their way, until they had a place to live and land to give them money for food and clothes. It's obvious, now. They were on their way to Australia.'

'That's exactly what I was thinking,' she said with an air of great satisfaction as she tucked into my box of chocolate drops.

'And did you question Pauline?' I asked.

'She denied taking the stamp, of course, that would be Pauline. A great talker, but more lies than truth, normally.'

'Did it have a postmark on it? Even if the stamp was removed, there would still be part of the postmark, wouldn't there?'

The elderly lady beamed at me like a proud mother. 'What a clever young man, you are. Well, there was a postmark, I saw it when I handed it over, but you know, Mr Collins, that letter had been lying in a damp drawer for about ten or fifteen years. And Pauline would have steamed off the stamp. She was very neat and careful about things like that. Her stamp album was a thing of beauty. Ever so proud of it, she was. Nevertheless, steam will affect an envelope whatever the reason. I know that it was very hard to read it, but I seemed to make out the word, 'Oxford' or something very like it. I only saw it for a moment, of course, just as I handed it over to her.'

'Oxford,' I said, feeling suddenly disappointed.

'That's what I thought that I saw, but I may have been wrong. Poor light, old age, any of these things could have led to making a mistake.' Mrs Peters had an annoyed look on her face, annoyed with herself, not with me. I guessed that she was not used to making mistakes.

'And you are sure that Pauline wouldn't have bothered steaming off an English stamp.'

Mrs Peters shook her head decisively. 'No, she wouldn't, letters coming every day, the waste-paper basket full of them. Why should she bother? No, if she did something like that, something that would have caused her dismissal, I'd say that it was because it was an unusual stamp, one that she didn't have in her collection.'

'Australia, perhaps? New Zealand, America, Canada, India, Tasmania, Singapore.' I thought of all the places that English people went to and then a sudden idea came to me, as I remembered the man last night. 'Or America, Georgetown, America,' I said slowly. That had been the place where Mr Doyle's rent had been paid from, according to his landlord. And, then more with hope than expectancy, I asked, 'What did the letter say?'

'I haven't the least idea,' she said composedly. 'I gave Isabella Gordon the letter, her letter. It was missing its stamp and most of its postmark, but it had been noted on the log by Pauline.' She paused and looked across at me.

'Anything else?' Now I was completely puzzled.

'Just that it was addressed to Miss Isabella Anne Gordon, daughter of Andrew Gordon and Anne Gordon; the ink was faded, Mr Collins, but I could read that very distinctly. Official looking, I thought it was. Professional looking. That's what I thought.'

I held my breath; held my breath and waited. But she said no more. *Isabella Anne Gordon.*

'Are you sure that you didn't read the letter?' I put a world of appeal into my voice, nothing that could be interpreted as censorious in any way. Just a young man appealing to an older woman for help. 'Just to make sure that it was suitable for a young girl to read? Do tell me that you read it, dear Mrs Peters!'

She smiled a little at that, but shook her head. 'No, I didn't; though I can't say but that I would have liked to know. But, there you are, I didn't,' she admitted. I thought that there was a note of disappointment in her voice, of regret that she could not tell me what I wanted to hear and waited patiently for an opportunity to question her further. 'You see, Mr Collins,' she explained, 'I was just handing over these articles. None of my business, really. The girl was over twenty-one. I could tell that by looking at her and I could tell it from the evidence of the register in front of me. She had a right to the two little items that her mother had left to identify her and she had a right to this letter that had come for her, although, as I said, it had been put there in error and should have been sent straight back to the sender.' She stared across at me and there was, I thought, an alert aspect of her features, almost as though she thought that I might come up with something else. I mused for a moment, my mind producing all of her words, one by one, across the memory sheet within my brain.

'Pauline steamed off stamps.' I said the words, half to myself, and half to her.

Mrs Peters beamed upon me fondly.

'That's right. Very neat, she was. Yes, she

would get the kettle, hold it just at the right distance. Would know how long to give it, I suppose experience would tell her, but it seemed to me as though she would always know the exact moment when the glue had melted. And it would do your heart good, Mr Collins, to see how neatly she peeled the stamp off and left never a trace on the envelope.'

And then Mrs Peters sat back in her chair and popped another chocolate drop into her mouth. I stared across at her, moving the facts around in my mind.

'As easy, or even easier to steam open the adhesive gum from an envelope than to steam off a stamp,' I said eventually.

Mrs Peters looked gratified at my little show of intelligence. I felt almost as though I were in the nursery playing a game of hunt the thimble under the fond gaze of my nursery governess.

'Indeed,' I said cautiously, 'it must have been very tantalizing for someone, once they had peeled off a foreign stamp, not to want to know what the letter was about. And very tempting, I'm sure, just to have a quick look to see what it said. After all, it must have been highly unusual, almost unknown, for an orphan in Greenwich Workhouse to receive a letter that was posted from foreign parts. A clerk handling these letters, especially one who had an interest in foreign stamps, would have been bound to have felt somewhat curious.'

Mrs Peters' bright eyes signalled to me to go on.

'It couldn't have been done, officially,' I said

257

slowly. 'In fact, as you've told me, Mrs Peters, officially, since the child was no longer resident, had, in fact, run away; well, officially, the letter should have been returned to the sender, even if he or she were in foreign parts.'

I left a silence. We were both, I knew, thinking hard. I had realized in a flash what she was implying, but knew that I would have to be careful.

'It occurs to me . . .' And now I did not look at her, just spoke looking across the room at the row of books on the shelf in the alcove. I left a little pause and then resumed, speaking slowly and as though to myself. 'Yes, I suppose someone who was well practised in steaming off stamps would be equally skilled in steaming open a letter.'

'Very poor glue in some of those ready-made envelopes. Not like the ones when I was a girl when you painted on your own glue.' Mrs Peters also looked across at her collection of books by Mrs Gaskell and did not meet my eye when I turned towards her.

'And, of course, it would be intriguing, a letter coming from foreign parts, addressed to a child.' I allowed the comment to hang in the air. Where did we go from here, I wondered.

'You're a nice-looking young man,' said Mrs Peters, unexpectedly. 'A bit too young, of course,' she continued, running an eye over me, 'but never mind about that. I'm sure that the river air has given you an appetite. It's just about lunchtime for Pauline. Now why don't you go down and take her out to lunch. I can recommend the

Trafalgar Inn. You will get a very good lunch there, Mr Collins.'

'What a very excellent idea,' I said, rising to my feet. 'I suppose I can't tempt you to join us, Mrs Peters, can I?'

I could see that she was tempted. There was a sudden glint in her eye. She would enjoy, not just the food and the company, but the unravelling of a mystery. But then she shook her head sadly.

'No, Mr Collins, you'll do better on your own, without me, or without your friend, Mr Dickens. You're a man that a woman would find it easy to talk to. Pauline was, is, a nervous girl and deep down, under all that talking, Pauline is a worrier. You, if I may say it, have a nice reassuring manner. You go now and enjoy your lunch. Don't say anything about me. Pauline would be upset if she thought that I knew.'

'Mr Collins!' Pauline was excited at my arrival and then disappointed when she looked past me and saw that I was not accompanied by my friend Dickens. Luckily her name was engraved on a neatly embossed and framed card that stood upon the desk as I was on the point of calling her by her first name and I swallowed it hastily.

'I've been sent by my friend, Mr Dickens, to ask you if you would trust me to take your books to him, Miss Harper. He will sign them and I will return them to you. What do you say? He would come himself, but he is so terribly busy at the moment. I will take the greatest possible care of them if you will entrust them to me. And

259

I know that Mr Dickens will write a little message for you also.' Dickens would not fancy coming to Greenwich this afternoon, but I knew him too well to fear that he would refuse to sign the books, though. His fans, though there were thousands of them, were very precious to him and he had a driving desire to unravel this matter of the death of poor Isabella Gordon.

'Oh, Mr Collins!' Pauline was in ecstasy at the thought. 'I'll fetch every single one of them during my lunch hour,' she said earnestly. She looked at the clock behind her. Ten minutes to one. The chances were strong that her lunch hour began at one o'clock. In any case, she had given me the opening that I wanted.

'I'm just off to have a spot of lunch, myself,' I said carelessly. 'Someone recommended the Trafalgar Inn to me. What do you think?'

'Oh, it has lovely food,' she said enthusiastically. 'Or so they say,' she added hastily. 'I've never been inside the place myself, you understand.'

Lived alone, I cast a quick look at her left hand, no ring; unmarried. I smiled at her. Too young for me, Mrs Peters had remarked in her sardonic fashion, but a youthful appearance would make me seem innocuous. I decided to proceed cautiously.

'Perhaps if you are leaving shortly, you could point me in the right direction,' I suggested. She followed my eyes to the clock. At that very moment, the long hand jumped forward a little and touched the figure of eleven. Pauline made up her mind instantly. She went to the door at the back of the office, opened it and called out: 'Mary Ann, I'm off to lunch now.'

'I'll wait outside,' I said hastily and was gone before the obliging Mary Ann appeared on the scene.

Pauline took very little persuading. Once she had accompanied me to the Trafalgar Inn and had inhaled the delicious aroma of steak and kidney pie, which eddied through its door, her protestations dwindled rapidly and she came eagerly into the coffee room with me.

Luckily most of the inhabitants of Greenwich and those who had stopped off to see the Royal Observatory were crowded into the tap room and the public room, so we had the coffee room to ourselves. I ordered recklessly: soup, steak and kidney pie and some port.

'Well, I never,' said Pauline. 'Goodness, gracious, Mr Collins! Port in the middle of the day! I never did hear of such of thing. The idea of me sitting here in an inn and drinking port at an hour like this!'

'Nice, isn't it?' I took a gulp to encourage her, and I must say that she downed a considerable amount from her mug, though doing so in a very ladylike fashion with one little finger lifted aloft as though to disassociate itself from the action. 'Now, Mr Collins, don't ask me to eat that amount of steak and kidney, just don't ask me!'

'Well, I won't ask you, then,' I said, heaping her plate and then tasting some for myself.

Judging by the way that Pauline was tucking into it, I decided that it would be no good to interrogate her about the letter until it was

261

finished. I chatted about my good friend, Mr Dickens, told her little secrets about the next instalment of *Bleak House* and then surreptitiously studied the puddings' menu chalked on a board by the door. That would be the moment, I decided. That would be the time when Pauline, relaxed by the port, filled with good food, would be in a suitable state to open her heart to me and to spill out any information within that mysterious letter. Bread and butter pudding? No, a bit too ordinary, something that a single lady might make to use up the stale bread in her basket. Blancmange? No, too messy, too difficult to talk while coping with the wobbles beneath the spoon. Gypsy tart – that would be the one. Superlatively sweet, crisp and delicious. I ordered it instantly with an eye on my companion, who threw up her hands and shook her head at me, but had a broad smile on her plump face.

'Lovely place here. Greenwich! Great spot to live in,' I said enthusiastically. 'I'd love to have a house here and look at the ships. I'd love to travel, go to foreign parts, wouldn't you?'

She almost choked on her gypsy tart in her eagerness to agree with me. 'I'm just the same, Mr Collins. I'd love to see all those countries . . .' She paused for a moment, and then she said, rather shyly, 'I collect stamps, Mr Collins. And sometimes, of an evening, I get my album out and I turn the pages and think about the countries where each stamp comes from. It's a lovely way to pass an evening.'

I stared at her in admiration. 'How wonderful. I started to collect stamps when I was a boy. We went to Italy for a few years and I had a big collection of Italian stamps, and then when we came home I got a bit discouraged because it seemed to be nothing but English stamps and the occasional French one. But then when I left school,' I said, leaning across the table and speaking to her in a confidential manner, 'well, my father forced me into a job with a tea importing firm, Antrobus & Company on the Strand. Didn't like it much, but I did get lots of stamps, from India, mainly, India and Ceylon. Lots of Ceylon stamps.'

'Ceylon,' she said eagerly. 'I have one stamp from Ceylon. Just the one. I love the sound of the name of that place. Sounds like music, doesn't it?'

'How did you manage to get it?' I made my voice sound like an eager collector of stamps. Ceylon, I thought and my mind went to the opium-drugged figure that I had escorted home last night. Could Jeremiah Doyle have anything to do with our quest?

She looked slightly embarrassed; said nothing for a few seconds, and then said dismissively, 'I got it from a sailor.' She had a slightly shame-faced look when she said the words. Perhaps because she thought it was unbecoming to associate with sailors.

Or perhaps because it was a lie. I took a bite into the gypsy tart from my spoon and revolved its sweetness within my mouth. Enough to put anyone in a good mood, I thought.

'Of course, you, a stamp collector, would be lucky, wouldn't you, working here. Letters

263

must have come from all over the world, from people enquiring after children that they had left behind.'

'Not much of that,' she said. 'Poor things. Once they were left, they were left. Were apprenticed out as soon as they could be. Didn't get much schooling, just get them out to work as fast as possible.'

'But that letter that came for Isabella Gordon,' I said casually. 'Where did that come from?'

She gave a guilty start. Eyed me carefully. I took off my glasses and polished them with my silk handkerchief. 'The river spray has got on to them,' I said in explanation and waited for her to swallow her mouthful.

'Isabella Gordon,' she repeated, almost mechanically. There was a wary look in her eye.

'Was that the Ceylon stamp?' I asked.

'No that one was from a sailor.' The answer came quickly and she sounded very definite, almost defiant about it so I allowed it to pass. There was definitely something slightly defensive about her now and I thought it might be wiser to wait, before any further questioning, until I collected the books. After all, the door had been opened now to allow a request to see the stamp album to seem quite natural.

'What about a cup of tea, Miss Harper?' I enquired and hoped for the answer which I received.

'I'll make you a good cup of tea, Mr Collins, when you come to collect the books. No point in adding to that enormous bill that you have run up here,' she said, sounding her former jolly and cheerful self.

'Do you know, I enjoyed that meal immensely,' I confided. 'As for that gypsy tart, well, I'll remember that!'

She giggled a little at that and I thought, not for the first time, how very good-natured, and happy fat people were. And so we got up to go and I bestowed a large tip on the surprised waiter. I had had my money's worth, I thought and the slow, intermittent service had made our conversation easier.

'Sun! In November! You don't know how lucky you are to be out of London,' I said, once I had paid the bill and we had emerged from the inn. We walked away together and I noticed that Pauline was now relaxed and happy. I resolved to be tactful and careful in my questioning. She, I felt sure now, might well hold the key to the murderer of Isabella Gordon.

Pauline's house was perched on top of the hill; belonged to her late father and mother, she told me as we struggled up the steep path. Her father had been a retired sailor and he kept a telescope, always, on his bedroom windowsill so that he could keep an eye on the ships as they went up and down the river.

'That was probably what made you take an interest in collecting stamps,' I said and she agreed so happily that I felt safe in adding, 'I do hope that you'll show your album to me, when we are having that cup of tea. You know you have made me feel quite nostalgic for the old hobby. I have no idea what happened to my stamp album; my mother probably threw it out on one of our moves – always moving house, my mother and my father.'

The stamp album was produced as soon as I was ensconced in an easy chair with a fine view over the river in front of me. It held an impressive collection, stretching over about twenty years, mainly English stamps, but there were also some German, French and Danish stamps, obtained by her sailor father from ships that came in and out of Greenwich, I guessed. A few Indian stamps, one from Ceylon, three from India; these ships would dock higher up in the river, nearer to London, but sailors would meet sailors so her father would have been the source for these perhaps. One American stamp and one Australian stamp. Dickens had told me about his American trip and how he and his wife had to take a train to Liverpool to reach their ship, so not many American stamps would come her way. As for Australia, well I had a strong impression that one had to go to Southampton for a ship to that faraway continent.

'Did your father ever sail to America?' I asked idly and she shook her head. She appeared nervous and uncertain. The flow of conversation had dried up. I felt ashamed to be playing guessing games with such a nice woman. I reached across and took her hand.

'Pauline,' I said earnestly, 'please tell me about that letter that came for Isabella Gordon.' I hesitated for a moment and then decided to be honest. 'I can't get the picture of her out of my head,' I

266

said, blurting out the words and feeling relieved that I could be sincere and honest. 'That man strangled her, beat her, her legs were broken, she was covered in bruises. I don't know how anyone could do such a thing to a young girl.'

Soft-hearted Pauline had tears starting from her eyes. She hesitated for a moment, looking an appeal at me and I answered the unspoken question.

'No one at your workplace will ever know,' I said. 'I just want a clue. She had dangerous information about someone, was blackmailing them, something about a brother. Does that make sense? Was there something in that letter that came for her . . . the letter that Mrs Peters gave to her . . . where did it come from, Pauline?'

'America,' she said after a long pause. She looked behind her as she spoke, her voice not much more than a whisper, almost as though she expected to find someone listening in to her confession. There was enough of a hesitation in her voice to make me uncertain of whether she was telling the truth.

'And was it about her brother?' My voice, too, was almost a whisper. I was on the verge of finding out something vital. I trembled with excitement.

She shook her head. 'Isabella didn't have a brother.'

'Didn't have a brother.' I repeated the words. I still held her hand and I felt how hot it was, almost fevered.

'The letter was from a lawyer, an attorney, in America,' she whispered.

'America,' I repeated. It was an effort to let go the idea of Yorkshire, but the word wasn't a surprise. I had been expecting something like this ever since I heard of the stamp being removed. What use to a stamp collector was one of those red penny stamps featuring the severe profile of Queen Victoria? But a ten-cent stamp of George Washington's intellectual face, now that would have been a prize.

'That's right, Mr Collins.' She squeezed my hand. She seemed to have recovered from her anxiety and embarrassment. 'It was ever so exciting, you'll never believe it, but it was about a will and it was about her father's will.'

'A will!' Now I was quite astonished. One did not expect to hear of a will in connection with someone who had been a street girl, a jailbird when Dickens had offered her a place in Urania Cottage.

'That's right, Mr Collins, would you believe it! The letter from the attorney said that Andrew Gordon, on the death of his wife, had made a will leaving all that she possessed, a half share in his property in Lumpkin and a half share in his property in Atlanta, and all of the money that he had in the bank in Atlanta. And Isabella didn't have a brother, Mr Collins. The will said that. I remember it distinctly. It said: "I leave all that I die possessed of to my daughter and only child, Isabella Anne Gordon." Those were the words, written down there. I couldn't believe my eyes. It was like *Oliver Twist* when he turned out to have a rich grandfather after all. I went to find if she was still with us but then when I looked up the records, it had "runaway" written beneath her name.'

'And so you put it with the things left for Isabella by her mother.'

'I thought that was the right thing to do. And when I found out a few months later that I should have returned it, well, I was frightened to say a word about it. I was only fourteen years old, Mr Collins. I was ashamed of myself. I thought I'd be blamed for it. And I thought I would lose the job because of steaming off the stamp and reading the letter. And I made a bad job of gluing it together again, when I looked at again, I could see where I had torn it when I was trying to peel it off. I told myself that they'd never find the girl anyway.'

'You didn't think to tell Isabella about what was in the letter, did you? When she turned up that time?' I tried to keep any blame out of my voice, but she flushed a rosy red.

'I never even connected her up with that letter, Mr Collins, didn't remember it at all. We were busy that day. I just told her to come back when Mrs Peters would be here.' She avoided my eye.

I thought about this. So, no Yorkshire, no brother. An inkling of the truth began to come to me as I pondered over the information that we, myself and Dickens, had been considering. There was one more question that I had to put to Pauline before I got the boat back to London, but first I had to reassure her. She was looking at me like an anxious dog who is not sure of a reaction and I felt sorry for her and quite protective.

'What a marvellous memory you have, Pauline,'
I said. 'Wills are fascinating, aren't they? I
thought of an idea for a story the other day and
it would all be based on a will, a will that gave
the most terrible shock to two sisters.'

'You are going to be like Mr Dickens, Wilkie,'
she said, using my name for the first time,
although I had proffered it a few times over lunch.

'Well, that's my ambition,' I said confidingly.
'My father wanted me to be a lawyer when I
couldn't stand the apprenticeship to the tea
importers. I thought that I would like it in the
beginning, but the law is dry stuff, you know,
Pauline, once you start to study it. But all those
court cases and all those wills, well they've got
the material for a great story in them.' I was
leading up to my question and it was important
not to worry her or to allow her to start feeling
guilty again. 'For instance, one of the things that
I learned is that a lawyer always makes you look
to "what happens if?" when you make a will.
And, I suppose in this case, the will would say
what happened if Isabella had died. Lots did, of
course, didn't they? Even the best cared-for children die. Our friend Dickens lost his little
daughter not long ago.'

That was a mistake. 'Oh, poor, poor Mr
Dickens! When I think how I cried over the death
of little Nell! And poor little Paul Dombey! What
a terrible thing for him.'

'Yes, it must have been,' I said. 'It was before
I met him, but it was a terrible shock, I think.
So, of course, Isabella's father would have been
reminded by the lawyer to make provision for

270

another inheritor of his wealth.' *A half share in two properties, all monies in my bank*; an extraordinary fortune for a girl who lived most of her life on the streets of London and in its prisons. 'I suppose,' I said aloud, 'it would be worded something like this: "In the event of the death of the said Isabella Anne Gordon . . ."' I allowed my voice to tail away and looked at her eagerly.

'That's right, Mr Collins, Wilkie, that's right. You've reminded me now. It was the partner. His partner was to get it all, because he had no other living relation.'

I held my breath and stared at her hopefully. 'His partner,' I prompted.

She nodded. 'That's right, his partner.' She smiled at me in a pleased fashion.

'What was his name?' The words shot from me, but it was no good. She was shaking her head.

'I knew that you'd ask me that,' she said rather satisfied with her own insight. 'Yes, I said to myself, just as I was telling you about the will, I said to myself, *Now, Pauline, what was the name of the partner?* But do you know, Wilkie, I just don't remember, funny name, strange, remember that all right, but can I think of the name? No, I can't, it's gone right out of my head, head like a sieve, but I do remember that it was all to go to his partner in the event of the death of the said Isabella. These were the words; now that you said them, I remembered them well.'

'And you can't remember the name of the bank, where it was, or anything like that?'

271

She shook her head, sorry to disappoint me. It had, after all, been almost twenty years ago, I supposed. 'I just remember that it came from a place called "Oxford" that's all,' she said hopelessly.

'Oxford!' I echoed. Mrs Peters had said that also. 'But you said it was an American stamp.'

'That's right,' she said, nodding her head.

Nineteen

For a moment Sesina thought that the fellow was just up to the usual, trapping her behind the closed door of the coalhouse, looking for a kiss and a fumble, but then when she saw his face for a moment under the gas lamp she knew the truth. And a second later he had slammed shut the door behind him and she was locked in there with him. She had made a terrible mistake. She had got it wrong. It had not been the schoolmaster. She had sent the letter to the wrong man and he had handed it over. In a second she understood all.

She had made a mess of it. Now he had come to kill her.

And she knew there was no way that she could get past him.

With all of her strength, Sesina flung the empty coal scuttle at him, aiming directly between his eyes. She heard the bang when metal met bone, but she didn't wait.

But there was a second way out of this place.

There was a stir from the floor, a crumbling of coal lumps. He was getting to his feet. Big, tall man, she hadn't a chance against him.

Knee them in the balls; that stops them for a while. The words came to her as clearly as if they had been spoken in her ear. That had been Isabella's piece of advice. Not much good her

273

screaming, she told herself as she brought her knee up with every scrap of muscle that she possessed. And it worked. He collapsed, screaming, groaning, clutching his groin, retching with the pain.

Ahead of her the small, round lumps of coal formed a ten-foot-high hill and she scrambled up it. For a few seconds sheer terror gave her the impetus to get off the ground. Frantically she clawed at the moving mass, scrambled up, hands clawing, knees desperately seeking to move up sliding chunks. She could see it now. Above her, ten foot up, a faint circle of light. Would she, could she, get to it before he grabbed an ankle? But for how long more would he be coughing and retching?

Now she was just below the coal hatch. Once a week, on a Monday morning, the coal man prised it open and emptied sack after sack of coal down through it. The mountain of coal was never allowed to get low. There was a brick protruding from the wall just below it, and she reached up to grasp it, clung on and levered herself up. On her feet, now, and her two fists were pushing against the heavy metal, her mind whirring.

There was no point in regretting that mistake now, thought Sesina, as she heaved with all her strength against the coal hatch. No more beating her brains to find out the truth. She had thought it through. She had thought about the birth certificate, about the fortune that Isabella had expected. Had weighed up each man and then moved on to someone new. And she had been wrong, wrong, wrong! She knew it the moment that she had seen him behind her. She had seen the flash in his eyes. Fury. Terror. Yes, she had been wrong, but now she might be about to die because she had not been clever enough. She had backed the wrong man. No more weighing up the rival attractions of ten pounds or twenty pounds. Now there was only one issue. Was she going to escape alive? Yes, she had been stupid, she thought, and now she would pay for it. Why did she write a letter to that schoolmaster, yesterday? He must have handed it over. Wanted to get her sacked. She had thought herself to be so clever, had thought that he would appoint a meeting place, had thought that she could pick and choose, could appoint a safe place. And it hadn't been him after all!

Isabella had tricked her, had kept her secret. But, of course, it now all made sense.

And now, perhaps, she was going to meet Isabella's fate.

Fear gave her extra energy and she clawed desperately at the metal edge of the coal-hole. She felt blood trickle down from her fingertips. The coalman opened it from the top, had an iron lever, enormous muscles and was a very big man. She was barely five feet tall, muscular, but thin and light. And she was shut into this coal-hole. She held her breath until her face swelled and her arms seemed to lengthen and then she made another effort. One side shifted, definitely shifted. She heard a shriek, a woman's scream. Someone under the Adelphi Arches. Some poor bastard. She pushed again.

Now she had got one side of the metal plate

lifted, but the other would not rise. Something was stopping the hatch from opening. It was jammed. She knew in a flash that she would have to take a risk, to allow it to fall back again. And then to push again from the centre. And then she had to get out, to climb through that hole. Lucky she was small and thin. But did she have enough strength left to lever herself up?

He was vomiting again. Thanks be! She had put quite some strength behind that upward jerk of the knee. Nearly felt like singing one of them hymns. *Praise the Lord!*

Now, listening to him retching, she could take her time, position herself a little more steadily, raise both arms and keep a steady pressure on both sides of the circular piece of metal.

He vomited again. Third time. Good. That would keep him busy. Another effort. If only she was a bit taller!

And then the metal plate gave way. Just at the same moment that he stopped vomiting. He spat out a stream of abuse, but she didn't care. She had her elbows on the metal rim and she began to lever herself up. The woman in the distance still screamed, a horrible, almost inhuman sound. And then, almost more appalling, complete silence.

Nothing for a moment.

And then success.

She had wriggled her shoulders through.

But from behind her, the vomiting had completely stopped. A sound of coal sliding, crumbling under him. Would he scale the coal mound? But he didn't.

276

The light flooded into the coal house. He had opened its door. And then the door slammed shut. The light was gone. For a second she hesitated, even slid a little, and then heard the click of a lock. He had turned the key on her. Now she redoubled her efforts, working intelligently now, scrabbling with her hand, sweeping the coal down, trying to create a platform, a place where she could kneel, and then stand.

As she got through the coal-hole on to the street, she heard the slam of the basement door from the house. He would be out within seconds. It was a race between them. And for both of them the prize was safety and to lose meant death. Death on the end of a noose for him and strangulation in the corner of a dark alley for her.

Twenty

Wilkie Collins, *Basil*:

The sense of bewilderment and
oppression grew heavier and heavier
on my brain.

'Not the schoolmaster.' I had a feeling that my
head was going to burst if I thought about the
matter for much longer. I put my feet up on
the upholstered stool and then took them down
again hastily as I glimpsed Greenwich mud
on their soles. Dickens was a meticulous man.
There was not one mote of dust in his study, not
a cushion ever lolled out of place. He was pacing
up and down, now. In a moment he would suggest
going for a walk.

I would be sorry to leave the comfort of
Tavistock House, sorry to leave the brightly-
burning fire and the soft cushioned chairs.
Dickens was a man whose mind worked in
unison with his legs, but I myself thought more
effectively when my body was comfortable. My
mind was still full of the schoolmaster. That
brutal face, that angry scar, I couldn't banish
them from my mind. And why did Isabella draw
such a clear picture of him if she had not believed
that he was the man whom she could blackmail?
In any case, I had an instinct that the fellow who

had beaten and strangled Isabella had been a rough, hard, man, used to violence. But if not the schoolmaster, then who? Could it be the lawyer? That lawyer, weakened by constant abuse of opium, effete, refined, gentlemanly; I could not believe that it could have been he who had savagely beaten the girl. Still he had a connection with abroad . . .

'Not the schoolmaster, Wilkie. He can't have anything to do with it. It's a different story entirely.' Dickens got up from his chair, walked across the room, straightened a mirror and then continued restlessly to pace the room. 'A brute of a fellow, Cartwright, but I don't think that he fits in. You don't think so yourself. That was the first thing you said to me when you came through the door five minutes ago. Even before you told me what those two women in Greenwich had to say to you.'

'But Isabella wrote about him, wrote about Cartwright – that scar, don't you remember, Dick? Said she had discovered something. And what about those cards? The notes that Isabella was keeping to write a book about the affair.' I frowned over my nails while I thought of the matter.

'Not Isabella.' Dickens' face was grim.

'Not Isabella!' I felt confused. Nothing to do with Yorkshire, nothing to do with schoolmasters, nothing to do with a murdered boy or a lost brother; I had accepted that after my conversation with Pauline, but it was all still rather confusing. 'But Isabella went to the Saracen's Head; enquired about the schoolmaster,' I said aloud.

'But did she, Wilkie? You heard the man, you heard the coachman yourself. He was unsure. And yet that sketch of yours was like her. A living likeness. Best thing that you have ever done. But the man was unsure when he examined it. He agreed, just to please us, but I'd swear that he didn't think that it was Isabella.'

Dickens walked up and down, his lower lip caught between his teeth, his eyes wide and unseeing. 'Sesina!' he exclaimed. 'It was Sesina who went there! I remember now that the coachman at Saracen's Hill called her "little". But Isabella wasn't what you would call "little" and the man himself was a small man. No, Isabella was quite a tall girl; I remember thinking that she might have been well-fed as a baby.' My friend's face was very grim and I knew that he was thinking of the well-fed and well cared-for child who had been left at the Greenwich work-house. What had happened after that?

'But why?' I said, more to myself than to him. 'Why did Sesina go there? Why go to the Saracen's Head? Isabella was still alive then; she must have been. The man would have said if it were only last week.'

Dickens shrugged his shoulders. 'I'd say that Sesina knew Isabella had a secret. That would be the way with these girls. Would tease each other, keep secrets, tell a few things and then say no more. They used to drive poor Mrs Morson mad with these sorts of games. Sesina may have guessed that Isabella had a secret, may have known that Isabella wanted to blackmail someone, but didn't know the name. She'd want to be in

280

on it, if I know Miss Anna Maria Sisini. She'd keep pestering for information, and Isabella would drop a few hints, false ones, probably. But I do believe that Sesina never knew the whole story and what she didn't know, well, she just made up. Well, well, well.' A slight smile dawned on his face and his eyes glinted.

'We were led astray,' I said. The whole thing was so unbelievable that I, also, felt a smile pucker my lips.

'And the cards, the clues, all that finding of them in that damp little bedroom. The titles for the booklets, she made it all up,' mused Dickens. 'Why, bless my soul, she's an inventive little thing, isn't she? Decided to go in for a little blackmail on her own account. As long as she kept barking up the wrong tree, otherwise . . .' His voice tailed out as we looked apprehensively at each other. It was now getting very urgent to sort the truth from the lies.

Twenty-One

Sesina heard the back door open as soon as she scrambled up from her hands and knees. Over the years it had sunk down upon its hinge and now it scraped over the flagstone with a distinctive sound when it was pulled open. She heard him shut it after him, also. A careful man. Heavy footsteps. Not going down towards the river. Coming her way. For a moment she despaired, but then some instinct of survival seemed to take over and, almost before she knew what she was doing, she was running hard towards the darkness of the arches. Some women were sheltering there, but she knew better than to appeal to them for help. There was no energy left in these poor wretches. They would stare at her and she would just lose valuable time. She plunged into the darkness beyond the archway and then turned sharply. There had been some damage there, she remembered. Yes, it was on that side of the archway, just where the wheels of a brewer's cart, heavily laden with wooden beer barrels, had skidded on the wet cobbles one morning. A trace had broken, the horse had fallen to the ground and the cart had knocked some bricks from the corner. By a miracle it had not been mended yet. Rapidly she put her foot into a space. It was very dark, but her instinct seemed to guide her feet to the protruding bricks as she climbed a few feet and then she wedged herself into the hollow space. Only a few feet above the ground, but if she stayed very still, he might pass without seeing her.

He was speaking to one of the women, now, asking her if she had seen someone go by. *Might as well be idle. Poor thing. Dazed she was.* While he wasted time at this, Sesina undid the knot of her white apron, rolled it into a ball and thrust it down the front of her dress. Black dress, black shoes, black stockings, black hair. She might melt into the soot-stained brickwork. Soot! In a moment she had reached out a cautious hand, clawed at the wet soot from the bricks and smeared it over her face, some more over her hands while he repeated his question in that loud voice of his. Not a word from them, of course.

'This way or that?' There was a chink of coins. Well, that might bring results. But the chances were that some would point one way and some the other. None of them would know. Didn't see me; I'd take my Bible oath on that. Heads down, shawls over heads, keeping a few little ones warm. They were past taking an interest in anything.

He'd move off soon. No patience that type. Wouldn't be feeling too well, neither, she said to herself.

And then a light from the darkness beyond. She strained her eyes, feeling her heart start a steady thud which she sensed pulsate against her ears and heard it echo in unison with hoofs, clop, clop, one horse, perhaps a donkey, but coming this way, led, she thought. Slow and steady. He was still trying to make sense out of the women, but now his voice suddenly stopped. He was waiting. He could see what it was and she could see also. A torch, a man holding a flaming torch, held high above his head and leading a donkey and cart with the other.

Her pursuer had seen it also. He strode away from the homeless women. Gave them up as a bad job. But this would be a different matter. A man with a cart, coming out from the dark depths of the Adephi arches. Surely he would have seen something, would respond to the prospect of a coin. The voice was loud, clear and authoritative.

'Hi, there! Seen a girl, a young girl, wearing an apron? A maid servant. Did she go your way, my man?'

He'd be holding up the coin.

There was a pause. The carter would want some easy money. Trying to think of something to say.

And then the carter's voice. Quick. Excited. Very high, almost a squeak. A young fellow with sharp eyes. Lifting up his torch as high as he could.

'There she is, sir. Look, up there. She's hiding up there! I seed her face.'

Twenty-Two

Wilkie Collins, *Basil*:

Everybody has read, some people have
known, of young girls who have
committed the most extraordinary
impostures, or sustained the most
infamous false accusations, their chief
motive being often the sheer joy of
practising deceit.

'She made it all up,' said Dickens. 'I just can't
believe it, but that must have been what
happened. Stupid! Stupid little girl. What was
she playing at?' He went to his desk, took the
cards from the corner of a tidy drawer and then
spread them across the blotting pad. 'That's it.
Sesina made it all up,' he said after a moment. 'I
should have known. I should have remembered
how these girls' handwriting looked alike. I just
took it for granted that it was Isabella who wrote
them. Sesina has made a fool of us, Wilkie. She's
been clever, leaving these to be found, taking us
to the place and allowing us to find some of them
for ourselves. How could I have been so stupid?'
  'I should have noticed, too, should have guessed
when you said that the girls all copied Mrs
Morson's handwriting. They both wrote just like
Mrs Morson. So it was Sesina all the time.' I

285

turned my face to the fire so that he wouldn't see me smiling. There was to me, even in the midst of our frustration, something rather comic about that little girl fooling the two of us to that extent.

'She's been listening, snooping, having conversations with us, dropping little hints, pointing us in the direction where she wanted us to go; she's been leading us up the garden path!' Dickens' face was still angry, but now he began to look thoughtful, knitting his brow and compressing his lips. He got up from his chair and began to pace up and down, pausing to adjust a curtain, almost automatically, while he brooded over the matter.

'But why?' I felt puzzled, now that I came to think about the matter. 'You know, Dick, I could have sworn that she wanted Isabella's murderer caught. You said yourself that they were great friends. Why did she mislead us?'

'Because she thought that she knew better!' Dickens' voice was angry, but the knot in his brows and the tight lips told me that he was worried, also. 'You see Wilkie, I'd say that even before Isabella was murdered, Sesina had worked out, or thought that she had worked out, that the schoolmaster was the one who was going to be blackmailed. And if I know Isabella, she would have encouraged Sesina along the wrong lines. That's the way that those girls were. Could be great friends, but never quite trust each other.' Dickens thought about it for a while, jumped up once more from his chair; went across to his desk, picked up the two duelling toads that stood on either side of his pen tray and held them poised in a fight position, one tiny bronze figure in each hand. 'God bless my soul, she thought she was cleverer than we,' he said as one toad was rapidly propelled against the other. 'That was the way of it, Wilkie. She thought she knew the truth and that we, poor stupid gentlemen, wouldn't have a hope of working it out unless she gave us a few hints. Great opinion of herself, that little girl. She pointed us in that direction because she thought, because she was convinced, that it was Cartwright, worked it out in that busy little brain of hers, left us clues, nothing said by her, just *Yes sir, no, sir, three bags full, sir.* Just left us to make fools of ourselves.' There was a broad grin on his face for a moment, but then it faded almost as though he had read what was stirring in my mind. He put the toads back and stared across the room at the baize-lined door. His face was deeply worried and he gnawed his lower lip before speaking again.

'I'll tell you what, Wilkie,' he said. 'We'd better work out quickly who was the real villain. That little Sesina might put herself in danger if she follows her friend's example. I'm a bit worried about her. Might walk over towards Adelphi while we talk, what do you think, Wilkie? But first of all, let me just check on something.' He went to his bookcase and took down the 'O' volume of the *Encyclopaedia Britannica.*

'Amazing, isn't it?' he said after a minute. 'You wouldn't believe the number of places in the world that are named after Oxford and we Brits think it's just one of a kind.' He closed the volume and replaced it on the shelf. 'An Oxford town in Georgia, established in 1838. Would you believe it, Wilkie?'

I drew in a long breath. But I was not surprised. My mind, also, had begun to turn in that direction. 'I know who you are thinking of,' I said slowly. 'And the property, the half-share left to Isabella by her father, they would have been hotels, I suppose.'

'And very, very valuable.'

'And the money in the bank.'

'They made a fortune, these two men. We heard the story, didn't we? We heard the story from him that night at dinner. But of course it was only half of the story.'

'So what happened?' I asked and then when he did not reply, I went ahead, spinning the story as carefully as if I were planning a novel in monthly numbers.

'Andrew Gordon, hard-working, careful man, Scottish, saved his money; like all the Scots, he was of an economical turn. Saved up enough for the journey to America. Some sailor brought a tale of gold and the thought of gold lying there in the ground is enough to turn the head of any man,' I said slowly.

'Even a married man,' put in Dickens.

'He persuaded his wife, told her the stories that he had heard, told her of a great future for her little girl. They would build a great house, dress the child in silks and velvets,' I said dreamily.

'And then, when she was hooked, he persuaded her to leave the child at Greenwich Workhouse.'

'*Only for a year, only for a year, and then she*

288

will be a little princess.' I almost heard the words in my ear, as I said them aloud. What a book this would make!

'Took all of their savings, perhaps sold their house. And, of course, it didn't work out. Didn't find any gold, got poorer and poorer. Wife in bad health, perhaps, and that was when they met our villain. A hard-working man, but had not got luck on his side. No gold, but a shrewd and clever idea that would be bound to make money in return for hard work. Needed capital, though,' said Dickens, ticking off the relative points on his fingers. 'And probably Andrew Gordon had a little capital left, wouldn't you say, Wilkie? That gave them a start and they became partners in the boarding house business, then bought some hotels. Wife died, but the money kept rolling in.' Dickens jumped to his feet and retrieved my hat from the top of a bookcase and tossed it to me.

'Come on, Wilkie,' he said urgently. 'We have to see Inspector Field.'

'Inspector Field!' For a moment I felt taken aback. Now it was no longer a guessing game, no longer a story. 'But shouldn't we see the man first, make sure that we are right.'

'We *are* right.' Dickens now had taken his own hat and coat from a closet. 'I'm always right when I put my mind to a matter. You're forgetting the girl, Wilkie. I don't suppose we are the only recipients of her literary efforts. She might well have moved on to blackmail and the letter could have been handed over. No, we'd better act quickly before Miss Sesina gets herself into trouble.'

Twenty-Three

Sesina had made up her mind in the space of a couple of seconds. The man with the cart had the donkey's bridle in one hand and the flaming torch in the other hand. He could not, would not, easily drop either bridle, or torch. And he would take a few minutes to tie up the donkey even if he found a handy place. The animal was overburdened and could not be driven any faster than a slow walk. But for now, at the moment, the donkey and cart were between her and the man who wanted to kill her. It was her only chance. Without hesitation she launched herself from her hiding place, running desperately through the darkness, away from the river, through the tunnel and towards the unknown. She ran with a blind faith that she could outstrip them, though she heard shouts coming from behind her. Once she glanced over her shoulder. The torch was bobbing in the distance, but its light did not reach her. One set of footsteps. The man had stayed with his donkey and its valuable load, but had handed over his torch.

After that one glance, she did not look back again. Best to keep going, her legs pounding, trusting to her sense of direction to avoid crashing into the walls on either side. The whole space between the Strand and the Thames was honeycombed with these tunnels, worming their way beneath the houses, giving access to lower basements and to underground warehouses. Now she was getting further in, well beyond where police officers did a perfunctory patrol, well beyond the dim light from candlelit basements. Darker and more dangerous. As she ran at full speed, Sesina did her best to banish from her mind the stories that she had heard.

Impossible, though. There was a murmur from ahead, a buzz of sound, not human; no words to be distinguished, but the hum was dangerous, menacing. A whiff of smoke. Criminals lived down here, cooked their stolen goods, or an animal which could not escape. Murderers, mainly, cast out by all except their fellow criminals. Deliverymen and boys told gasping housemaids horrific stories about these denizens of the underworld beneath Adelphi. 'Roasted and ate a girl like you,' the butcher had said with relish one morning when the hue and cry was up and squadrons of armed police had charged past the basement door. Sesina paused. Between the menace from behind and the menace from ahead, she chose the comparative safety of one middle-aged man, even though she knew him to be a brutal murderer.

And then, on her right cheek, a slight breeze, a smell, a familiar smell, the smell of stinking river water, the unmistakable stench of the Thames, rising above the wall built to shut out its odours from the wealthy. Another underground tunnel, leading away to the right. '*You could go from York Buildings to White Friars without ever seeing the sky.*' It was the coalman who had told her that. Perhaps she could escape after all. He had a torch, but its light would not stretch far. She glanced rapidly over her shoulder, one glance, yes, she could see it. A second glance. The light on the ground only reached about ten feet in front of him. In the hollow darkness she could hear him pant, but she felt safer now. There was no way that he could see her and she could tell, by the sound of his boots striking the road surface, that he had slowed to a walk. Big, fat fellow. Ate too much. Out of breath, probably, and afraid that the torch would blow out. He, like she, would have felt the breeze coming from the river. It was getting stronger by the minute.

There must be another tunnel, joining this one at right angles. The river smell, and the breeze had become stronger. She risked another glance over her shoulder. The wick of the torch must be flickering, but the light itself was stationary. He had stopped. Why? And then she knew. A shout from behind. That familiar war cry to excite the mob. 'Stop thief!' and then, worse still, his voice; no doubt about that accent. 'Ten shillings for the man who catches that girl!' That would rouse the most sluggish; coax forth even men fearing a scaffold. Nothing, she thought, as she began to run again, nothing was as urgent as the feeling of hunger, the instinct was to survive the next few hours and allow the future to take care of itself. These men would come out from every hole in the ground in order to have ten shillings in their hand.

So now there was a response, a reply, a distant howl, men yelping and men whistling, feet banging on the ground, a man-hunt. She had heard that once before, had heard it from the safety of the basement door. And even then she had shuddered as she closed the door rapidly.

Her instinct was to get back to civilization again, to get back to that warm kitchen and to the thick walls and heavy doors that kept a man-hunting mob at bay. She would take a chance.

She began to run as fast as she could. She would get back to the river. There would always be someone along the foreshore, searching for wood, for pieces of coal, for drowned bodies that might have a few coins in their pockets. Somehow she could perhaps lose herself among them until she could get away. There was a faint gleam ahead on the right-hand side of the tunnel. Not a light, too dim for that; the fog was heavy today. But there was the smell of river, getting stronger than ever. She rounded the corner and fell heavily to the ground, tripped up by what lay there.

Twenty-Four

Wilkie Collins, *Basil*:

There was a fight—the police came
up—I was surrounded on all sides by a
shouting, struggling mob that seemed to
have gathered in an instant. Before I
could force myself out of the crowd,
and escape into the road, Margaret and
Mr Mannion had hurried into a cab. I
just saw the vehicle driving off rapidly,
as I got free. An empty cab was
standing near me—I jumped into it
directly—and told the man to
overtake them.

'An American,' said Inspector Field dubiously.
'A rich American.'

'Why not? You don't just arrest English people,
do you, you English policemen? Come on,
Inspector Field, you know you do. I saw you
arrest a black man the other day.' Dickens was
sharp and impatient. A sign of his anxiety, I
thought, though his face was not easy to read.

'But, this man . . .' Inspector Field thought
about it for a few moments and I could almost
hear the words that ran through his mind: *This
very rich American; this property-owning magnet;
this man who may well have dined with one of*

the bigwigs in Scotland Yard. 'Are you sure, Mr Dickens?' he said eventually.

'As sure as you would be yourself before you arrest a man for questioning. That's all that is necessary. Arrest him; caution him; question him. Come on, Inspector,' said Dickens impatiently. 'The evidence is there. Isabella Gordon's father went to America to make his fortune. He finds that it's not as easy to get gold as he had expected. He uses the remains of his little fortune to assist a man who has an idea of setting up boarding houses for the hopeful prospectors. And this man, I would wager any sum on it, this man was Donald Diamond. You heard all of his stories yourself. Ten years or so later, Andrew Gordon, perhaps he was dying at the time, in any case, Andrew Gordon goes to a lawyer to make his will. All drawn up, neat as anything. "I leave all that I possess, my two hotels, and all monies in the bank, to my daughter and only child, Isabella Gordon, resident in Greenwich Workhouse. Should the same Isabella Gordon have died, then the above named properties and monies go to my partner, Mr Donald Diamond."' A few of Inspector Field's men had crept into the room and all were listening in silence. Ignoring them, Dickens rattled off that rather imaginative version of Andrew Gordon's will with great aplomb and not a man in the room was ready to argue with him. When he finished there was a dead silence.

Dickens cast a quick glance around the room. All were silent, all gazing at him with mouth ajar. Every word of what he had said was believed. All heads were nodding. I sat very quiet and

295

studied Inspector Field's worried face. For him, the problems of arresting a rich American went beyond all convictions of his guilt and I guessed that Dickens was too clever not to come to the same conclusion and not to waste any further efforts of convincing him of Donald Diamond's guilt.

And I was right. Dickens changed his tune.

'Call it a whim, Inspector,' he said softly. 'The whim of a man fussing over a girl who was once in his care. And remember what happened to the other girl, the one that shared a room with this girl. I'm just a bit concerned, Inspector, just a bit worried that something of the same sort might just happen to this little Sesina.' Dickens paused a little and looked pensively through the grimy window and then quickly back again. 'I'll tell you what, Inspector. What do you say to you asking this man Donald Diamond to come and talk to you in your office? Just to have a chat. Fetch him in a taxi, all very informal. You can make up a tale,' he said, giving the inspector one of his most seductive smiles. 'You can make up a tale. A letter from America, from Georgia, trying to trace the partner of one Andrew Gordon who is thought to be in London; wonder could Mr Diamond be of assistance; well-known by all that Mr Diamond plays host to many Americans in his house and you do remember him talking about Georgia that night when we all dined together at Rules. What do you think, Inspector? Have a chat with him in his own house, all very informal. But a man of your insight, a man of your experience, will be able to tell if there is anything in this wild story that my friend Collins and I have brought to you. Question him about the two hotels. Ask him about the wife of his partner, about Anne Gordon. I'd lay a bet that a man of your experience will manage to worm some information out of him and remember, Inspector, I'll be at your side and over the years I have listened to a lot of Don's tales.'

And I'll be there, too,' I put in. After all I was the one who had got the vital information out of Pauline and I didn't see why I should be left out at this stage.

'We'll get you a cab,' said Dickens without replying to me. He put his hand on my shoulder and made his way to the door, then looked back and I followed the direction of his eyes. Inspector Field, slowly and deliberately, was opening the drawer of his desk. He extracted a pair of handcuffs from it, and placed them inside his trouser pockets. A small pocket pistol followed it and Dickens gave a satisfied nod. Seizing me by the arm, he pulled the door shut behind us.

'Wilkie, my very dear friend,' he said with unaccustomed earnestness, 'I don't really want you to come with us into the American's house. You can get out of the cab there, but then I have a much more important mission for you. I want you to go to number five, get hold of Sesina, put her in a cab and bring her to my place, to Tavistock House. Stay with her there. Wilkie. Don't let her leave until I come.'

'Wouldn't it be better if you went,' I said rather sulkily. 'She's more likely to do what you say.'

He gave a grimace. 'No, my friend, you're the

297

one with the flair with women. What was it that Eliza Chambers said, wrote to me the other day? "I was sitting beside dear Mr Collins and that alone is enough to ensure having a brilliant time of it. One always feels so well-looked-after by him." All my lady friends are the same. I have to promise them that you will be there before they condescend to come and dine with me.'

I gave in. It was rather flattering to think of being used as an attraction to one of my friend's celebrated dinner parties and even more flattering to imagine the literary world of London discussing me, even if it was only about my merits as a dinner partner.

Twenty-Five

The body on the ground was cold, stone cold, but not that long dead, thought Sesina. There was no smell of decay, nothing other than the normal stink of unwashed body and unwashed rags. Sesina got to her feet and then paused. The light was better here, but it was still a long way down to the riverside. The mob was coming on at a fast rate. There was no certainty that she could outrun them, reach the end of the tunnel before them. And, of course, there was no knowing whether anyone down there on the riverside might come to her rescue. Perhaps they might join in with the howling, shouting crowd, each of them striving to earn the ten-shilling price placed on her head. Too much to hope for that any police might be sauntering around. Too fond of their own comforts and their own skins. Plenty of them up on the Strand, of course.

Rapidly Sesina snatched the white apron out from beneath her dress. She slipped the strap over the dead woman's head, forced herself to feel below the dead body and to fasten the waist strings. And then she pulled the cap from the apron pocket and placed it on the head. The starched whiteness would act like a beacon to the light from the torches. The noise was getting louder. They were almost upon her. She had no more time to set the scene. Chances were that

299

most of them were drunk on cheap gin. She dragged the body right out to the centre of the archway and arranged it there. Jenny, she said to herself. That's who it is. Poor old Jenny. A prostitute that lived rough in the Adelphi Arches, begged for food from time to time when customers were not forthcoming.

Dead now.

Strangled, probably, but Sesina did not have the time to look properly. The important thing was to have a body. She moved away rapidly, but glanced over her shoulder as the shouts came nearer. Even in the dim light, the arranged figure was immediately noticeable as the body of a girl. The white apron and cap showed up really well. And then she went and huddled into the little hollow where Jenny had spent her last minutes or hours of life.

A second later the torches flared against the dripping walls of the arches. The strong smell of bitumen emanated from the pieces of wood broken from roadmen's cabins. A whoop of delight; they had seen the body. Fierce voices, hasty curses, arguments, sounds of blows. And then a sudden silence. Lasted a few seconds until the chorus of disappointed voices.

'Shite; she's dead!'

'Hell's bells.'

'I was the first that see'd her, sir.'

'Might be just shamming, sir.'

'Stop kicking her, you fool. Don't you know a dead body when you see one?'

'OK, men. She's dead. Dead, fair and square. Here's some coins for you.'

Sesina closed her eyes in thankfulness. He was going to accept that she was dead. The light was too poor to see a face and he had been fooled by her quick wits. A little thrill of excitement ran through her. What a story she would have to tell. She forced herself to stay rigidly still, although a cramp was beginning in her left leg. There was a loose stone jutting out from a broken edge of the archway. Someone should check on them arches, she said to herself, bring the whole lot down if they collapse. She distracted herself from her cramp by going through the streets above: Adam Street, John Street, James Street and then there was York Buildings and Robert Street: they'd all collapse and, of course, the terrace itself with its eleven houses. She tried to imagine Mrs Dawson's face as she felt the building collapse and that made her feel a little better. A suppressed giggle seemed to warm her. One thing anyway. Mrs Dawson'd never escape. Too fat!

The mob of men had disappeared from her sight. He had flung the handful of coins back into the darkness of the tunnel which they had come down and the men were after them instantly. Sesina could hear them. Wild animal howls, fierce fights, and struggles for possession of one of the torches. Soon they would all be drifting back to their fire, to the bottles of gin that they had managed to steal or whatever they had roasting above the flames. Rats, cats, even dogs; these men would eat anything if they were hungry enough. They'd be disappointed though. Would have expected more from the man in pursuit of a girl. Even after the first word that he spoke, that American accent would have told them that he probably had pots of money.

And he, of course, was clever enough to know that. He'd guess these men might be dangerous. Now that he had a dead body, instead of a living girl, well he just walked off, smart as you please, away in the opposite direction, out towards the river and then, she hoped, back into his home. For a second she saw him, outlined against the light coming in through the arch at the end of the tunnel and then he was gone, turned back towards Hungerford Stairs.

Sesina drew in a long breath of relief. He had been nicely fooled. But he had the sense to know that these men were dangerous. They knew that he had money and they would be off after him. He'd do well to keep away from that mob. He had done the right thing when he had walked hastily towards the end of the tunnel. By now he would have emerged on to the foreshore of the Thames and would be among fishermen, coal barges, and those who scanned every square foot of sand and low water for anything that might keep the life in them for another day.

Sesina gave him five minutes, forced herself to count the numbers from one to three hundred and sixty, just like that poor girl at Urania Cottage, the one that Mrs Morson persuaded to count up to a hundred every time that she was in a passion. And then she struggled to her feet and edged her way along the side of the tunnel. Blinking slightly as the light, even on this foggy day, became stronger against her eyes, she stepped warily out from the shelter of the tunnel and scanned the foreshore.

No! He was still there! He had fooled her! He had known she wouldn't have trusted herself to go back among that throng of wild men that he had summoned up. There he was, waiting patiently, leaning his back against one of the iron mooring posts and surveying the scene as if he were about to begin a painting.

He saw her instantly though. She felt a sensation as though his eyes were boring like gimlets through her. Now she would be at his mercy. She would be stupid to think that any of those people on the rivershore would interfere to protect her. One look around at the skeleton-like figures, at the hopeless faces, at the dead eyes, one look told her that. Even now they were edging away. Distancing themselves from the richly dressed gentlemen who was looking intently at the dishevelled maidservant who had emerged from the tunnel.

Twenty-Six

Wilkie Collins, *Basil*:

The awful thrill of a suspicion which I
hardly knew yet for what it really was,
began to creep over me – to creep like
a dead-cold touch crawling through and
through me to the heart.

Inspector Field was very silent in the cab, silent
and worried, wearing the air of a man busy
concocting an explanation for his seniors. Dickens
did not interrupt him, but gazed through the cab
window with a casual curiosity as though the
busy scene on Trafalgar Square was new to him.
I was not deceived though. He had thrust his
hands into his pockets, but protruding from the
top of each of the side pockets of his loose-fitting
trousers was a set of white knuckles. Dickens
was on edge with worry and apprehension of
what might be going on while the cabby guided
his horse through the heavy traffic on Trafalgar
Square and came to a temporary full stop at the
entrance to the Strand. Inspector Field, also, bore
a sombre look and above our heads the driver
whistled a merry tune as if to fill the gap in our
conversation. I, too, began to feel apprehensive.
Sesina, who had been merely a useful finder of
clues, might now be another victim. Inspector

Field had his handcuffs and his gun. Sesina had nothing, but her own quick wits and indomitable courage.

And so, when the cab drew up in front of number eleven and while Dickens was fishing loose change from his trouser pockets, I slipped out and strolled nonchalantly along the pavement, looking over the iron railing from time to time and surveying the full tide washing up on the river beach in front of the Adelphi Arches. Some boys and girls were standing in the river, sacks in hands, some of them with a few coal pieces in them. They were curiously still, I thought, looking at them; not bending and dipping as they would usually, and for a moment I felt a slight uneasiness. They were looking further down the river, down towards the Savoy Steps. I could see nothing but hastened my footsteps, almost ran the last part, crossing the now empty road in a couple of seconds. I pounded on the doorknocker of number five. No answer. I knocked again. And again, feeling almost like breaking the fanciful glass panes. And then the door opened eventually and Mrs Dawson stood there, looking rather sulky.

'Oh, Mr Collins,' she said. 'I'm sorry that you were kept waiting. Can't think what happened to that girl. Oh, here comes Mr Dickens and another friend, getting out of a cab. Look, just behind you, Mr Collins.'

'Not at home; not a sign of him,' said Dickens at my ear. 'Let's at least make sure of the girl. Good afternoon, Mrs Dawson. Might we have a word with your housemaid, Sesina, please? This is Inspector Field.'

Twenty-Seven

For a moment Sesina almost gave up. There was no escaping this man. She looked around the foreshore. Every face there looked away from her, backs were turned. No one was going to interfere between a servant and a well-dressed gentleman. Sesina stared longingly up at the terrace of eleven houses, the magnificent Adelphi Terrace, all the houses built on to each other, looking like one enormous mansion. She then looked along the upper road running past the front doors and then at the lower road, running past the entrances of the tunnels that led to basement entrances of each of the houses. If only she could climb up there, and get to the back door before he grabbed her. She thought of the fat Mrs Dawson, of the lodgers: the lawyer, the schoolmaster and the two newspaper lads. Surely he wouldn't try anything on once she got back inside the front door. She would take great care that she was not alone with him for a second, not ever again. It was no good, though, he would get her before she could ever climb up to that level.

And then she saw something, something that gave her hope.

At the end of the lower road, there was a standpipe and a two-tiered granite trough from which horses could drink at the upper level and dogs at the lower level. Bob, the butcher, had stopped his cart there and allowed his horse to drink from this free supply of water. Sesina did not hesitate.

'Bob,' she screamed. 'Bob, I'm down here. Help me up, Bob!'

He'd do it. She knew that. Had been sweet on her for ever so long. In a moment he had dropped the horse's bridle and sauntered over to the edge of the railing and looked down at her with a grin on his repulsive face. She went as near as she could and began to scale the unstable sandbank.

'Well, well, look at that. Can't wait, can you?' There was a sneer in his voice and a fat smile on his stupid mouth. She didn't care though. He had taken a rope from the back of the cart and now he dangled it enticingly over.

'What would you give for the rope? Save your shoes, wouldn't it? Otherwise you'd be all mud when you gets back. What'd'ye give for a leg up, then, Sesina?'

She gave a hasty glance over her shoulder. *He* was still there. The murderer was still watching her. Wouldn't come any nearer, though, while a hulking great brute like Bob was leaning over the parapet and talking to her. She'd keep him talking for a minute.

'Well, I'd shake you by the hand,' she yelled out.

'And a kiss or two.'

He was sure of himself now. Still, there was lots of coming and going on that lower road, carts coming out of one tunnel and she could handle an idiot like Bob. She did not reply but pursed up her lips invitingly. That should do it.

The next moment, the end of the rope dropped down, neatly hitting the ground beside her. He was grinning widely as he tied the other end to the iron railing. She raised her arms, took a strong grip on the rope and began to scramble up the steep bank of sand. Hand over hand, quite easy, really. She didn't care. Let him kiss her. She could keep a fellow like that under control. And Bob had his deliveries to do. Couldn't hang around pawing girls for too long. She looked once more over her shoulder. No sign of the man. Now where had he gone? A shade of worry passed over her. Had he gone up one of the tunnels and would she find *him* waiting for her when she got to the top. Half a crown from *him* would get rid of Bob. She climbed even faster, her calloused hands gripping the rope firmly and now she kept her eyes fixed on the railing above.

She was up in a few minutes. Didn't hesitate. Flung her arms around Bob, kissed him heartily. *Take the advantage, don't let him chase you. That got men worked up.* Funny how Isabella's words were always still in her ear. He was a bit taken aback, big bully and loudmouth as he was. Not as much of a ladies' man as he pretended. She glued herself to his lips for another moment and then detached herself with a casual wave of the hand.

'See you tomorrow, Bobby,' she called over her shoulder and ran full pelt along the lower road. A cab was going along the upper road and she kept to the far pavement so that she was

308

clearly visible by the driver perched up high, above its roof. She even gave him a little wave and knew that Bob had seen her do that. He wouldn't follow her. Had been in trouble with the police last month. Wouldn't want any bad reports going to his master again. She half-giggled to herself, weak with relief at her narrow escape. Her mind was filling up with ideas. Steal a few pages of the lawyer's writing paper. Very good class of writing paper. Do a few references in her best hand. Pack her bags early in the morning, very early, before any rich gentleman would be out of bed. Just scarper. Get a room somewhere cheap. Soon get another job. Leave no trace. A bit sorry to leave poor little Becky, but Mrs Dawson wasn't a bad old tallowketch; she'd keep the girl. Now she was through the arch and then beside the basement door to number five.

The door in the lower basement opened readily to her key. It seemed like an age since she had been inside the dark, damp hallway. Almost impossible to think that it had probably been just an hour or two. She hoped that Becky had kept the fire in while she had been gone. She pushed open the kitchen door. A nice bit of heat wafted out. Filling her with thankfulness. She'd have a little sit down before writing her references and slipping out – by the front door, she decided. Much safer than those tunnels.

And then, even before she could close the door, her breath was suddenly cut off. She was clutched in an iron grip. He was behind her, pressing her against him, the back of her neck pressed against his waistcoat buttons. Strong fingers pressing into her throat, nails digging into the skin. Dizzy, nauseous. Not a word spoken. He had sneaked through the hall door. She had forgotten about his key. This, she thought, is the end, the end of all my dreams. I'm dying. She squirmed, freed her nose from his arm. A strong smell. Goose fat. Becky! Get out! Save yourself. He'd strangle the child next. No possibility of . . .

Panic swept through her . . . can't breathe . . . heart thumping . . . strange sounds. She kicked at his legs, but it was useless. That man was immensely strong. She tried to move her head, tried to bite him, but her senses were ebbing, a mist in front of her eyes, the thudding of her heart had begun to slow down, to beat in her ears . . .

And then bells, bells jangling in her ears . . . Church bells? No, they were just above her head. Heaven . . . Perhaps Mrs Morson was right about Heaven, though neither she nor Isabella had ever believed in that stuff.

Bells, not church bells. Bells. Every bell in the house clanging loudly, ringing frantically. A sweeping brush, tearing at the wires, bells jumping and swaying; deafening clamour.

Something wrong with her eyes . . . head bursting . . . she could see nothing just a circle . . . terrible mist . . . all ending . . . she was dying . . . a round gleam . . . an eyeglass . . . St Peter . . . widening a little . . . gold-rimmed . . . Becky crying . . . men shouting . . . metal click . . . the circle in front of her eyes widening and widening. The stove . . .

And then Mr Dickens' voice. 'That's it, Sesina. Take your time. Take her arms, Wilkie. Where's that woman? Mrs Dawson, Mrs Dawson.'

The red mist began to roll back from in front of Sesina's eyes. And there he was, the landlord. Looking odd. Face strange. Hands stuck out stiff as a clown, stuck out in front of him. Handcuffs. And Inspector Field with a gun. Mr Donald Diamond. Sesina thought that she would spit in his face if she had the energy.

Mr Dickens was shouting. 'She's fainting. Hold her, Wilkie.'

But she wasn't really. It was just a nice feeling to let herself flop down on the mat in front of the stove while Mr Collins held her in his arms. Mrs Dawson, herself, putting a cushion under her head. Mr Collins, kneeling beside her, holding her hand, his gold-rimmed spectacles twinkling at her.

'I thought you were St Peter,' Sesina said to him, hearing her voice hoarse and raucous, like the voice of a stranger.

'I often have similar thoughts about myself; especially after a dose of laudanum,' he said. 'Now just you relax, little Sesina. Nothing more for you to worry about.'

It all seemed a little strange, a little misty still. She watched the landlord being dragged out of the room by the police inspector. Mr Dickens went too. Little Becky came and sat down on the mat beside her and touched her hand.

'Was it yourself, Becky, making that row with the bells?' Sesina had a lump in her throat. Didn't know whether she was going to laugh or to cry.

Becky stared at her wide-eyed, startled by the hoarse and husky voice. Mr Collins went over and got her a mugful of water.

'Prefer gin,' she croaked and he winked at her. But she was glad to swallow the water down. Gin would have burned her throat.

'Why did he do it?' Sesina managed to get the words out after the water. She thought that she would prefer to hear voices than to find her mind wondering what might have happened if the policeman, Mr Dickens and Mr Collins hadn't been upstairs and if Becky had not rung those bells.

'Isabella had found out that he was the partner of her father,' explained Mr Collins. 'They were partners out in America. Made tons of money, Sesina. Poor Isabella should have been very rich, but Mr Diamond kept all of the money that was due to her.'

Dirty, rotten monster. Hope they hang him high and that he burns in hell. Sesina took another sip of water and decided to stop thinking about it. Would there be a reward? she wondered. She shut her eyes for a moment and then opened them. Mrs Dawson was looking upset. Red as a turkey-cock. Needed a swallow from the gin bottle. Opening and shutting her big mouth like a stranded fish. Hands on hips, too. *Oh, well, just spit it out, missus!* Sesina closed her eyes and then opened them again. Might as well let her get matters off her chest while Mr Collins was here to smooth her down.

'And, I know what it will be like, Miss Sesina,' said Mrs Dawson, trembling with rage. 'You've

house would go on having lodgers and taking it all in all, it was a good place to work in. She gave Becky a wink. They'd have a good time here, the two of them. She'd persuade Mrs Dawson to send the washing out, make that a condition of staying put. Strike while the iron is hot; that's what Isabella used to say and she was right. Once Mr Collins was gone, she'd have a chat with Mrs D.

Anyway, she had a nice bit of privacy here in Adelphi Terrace. Becky would be no trouble and she'd train her to stand up for herself. Make Mrs D. keep on that scrubbing woman. And a boy to do the coal in the morning. That would give her a little more time to herself. She thought that she would like to write a book. Mrs Morson had told them that Mr Dickens sold 34,000 copies of the first number of *Bleak House*, each one of them costing one whole shilling. Imagine having a bag with 34,000 shillings in it! Sesina shut her eyes and began to plan her story.

London. November. Fog everywhere. Dead tide. Two men. And one very beautiful girl.

'Sesina,' says one of the men. 'We need your help. We have a mystery to unravel.'

314

got our landlord arrested and now these houses will be sold or something and none of us will have jobs.' She applied the corner of her apron to her eyes and wept piteously as she got herself out of the room. Becky looked on with eyes filled with apprehension.

'Don't worry, Sesina,' said Mr Collins. 'I'll look after you and Becky. I'm sure that my mother can employ you both for the moment and soon I plan to set up some rooms for myself and I will need someone to keep me in order. Thinking of turning over a new leaf, Sesina. I have all sorts of plans. You and me will get along fine.'

Making all sort of plans; she knew where that would lead, thought Sesina. She'd be working herself to the bone, doing all the cleaning and the cooking and the lighting of fires. He'd be having little dinner parties and expecting her to do the food and the serving. And to turn up with his breakfast and his hot water in the morning. And that wouldn't be all, she guessed. *You know what men are like; you'll end up with a baby under your apron.* She could just hear Isabella say those words. She knew what men were like. No thank you, she thought.

Still, she had a soft spot for him and his funny little glasses so she'd let him down easy.

'You're very good, sir,' she croaked, 'but I don't think that I can desert Mrs Dawson. I'd better stay here.'

They'd have a lawyer to manage the house while Mr Diamond was in prison, she guessed. And afterwards the houses might be sold. The